Hart De Lune

When Sinners Hate

House of Skin
Book Two

by

Charlotte E Hart and
Rachel De Lune

Hart De Lune

Hart De Lune

WHEN SINNERS HATE
HOUSE OF SKIN – BOOK TWO

Prologue

Alexia

The jet touches down, and I'm thrown forward in my seat as the tyres screech on the tarmac. "What the fuck, Tim," I shout to the pilot.

"Sorry, ma'am. It's a short runway."

Why Father insisted on flying me into a small runway out of town over any sensible choice of a central airport or landing strip is beyond me.

We stop abruptly, and the jet taxis to a small hangar that looks like it's seen better days. In fact, the whole place looks like locals with their radio-controlled planes use it.

I unbuckle as Tim's assistant – some guy I can't remember the name of – comes into the passenger cabin and sets about opening the doors. I check my hair is neat, cover my eyes with my sunglasses and grab my Birkin. Tim, or whatever his name is, can bring the rest of my luggage.

The heat in Miami is thick with salt from the ocean, and there's often a breeze. At least there is in my building. The same in San Diego. But here, in Texas, God, it hits me like a bus as I climb down the steps. It's cloying and already has me wishing to retreat into the air-conditioned jet.

The black Range Rover, which I assume is Father, idles at the side of the hangar. I'm not walking over to him in these heels. So I stand to the side of the jet, cross my arms and wait. My luggage arrives next to me, and I take a disinterested glance to my side before tilting my head at the car.

Finally, the engine growls to life and rolls slowly towards me.

I grab the handle and swing the door open. "How gallant of you, Father."

"I see you enjoyed your flight."

"There was nothing wrong with the flight. It's the false veil of secrecy it offers, as if you've just flown in your latest haul that offends. I hope someone is dealing with my luggage."

He smiles and chuckles to himself, which lifts the sagging skin around his cheeks, and I watch as he slicks his nearly all-white hair back and looks at the driver, who exits. "We'll take you back to Nicolas' house."

"He owned a house here?"

"We are going to be working in San Antonio and so needed somewhere to stay. He liked his luxury. I'm sure you'll approve. He didn't have long to enjoy it."

"And what about the operation he was setting up?"

"It's under control. You don't need to concern yourself with that."

"Really?" I twist in my seat and look at him, but his gaze is locked out into the dusty landscape around us.

"Really. We all have our jobs to do," he mumbles.

Yeah.

The drive to Nicolas' is in silence. I'm used to long periods of quiet where my father is concerned. He doesn't see me as a confidant as he did Nicolas. They fuelled each other's ambition. I'm simply a prize for Father to share out to whomever he needs to win over.

A tool.

A plaything.

A bargaining chip.

Much like this deal.

The car pulls up, and I wait for someone to open my door. Finally, the driver comes to my side, and I see the stack of luggage from the trunk ready to be taken in. At least the house is nice. Quite stately in a way. A short, gated driveway leads to the turning circle we're in now. The double-fronted arched doorway must lead inside. The whitewash gives it a Mediterranean flare I approve of.

Wooden floors clack under my heels as I enter, and more arched windows help to cool the property. For that, I'm forever grateful. "Who's working here?" I look around the empty rooms expecting someone to come out and move my bags up to my room.

"Just my driver and the housekeeper," Father says from behind me.

"Are you serious?"

"What more do you need? It would do you well to fend for yourself. You have the meeting with the Cortezes tomorrow. Do you think you'll be spending all your time here or getting to know your soon-to-be husband?"

"I'm still an Ortega, even after they take my name from me. And until then, I'd like to be treated as such. You can have your driver deal with my bags. I'll find my own room."

Ten minutes of searching and the eventual room I pick, from the half dozen available, is quite lovely. Decorated in neutrals, with plenty of space and light, there's nothing to complain about except being stuck here with my father. It's been a long time since we've lived in the same house, and my nerves are already fraying. I suppose it's a lesson in patience.

The driver does deliver my bags, and I take a shower and clean up before dinner.

As anticipated, Father hasn't discussed the finer details of the plan he's been working on to align us with the Cortez family. Although, what more specifics do I need other than I'm meant to marry one of them as a sign of commitment and allegiance?

An hour or so later, a meek, older woman appears at the door, announcing that dinner is ready. I nod, and she retreats quickly, giving me time to check my outfit in the floor-length mirror before heading down. The staircase is certainly a feature of the house; at the bottom, the housekeeper is waiting to show me through to the dining room.

Father is sitting at the head of the table with a place setting on either side of him.

A little macabre for my liking.

I don't sit on his right. That was Nicolas' seat and clearly still is, even though he's dead.

As I take my seat, he pours a glass of red wine.

"I'd like to go over the arrangements I've put in place with Melena."

"Ah yes, my mother-in-law. How is the witch?"

"You'll watch your tongue around her. I know you joke, but she isn't to be underestimated." He doesn't look at me but simply picks up his silverware as the plates are laid in front of us.

"Will you please stop treating me like some weak woman. Melena Cortez is the matriarch of the family. Don't worry, I'll watch my back."

"Once you're married, I'll begin to explore the haulage and transport options that Cortez will open to us. They'll have their own arrangements for us, I'm sure. But with us as a united front—"

I roll my eyes. He only sees one side of this plan. "Your short-sighted ambition is your downfall, Father. You and Nicolas spent far too long trying to conquer the world in your own ways. But you never could see the right way to do it."

He slams his knife down on the table, rattling the glasses. "And you have come to this conclusion, Alexia? You, who has had so much experience."

"Yes. You want an alliance with the Cortez family. Expand our strength with theirs."

"Yes. That was my plan and the one you'll help me achieve. Although Nicolas didn't see it as I do."

"And even after what they have done to your precious Nicolas, you still want to honour the agreement?" I test him, wondering if he'll ever see what is coming.

"We will never be a rival to the Cane empire alone." He raises his voice as if that can intimidate me.

"And Cortez won't either. They don't want to take that on. Why would they?"

"But us together – no one would challenge us." He boasts as if simply joining our business empires will suddenly threaten our biggest competition.

"Possibly. Possibly not," I muse, slicing through the grotesquely under-cooked steak on my plate and taking a bite. "It's still a risk. And will depend on how much influence you can gain over Melena. That's on you."

"You doubt me?" he questions.

"If we play this right, we'll get everything we want and more." He narrows his eyes at me. "Revenge." I purr. "Simple. Calculated. And it will be the undoing of the Cortez family and our making."

He studies me for a moment as if I said something that genuinely made him think. "You want revenge?" His scoff turns my stomach.

"Why don't you?" I spit. "He was your son. You're willing to risk another heir?"

"You aren't an heir, Alexia. You're my daughter and will do as I say." His fat fingers wrap around my arm as he grabs me and squeezes, but I'm past that. I shrug him off.

"You will be sorry you don't see me as more because I'm going to hand you both the Cortez business and our revenge on a plate. And they won't see it coming."

I pick up my cutlery and take another bite, waiting for his next retort.

"Maybe I underestimated you, Alexia. If you can deliver as you say."

"Oh, I will. You can bet your life on it. The Cortez family won't know what's hit them."

I pick one of my favourite dresses – a skintight leopard print with lace bust details. It's closer to a second skin than a dress and will help make an impression. The black Pigalle Louboutin pumps complete the outfit and give me the extra few inches. I never like it when a man can tower over me.

My footsteps punctuate the air as I glide down the staircase. I'm due at the Cortez house in a few hours, but I want to make sure I can have a little heart-to-heart with Melena before anyone else arrives.

Father is waiting at the car, but he doesn't have an invitation, and I certainly don't want him there, especially as I want to be on the right side of Melena Cortez. After our conversation last night, I'm hopeful he might actually start seeing the potential in all of this. Time will tell, although there's a nagging at the back of my mind.

He opens the car door for me. "I'll ride with you." I stop and look at him, taking in the father figure he's been to me all these years.

"No, you won't. This is on me." I slide into the car and pull the door shut, ending any further line of questions. "Go!" I summon the driver, and he pulls off down the drive.

The Cortez house certainly is a spectacle. A mansion with white pillars holding century at the front. It's glorious and puts Nicolas' house to shame. Security is tight, and we go through two checkpoints before I'm greeted by some staff member. They dismiss my driver, and it's then that I realise just how far into the lion's den I've strayed.

Oh well.

I take a breath and check my hair.

Better get this show started.

The buttoned-up help leads me through the house and out into the gardens. An older woman smoking a cigarette is sipping a tall glass of something in the shade. She looks smaller than I thought – dainty, perhaps? Her reputation reminds me that I shouldn't judge her by her looks.

"And you must be Alexia Ortega."

"Yes, ma'am." Her accent is thick, but as I meet her eyes, I see there's nothing frail or dainty about her.

"You'd make us a lot of money," she drawls. Her comment doesn't strike me as a compliment, but I take it as such and nod my approval. "I'm pleased you chose to come here early. Come." She beckons me with her hand, waving her polished red nails towards me.

I approach and perch on the seat at the edge of the shade, placing my purse on the wrought iron table.

"Yes, you'll do. Of course, they'll break you in. I've taught them well, my boys." She smiles as she takes a drag on her cigarette and blows a stream of smoke towards me.

It's all a game. A power play. And one that is easy to play. Because her threats and words of warning can't harm me, nobody can.

"And which of your boys will I be marrying, Melena? Or should I call you Mother?"

She stands and grabs my chin with her hand so fast I'm helpless against her assault. Her bony fingers squeeze against my jaw, and I can feel the throb of pain begin to pulse.

"You'll watch your mouth with me, girl. Do you hear? You put a foot out of place, and we'll be more than happy to introduce you to your brother." She elongates the word, pulling out each syllable.

I grab her wrist with my hand and bend it back, forcing her to free her hold. "I understand. I know my job. Can you say the same about your boys?"

Her eyes search mine, and for a moment, I think I might be able to understand where she's coming from. Protecting her family – protecting her business. She's right to threaten me.

She backs off and goes back to her seat. "We have a family meeting in the lounge. They will all be here, and I'd like you to wait before we introduce you. They know what they are here to do."

"Wonderful. If you can look to get me a glass of iced tea, maybe, I'll wait here." I take my compact out of my purse and check my lipstick and make sure my jaw isn't bruised from her little stunt.

"Very well." She gives a little clap, and someone approaches. "Give Miss Ortega anything she wishes. And bring her into the lounge when I give the signal."

The waitstaff doesn't say anything, just nods and looks to me.

"Oh, iced tea." I smile.

Both Melena and the waitstaff disappear, and I shift to sit in the full shade. The heat is so dry it feels like it will burn my throat as I breathe it in.

A tray of cold iced- tea arrives, and I muse to myself that it might have some advantages marrying into this family. They certainly know how to staff a house.

My nails begin to tap, my leg bounces, and my overall impatience crawls up inside me as I wait. Wait to meet the man I'm meant to marry. Wait to meet the men who killed my brother.

Finally, another servant appears and nods in my direction. I stand and follow her into the house and to a set of doors. She nods and leaves. So with a deep breath, I push the golden handle down and let the door swing open. Pulling myself up, I stand as tall as possible as I enter the room.

My eyes do a quick sweep but don't really recognise any of the men in the room.

"Hello, Melena. Boys." I watch as they all glance and take their fill. Judging by some of the reactions, they weren't expecting me. Interesting. "So, who's it going to be?"

CHAPTER ONE

ABEL

There's silence in the room for a while. I let it linger, waiting to see how Alexia Ortega reacts to a Cortez welcome. Even our mother sits there unsure which way this will go because I haven't told her yet either. I was waiting for this moment before I confirmed it, perhaps wondering if Knox would show enough interest. He hasn't.

Unsurprisingly, Shaw can't keep his eyes off the newcomer, and makes his way over to introduce himself. I understand that from his perspective because she is stunning. Unfortunately, she's also stunning in a way that makes me question if there's any reality left in her. That's not the kind of woman he can handle on any level.

I've been watching her for nearly six months. I was about set to make a choice for this family, but then Dante decided he wasn't going to play ball and found himself something special. Screwed my plans, because he was the only one of my brothers that could have managed her successfully. Shaw was always a pointless discussion. She'd eat him alive unless we constantly fed him instructions. Knox? I could push him – make him, and he'd do it. He'd also probably manage her with the precision of a blade. However, the moment her family took on mine this became my problem to deal with.

Mother eventually stands up in greeting, as if bowing down to some unwritten rule between our two families. That might have been true before, but there are no rules now as far as I'm concerned. Whether Alexia agreed or not, or knew or not, that family came for us. They took something precious to one of us and they threatened it. Dante may have made sure Nicolas never got a chance to breathe again, but now it's my job to send a message back loud and clear to the Ortega family; we will not be fucked with.

I watch the greeting between the women, and then catch hold of the newcomer's eyes. She stares without an inch of backing down. In fact, she lifts her chin in defiance. Perfectly poised. Perfectly dressed. Perfectly fucking aimed at anything her father wanted to aim her at. Miguel Ortega trained her well. She's been moulded enough to drive any man to distraction.

A low rumble of chaos runs through me. It winds my dick into a frenzy of outrage. I smile at what's coming, as Dante looks back at me. He's still got that scowl embedded in his brow, confusion marring his thoughts presumably. I put a hand on his shoulder and nod, pointing at the rest of the family in the same breath.

"You can all leave. We'll be fine on our own," I offer.

There isn't one flinch or show of interest on her, barely even a movement in her lips.

Dante's body spins fully to look at me, his glare questioning what the fuck I'm doing when we could be using Shaw for this. I nod at him again to get out of here. He's got a life to live now – a lover to enjoy. I was still curious about his commitment to her until Nicolas interfered. I wondered if I could turn him back to us – make him do this – but I only had to see his fear to know exactly where his loyalty was. The only way we keep him now is by me giving him everything he needs, because if he has to make a choice between us or Wren, I'm not sure it's going to be us that win.

"It's alright, Brother," I murmur. "Go."

He frowns, but turns and walks towards the others until he's

17

leading Mariana out behind the rest of them. Frankly, I pity him the responsibility and feelings involved in a relationship, but his choice is made. I respect it. In fact, I'm relatively pleased with it given the woman he's found. It's a shame she has no idea what we do yet, because I'm damn sure that's going to sting like a bitch when she does find out.

The noise of feet and low talk slowly quietens to nothing, and I turn to the sideboard to fetch some Champagne. The liquid pours slowly, giving me a few seconds to think. There isn't much need for thought. I doubt fucking her will be a chore, but there definitely will be a standard to set clear if this is going to end up relatively amicable.

By the time I turn around she's out on the veranda, her long, lean body standing tall in the middle of the space. Platinum blonde hair, no doubt fake, hangs loose down an exposed back, and leads to deeply tanned legs perched taut on black heels. Appropriate clothing for her wealth. Clinging to her shape, and just on the line of slutty. Can't say I mind that at all.

"You chose yourself, Abel," she says, as I approach. "I'm honoured."

Her face turns to look at me, red lips smiling broadly. I hand the Champagne over, looking at the intensity that perfection gives her. I doubt anyone's ever said no to her, or imposed rules on her privileged little ass. That's about to change.

"You shouldn't be. I'm far from the life you're used to living. This will be more like a prison sentence for you, Alexia."

I let her name linger in my mouth, as I look at hers, unsure of its familiarity. We're not familiar. I doubt we'll ever be past fucking because this is just a convenience – a union. And, whether she likes it or not, I am more of a monster than either her brother or father have even been. She just doesn't know it yet.

"I don't know. This place is nice enough. A little small, but it will do for us."

I chuckle and stand beside her, casting my stare out to the view rather than her. "This is my mother's house. I don't live here."

"You don't?"

"No."

"Where do you live?"

I turn and lean on the rail, choosing to look back at her instead of the same grounds I've seen a thousand times. "Where I live is of no concern to you."

"Well, that'll be rather hard. We're to be married but we won't sleep together?"

"This isn't love, Alexia. I doubt either of us has any sentimental ideals."

"Ah." She snickers to herself about something and begins walking back into the house. "You're frustrated. Did I ruin a plan of yours, Abel? Do you have someone special out there in the wilderness who pines for you? Do you pine for her?"

She sips her drink and wanders around the room, sneering at certain objects as she goes, before she leaves the room and takes herself through the corridor. I follow, trailing her with little else said. It's a nice enough view of her ass that I'm comfortable with the silence, and when she does eventually look back at me I don't conceal the interest. "Do you like what you see?" she asks.

"I'm sure you'll be useful enough for fucking." I move past her to walk the stairs to her suite. "Come." Or maybe it's our suite. I haven't decided yet, but one thing I do know is she won't be going anywhere near my home. That's my space – my refuge. Only family has access to it other than me, and that requires palm prints from each of them and a damn good reason for bothering me.

The door opens to the far west wing, and I walk us into the large, three–room space. It was mine for a while, but it's been renovated as a guest suite since I left. One open plan lounge area, one master suite and one bathroom. Blue and gold now. Not my preferred taste, but I won't spend any time here other than necessity.

"These are your rooms," I say, closing the door behind her. "I expect they can be redecorated if you want."

She looks around, inspecting the area and the glass bowl on the side table until she's back in front of me. "Adequate. I'll bring some of my own things with me when I return."

"Return?"

"I'll be back in a few weeks once I've settled some matters at home." I back step until I'm leaning on the door and drink what's left of my Champagne. "Is that a problem?"

"It is for you, yes."

"For me? Why?"

"You're not leaving, Alexia. You're in now. The doors are locked unless I say otherwise."

For the first time since she's been here, the mask slips. She glares at me from under it, her shoulders going rigid. I chuckle to myself, amused with her internal tantrum about control. Whatever control she thought she had left the second she arrived. I may seem calm, tolerable even, but I'm far from it when pushed, and I am repulsive when challenged. She won't like me much at all.

"Let me make this clear so you understand what you've agreed to. There is no leaving unless I sanction it. There is no opinion of yours that's relevant. There is no option available to you other than what I say. And there is no way out, Alexia." The first glimpse of her real nature starts to emerge. It's filled with all that hatred I know she harbours for some reason. Her smile cracks, her eyes harden, even her nails seem to grow in the minute I take to lay down the rules. "As my wife, I'll expect you to do exactly what I ask, when I ask it. Any form of denying me will end in your harm. Do you understand?"

"You're threatening me?"

"If you disobey me, yes." Her chin tips up again, and all those pretty features stay flat, as if to make her first challenge known.

"Take a minute to ensure that message lands clearly in your head. This is my only warning. There won't be another."

She does take her minute. She analyses me. She looks me up and down. She even dares opening her mouth to attempt arguing with me. It would be unwise, which she clearly catches on to because that mouth closes again.

"For clarity's sake, tell me you understand."

She nods. Nothing else.

"Use your fucking mouth."

She frowns at that and attempts berating me with a covered glare again. "Yes. I understand."

I kick off the door and walk closer to her, taking her empty glass so I can refill it downstairs. "I'm glad that's settled. Will you arrange for your personal items to be delivered or should I contact your father?"

"I'll see to it."

"Good. I'll meet you by the pool in half an hour," I murmur, walking for the door. "I'm sure you'd like some time to adjust to your new home and clean up." She stays quiet. No recourse. No attitude to deal with. "And Alexia, lose the lipstick. I don't like it."

Easier than I thought.

CHAPTER TWO

ALEXIA

A rrogant fucking bastard. He caught me off-guard with that little play, but now I know he wants to make sure I know my place, I can play along.

Abel Cortez. Well, I wasn't expecting him. He's the one with the record, the one that seems to steer the decisions and keep the rest in line. A catch to many. I should be flattered that the simpering younger brother wasn't the plan. But then, I'd be able to wrap him around my little finger by sucking on his tiny cock and making him do my bidding.

For some reason, I can't picture anything about Abel as being small.

I take a closer inspection of my new quarters. The décor is obvious and, I suppose, of a certain quality. My fingers itch to smash the stupid bowl. It's ugly and might help relieve some of the tension that's built up. Being on my game with Abel will be challenging, but I won't let him best me.

He's the alpha of the family. He's been put in this position – as have I – and he's making sure he gets his kicks. Well, it's just another job. Just a means to an end. And if I have to play the obedient wife for all to see, then I'll oblige just as long as he realises that I don't give up my control. I can act and play pretend, but real control – never again.

The bathroom is splendid and probably the nicest room in my new accommodations. I stare at my reflection and study my features. Pristine hair, although coloured, looks flawless with shine and the tone makes my naturally bronzed skin look even darker. My fingers reach and trace the shape of my lips – a shame. Red would have looked good on Abel.

I run the faucet, dampen one of the washcloths so conveniently placed on the marble countertop, and run it under the water before bringing it to my lips and smearing the flame-red lipstick.

After I'm done, I look at myself again and with some care, ensure everything else about my makeup is still in place. My lips look puffy and full, tinged with colour still. In fact, rough up my hair a bit, and it looks like someone kissed the shit out of me. Or I sucked the crap out of them.

Fortifying myself with a deep breath for what's next, I smooth down my dress and leave the room, following the same path we took up here. Then I head in the direction I was escorted out towards when I first arrived. I didn't see a pool last time, but it can't be hard to locate.

It seems everyone in the house has left as there's nobody around, so I take my time finding my bearings. Keeping Abel waiting won't hurt.

Finally, I catch a glimpse of him. His back is to me, but no one else in the Cortez family could pass off that silhouette. He's built wide across the shoulders, and I'm impressed his suit fits so well considering his size.

I approach him and lean on the railing overlooking the pool. "Better?" I wait until he gives me his attention and slowly trace my lips with the tip of my tongue.

"For now." He makes a show of looking me up and down, but I can't decide if the disapproval is genuine or part of the act we have going on – and it is an act. We are both here for an ulterior motive. Be it family honour or responsibility, neither of us would choose the other to happily marry otherwise.

"Are you going to show me around – as you made it quite clear this would be my new home?" I emphasise the word 'home' before smiling at him. "I'd hate to get lost being here all by myself."

"You won't be here alone. As I've said, this is Mother's home, and she's well protected. I don't think you'll appreciate venturing too far from your suite."

"The pool. I will need to cool off in this heat." I switch directions as I digest the fact that I'll have Melena Cortez as a housemate until lover-boy feels he can trust me. I walk around Abel and down the steps to the pool level. It's a curve ball, like many things I'm sure will come my way, but I will make it serve my purpose.

The pool looks far too inviting, and the idea of peeling out of this dress to start my seduction of Abel Cortez springs to mind. But it's too early for that. And I want him to work for it.

I take a seat and lean back on one of the loungers, kicking off my heels. "You know, I have to say I was expecting something a little more romantic from my betrothed." A shadow blocks out my sun, and I squint and look up at Abel standing over me, his arms crossed. "You're in my sun."

"And you'd like me to move?"

"Oh, don't worry. I know you're not going to do what I ask, Abel. Not yet, at least."

He scoffs and turns away.

"Oh, if I'm on house arrest, I'll need someone to go and shop for me while I wait for my belongings. If I'm going to make use of the grounds, I need to be dressed appropriately. I can't imagine you'd be too happy for me to wear this, and only this for the foreseeable." My fingers trail down my curves, indicating the dress that I chose for the meeting.

"Make sure they arrive soon."

"So, are you going to show me around, or shall I ask your

mother to put on her best Southern charm?" I grin up at him, leaning forward so he has a perfect view of my cleavage. "And I'm assuming there's a chef or housekeeper? Am I supposed to book my own meal requests?"

"And if I were to tell you to make your own dinner?"

"Then I'd question your intentions in this arrangement of a marriage. I'm not living with my fiancé, I'm left here to fend for myself. Seems to me this agreement isn't what we agreed to, and I'm sure my father will be interested to hear that." I stand up, but Abel doesn't back away. My chest brushes the lapels of his jacket. In the shade from the sun and this close, I can appreciate him a little better.

He seems to be assessing the situation just as I'm sizing him up.

Finally, just as I'm imagining what kind of kiss should be our first, he stands to the side and offers me his arm. With my shoes abandoned, he towers over me, which sends a shiver up my spine, but I take his arm.

"Dinner," he simply says.

"A little early, isn't it?"

"Not for what I have in mind."

Promising.

I pause and snatch up my shoes, and he walks me back through the house via a different direction. He might insinuate I'll be keeping to my area of the house, but I'm not going to be caged like a toy – only to come out when he wants to play.

No. My agreement to marry is based on strengthening our side of operations, and I intend to ensure that happens.

We pull up to a rather swish-looking venue, and I wait for Abel to open my door, which he does. Again, he offers me his arm, and I take it as he leads us inside.

"I like this. Very smart, Abel. Much more in keeping with my expectations of everything I've heard about the Cortez family."

He scoffs a little as we wait at the maître d' stand.

"What's so funny?" I ask.

"If you think this," he looks around at the entrance and all of the polish and finery on display, "is what the Cortez family is about, you might not have the full picture."

The maître d' chooses this time to glide to his station and cock his head a fraction to the side before smiling and beckoning us into the restaurant with a sweep of his hand. I follow, still holding onto Abel's arm until we arrive at a small table for two in a secluded section of the restaurant.

The pale neutrals and glassware on the table all work in harmony to give an exclusive and expensive vibe that I honestly appreciate, and despite my earlier comment, I know that the belly of Cortez lies in much more sinister endeavours just as ours does. It doesn't hurt to play pretend every now and then, though. After all, isn't that what we're doing now – playing pretend?

"We'll have a bottle of my Teso La Monja," Abel orders.

"What, no Champagne?" My pout is forced but effective, at least to the waiter who seems to have halted his retreat.

"Champagne for what? Are we celebrating?"

"We are." I look up at the waiter and put on my best innocent-looking face. "We've just gotten engaged, so in my book," I place my hands against my heart, "that deserves bubbles." I smile.

"Congratulations, sir. Ma'am. I'll bring a bottle with the wine." He tilts forward towards Abel and then glides away.

"Oh, that was fun."

"I can see."

"Well, Abel, a girl's got to try and get her kicks somewhere." I turn to him and wait for how the rest of the evening will go. So far, he seems only too happy to call the shots – dictating the living arrangements, where I can go, what time we eat, what wine we'll drink.

He doesn't bite and just sits back in his chair as if waiting for me.

I steeple my fingers and lean forward, waiting.

The minutes tick on with neither of us saying a word, both of us staring at the other. There's a friction between us — more than just the obvious — and it's building, like electricity charging in the clouds before the lightning strikes. But, we'll have to settle for the buzz of the charge because a new waiter scurries over to us with wine and my Champagne.

He makes a big show of popping the cork, and I play along, happy to clap and cheer as he tops off my glass. Abel just sits, watching. He even shakes his head when the waiter offers to fill his glass.

"Oh, come on, I'd like to toast with my future husband." The sweetness of my tone should make my teeth hurt.

"Are you ready to order?" the waiter asks.

"Yes."

"No." We both speak at the same time. "I've not seen the menu yet, darlin'." I continue.

"We'll have the scallops to start, followed by the beef tenderloin with braised greens," Abel orders for me, and I feel the heat rise to my cheeks.

"No. I'd like to see the menu."

"Believe me, this is the best thing on the menu, darlin'," he mimics my words from a moment ago. All it makes me want to do is crack his seemingly composed exterior all the more.

"If you wanted an obedient little wife, you should have considered the match a little more carefully," I seethe.

"From here, there's nothing wrong with the match, and the quicker you learn that you have no say in any of this, the better."

On his knees. Begging. Desperate.

The vision calms my riled nerves, and I drain the Champagne, quenching the fire that's burning to get out. Abel, seemingly forgetting the gentleman act from earlier, doesn't fill my glass when

I place it back on the pristine table, so I grab the bottle and do it myself. Something I should simply get used to.

Annoyingly, the food, when it comes, is sublime. Succulent and juicy scallops melt in my mouth. The beef is delicious, and despite it being early for dinner, I'm starving. Abel wears a smug smile the rest of the night, but I let him have this one. There's no benefit to screaming and shouting at this man. He'll take no notice, and I refuse to let him see how much he's getting to me so far.

I'm the one who's lost ground. Each decision, every move has been his so far, and I need a win.

The conversation on the ride home is non-existent. I text my father and insist that my things are delivered before the end of the night - I won't have another day without my wardrobe. He confirms promptly, and I put my phone away.

"So, is tonight the night?" I ask, wanting to know what the living arrangements will mean for us as a couple – even a fake one.

"The night for what?" He doesn't move his eyes from the road.

"For us to get to know one another more … intimately. I don't know about you, but I'd like to work out some of my frustrations."

"When I want to fuck, I'll let you know."

"And you kiss your mother with that mouth. Well, hopefully, you won't be some pussy-ass limp dick who can't get hard enough to fuck me right."

He doesn't answer, and I have to wonder if anything will get a reaction from Abel Cortez.

We pull up to the gatehouse of the mansion, the barriers draw back and Abel drives on up. He keeps the car running and shows no interest in getting out.

Very well.

"Make sure security knows my things will be delivered tonight. I don't want to be disturbed once I've gone to bed."

"Anything else?" he asks, almost sounding sincere.

"No. Is there anything you have planned for us tomorrow?"

"Yes. But I'll let you know in the morning." He revs the engine of his Dodge.

I get out of the car and slam the door. The second it's closed, he drives off.

The scream rips from my throat in a high-pitched siren. It, like the spark and tension, has been building, and I feel unable to keep it contained. It feels good, too.

Well, if Abel's going to treat me like shit, he better be ready.

CHAPTER THREE

ABEL

Dante is, amusingly, nervous. I chuckle to myself about it and watch him from the kitchen as he walks towards the lounge with his little Wren. She's all smiles and greetings. First with Mariana, and then Knox. Although, the latter is less happy and more cordial. Either way, seeing Dante with some anxieties attached to him is comical. The only time I've seen that was before I went inside. He was a different creature by the time I came out. Forced that way by me and mother perhaps, but neither nerves nor apprehension are traits anyone associates with him these days.

"The Dragon. You're the one who killed my brother," drifts back at me. My back straightens at the sound of Alexia, and I leave the kitchen to intervene in whatever this might become. "For her, presumably." By the time I'm around the corner and into the hall, Dante's blocking Wren and Alexia is still wearing that same fake smile she holds so well. "Oh, don't worry. I'm not overly bothered. What is done, is done." Wren keeps hold of Dante's hand like her life just got rammed into hell, and my brother, well, he's turning red. Never a good sign. "Besides, I'm looking forward to planning a wedding now. That's what you're here for, yes?"

"Yes, it is," I cut in, looking at Wren. "Outside?"

She looks up at me, and then back to Dante before letting go of his hand and following me. I don't know what's said between my brother and Alexia after that, nor do I care. He'll make his point felt in any way he chooses. With any luck, it'll resemble a threat, one he'll carry out if I agree.

By the time they both come out and join us, Wren has her iPad out and is busy making notes. They sit down with us – them on one side, us on the other. It could be seen as affectionate if I wasn't with someone just for the sake of a union. Instead, what should probably be serene becomes business-like and methodical as the conversation continues, especially with Wren's curt words leading the talk. Unsurprising given Alexia's opening conversation, I suppose.

Dress – Ivory. Venue – Bellini's perhaps, considering I own it, but Wren will look into other places, too. Flowers – I couldn't care less. Alexia can deal with it if she wants something specific. Guests – over two hundred, only twenty of which mean anything to either of us. Timescale – six weeks from today.

One of mother's servers comes over with a tray of drinks, and Wren continues to discuss the arrangements, but at some point during the last however long, Dante's eyes got fixed on mine. I know what he's thinking. He's still questioning me and what the hell I'm doing. Probably because he believes I've got a heart like him. I haven't. What was left of mine got taken from me when I was inside Huntsville penitentiary.

I blink under his intensity, letting my mind go back to that time. His life might have made him numb to his job, but I know the boy he was. He always did have hope. It wasn't taken from him or sucked out of him. He wasn't left to rot in a hole. He wasn't held down and beaten on by nine guards, or worse, just because they could. He wasn't put into isolation for weeks because the governor thought it necessary to curb the rebellion. And he wasn't starved for days either. No, he chose to suppress his feelings. He found a way to push them aside while he did as I asked. They can be pulled back up when you do that, but any hope I had for something better, something enjoyable – regardless of me finding my way out and building a life out here – is still back there in the wall.

"Abel, Alexia. How are the plans going?"

I break eye contact with Dante and look across as Mother sits down. She smiles at all of us, as if she's happy about this, for the sake of our welfare. I suppose it is welfare related in some ways. Alexia will stay alive if she's with me rather than being used as a threat by another cartel, and my family will take what's Ortega's, near tripling our reach, by the time I'm finished.

Dante suddenly gets up and walks away, shoving his chair back with enough malice that I know he's got something to say. I smile at Wren as she goes to follow and put my hand on her shoulder to keep her down. "Stay. Finish this up. I'll go speak to him." My gaze finds both Mother and Alexia. "Play nice."

It doesn't take long to find him. He's over by the orange trees, smoking and standing firm to try containing himself. "This is fucking bullshit," he says, as I approach.

"It's bullshit that stabilises us."

He throws his smoke on the grass, crushing it down. "Why the fuck didn't you speak to me about it?"

"By the time I was going to, Wren was here. Would you rather I'd forced you into it?" Those eyes of his harden. "And that's exactly why I didn't. Calm the hell down."

"Yeah, well, it's still bullshit. Shaw would have–"

"This is my problem to deal with. It's done. Behave, Dante."

"Fuck you."

I chuckle and slap him on the back. "I appreciate the concern, but I'm fine. Besides, she's an Ortega. We still have a score to settle."

He frowns and flicks his stare back to the ladies, who seem to be continuing cordially. "What does that mean?"

"You got your revenge, Brother. I'm gonna find a way to deal with mine for a while."

A slow smile starts spreading on his face. It's enough to show he just caught up with the program and stopped thinking with that heart of his. So I start walking us back to the table.

"You gonna play nice now?" He nods and lights another smoke. "Good."

"So, Wren, now the greetings are out of the way, tell me how you got into planning weddings for a living," Mother asks as we retake our seats. "Fairy-tale dreams, was it?" Dante chuckles and looks over at Alexia, shaking his head about something.

"No, not really," Wren says. "Well, maybe a little. Creating something special from nothing is kinda magical, even if what I create isn't always what I'd choose for myself." She gives Dante a quick glance, and it makes me wonder if Wren is as innocent as Dante makes out. "Making someone's dream and special day come to life can be exciting and rewarding. Plus, I'm efficient, hardworking and well—organised, so event planning was a natural fit. I'm very good at what I do." She levels a hard glare at Alexia. It's good to see the fire still shining brightly. Doubt she'll last without it.

"How sweet. Sounds idyllic," Alexia drawls, reaching for more Champagne. "That must be why you're so charming." If words could cut any sharper, I'm not sure how. Wren's fire seems to diminish, and she looks affronted instantly. Mother's using her usual condescending smile to make sure she's feeling the impact of two bitches in heat.

"I'm charming to all my clients at the first meeting, but that won't continue unless you deserve it. As yet, I'm not sure you do," Wren replies.

Dante keeps chuckling, and even I can't stop my own smile as I remember her attitude from that night we had together. She might be small, but damn she's got some front about her. "Anyway, honeymoon?" she continues. "I know some great venues in the

Maldives. Or perhaps Europe? Italy is wonderful and–"

"We won't need that," I cut in.

"Abel, you must," Mother announces. "Richard and I went to Italy. It was–"

"I said no."

The table goes quiet, and I watch as Mariana comes across the lawn. She squeezes herself in–between mother and Wren, smiling about something.

"Well, this looks lovely. Where are you up to?" She leans in towards Wren, letting their shoulders meet, probably for support.

"We're discussing the fact that, apparently, there will be no honeymoon," Alexia says. "I don't know why. My betrothed seems to think I don't deserve one."

She doesn't.

I look at her, watching her challenging nature trying to flirt me into something. It won't work. The only thing I want from her is obedience, preferably with her mouth closed unless it's around my dick. "I won't have the time. Maybe next year," I concede.

She rolls her eyes at me and looks away, yet again trying to push my mood somewhere she hasn't seen yet. "Maybe next year I'll be allowed out of the house, too."

And that's just plain antagonistic.

I lean in, making sure only she hears what's coming for her if she doesn't stop. "Be careful with your tone. This is my family. Respect it, and me."

No response, but at least she's shut her mouth rather than try pushing me some more.

"And what about dress code? I'll need it for the invites," Wren says. She looks at me rather than Alexia, having now worked out that this is happening the way I want it, not her. "And who do I get the guest list from?"

"I'll do the guest list," Mother says, rising from her seat. "And, if Abel agrees, the dress code. Perhaps you and I could meet next week to organise that, Wren." She looks back at me, waiting for my confirmation. I nod.

"That's fine."

"Do I get any say in my own wedding?" Alexia questions.

My gaze comes back to her. "Other than the flowers, no."

She stands and glares at me, still managing to keep herself pristine in appearance regardless of her fury. I chuckle at her and pick up my Champagne, amused with yet another tantrum about control.

"Shall we go back up to the house?" Mother says.

Mariana giggles in the background as Mother waves Wren up, and they all end up leaving us to it. I listen to the slow run of chatter as they make their way across the lawn, keeping my stare aimed at the woman who dared show a fucking opinion that wasn't wanted.

"What is this?" she seethes. "Am I to be humiliated constantly?" I stay quiet and keep watching, perhaps waiting for her to take this too far so I can do something about it. "Why should your mother manage the guest list? Or deal with the dress code?" Presuming this is a chance for me to make a point felt, I let her continue. "This is becoming intolerable. I am Alexia Ortega, and I will not be sidelined and ignored."

I stand and move closer, making sure she's looking up at me rather than down. "What you don't seem to understand is who you're going to be. You will be Alexia Cortez in two months, and as far as I'm concerned, you already are."

CHAPTER FOUR

ALEXIA

I hold his stare – his threat.

Because there is no question as to what Abel just laid out for me.

Blood rushes through my veins, charging me with anger and frustration at the situation I've walked myself into. Manoeuvring with Abel Cortez is certainly proving more challenging than I thought, but if I'm to be married in a sham wedding, then what's the problem if it's in front of people I despise or don't know? In a dress I haven't chosen myself? This is for my family – not myself.

"I'm feeling a little tired. I think I'll go back to the house." My head is high, and my pace graceful and calm. Nothing like the storm that's building inside of me. Part of me would relish Abel calling after me or following me, but he doesn't.

There's no sign of Wren or Mariana back in the house as I head straight up to my rooms. I close the doors behind me and look around the room. My eyes land on the stupid, decorative bowl. Its smooth surface is in my hands before I can stop myself, and I raise it over my head before throwing it to the floor, watching it shatter into a thousand shards against the hardwood.

As the crash reverberates around the room, a fissure of tension is released from my chest, and I can breathe again. I wanted to do this when I first saw the thing, and now I'm smiling down at the mess I've created.

Taking a satisfying breath of air, I march to my wardrobe. My things have arrived, but I still have half the contents of my bags scattered over the dressing room, and it's time to put that right. After all, how can I think clearly when my only belongings – my only real connection to me – in this house are in disarray?

After a few hours of organising, I feel a hundred times better than when I came here, like I've replenished my armour for battling with Abel. And there is a battle coming. He just might not know it yet because he's not touched me or shown any interest in me since I walked in. That can't last if this fake marriage is going to keep me entertained.

Sex has never been about love or emotion for me. It's a way to keep control in a world where being a woman often puts you on the back foot. I've been second to my brother, been the quiet and obedient daughter and kept to the shadows, but that's not who I am. And if Abel wants me to remember I'm going to be Alexia Cortez, then perhaps he needs to show me some motivation.

If nothing else, it will help with the frustration of being trapped here.

~

I stay in my 'chambers' for several hours. Small talk, or any kind of talk, with Melena isn't high on my wish list. But it's boring beyond contemplation.

Besides, I've licked the verbal wounds from this morning and now feel suitably calm.

With my house arrest, I'll need to ensure someone can come to visit for manicures and such. They need redoing already, and my hair won't last much longer without a stylist to colour and style it, especially in the heat. I consider the cost of flying Jamie out every four weeks. I send a quick message and wait for the reply, already knowing she'd love to do it and, actually, looking forward to some non-hostile company.

I go out and sit by the pool, knowing it's the quietest part of the house, but I'm distracted by the site of Abel in the corridor on my way.

"Ah, husband. You came to check up on me?"

"No, actually, I'm here to speak with my mother." He walks right past me.

The calm I'd taken hours to find evaporates.

My steps are heavy and purposeful until I slump down into one of the loungers. "Jerk," I mutter under my breath.

My phone buzzes in my hand, and the message on the screen helps bring a smile to my lips.

You better not be kidding around. I'm so excited, and your hair will thank me later.

With my entourage booked, I lie back and enjoy the sun for a while and wonder if Abel will come and look for me when he's finished with his mother.

Of course, he doesn't, so I grow restless and agitated and finally go and look for him.

He's in the dining room with his phone out, so I decide to make a nuisance of myself.

"I thought we could stay in tonight. Get to know each other." I trail my finger over the back of the chair he's sitting in and come around to take mine next to him.

"We'll go out. I've had enough of being here for one day." He stands immediately, as if being this close is too close.

His attitude is the final straw in my bad mood for today. "First, I don't get to stay with you. Then we don't get a honeymoon, and now you're not even letting us get to know each other. How is this marriage going to work?" I look up at him to see if I need to push a little harder.

"I thought you heard me earlier. You'll be a Cortez and do as you're told."

"Will you tell me to fuck myself, or will you be stepping up to fulfil that role at any point?"

His brow cocks. "Is that what this is about? You want to fuck?"

I stand and close the distance between us, wanting to be close enough to touch him – to kiss him. "Well, as my husband, I want to make sure you can satisfy me. I enjoy sex, and as you seem to be stopping me from enjoying anything else in this relationship, it's my last hope." My lips pop as I emphasise the last word, and I look up and wait for him to react.

He's hard to read because he's so still and shows no emotion. Not like his other brother, who seems brimming with emotional tension.

Most men I've been with haven't even waited to try taking advantage. They jump the gun, and before they know it, they're on their back and I'm having the fun I want. This man is different. And it's strangely attractive. There's an unknown between us that sets a quicker beat to my heart.

My hands rest on his chest and slide up and over his shoulders. I telegraph the move and wait for him to catch up, but it's like I'm seducing a statue.

"Come on, Abel. One kiss," I purr at his neck.

My tongue slips free, and I lick at his throat. Salt and musk mix and spark on my tongue, and the urge to sink my teeth into his skin swarms over me. So, I do.

My teeth press firmly against him while my hands grip his shoulders, and he finally reacts.

He seizes my wrists in a harsh grip and flings me off him. "Bitch!"

My smile is triumphant as I've finally pushed the right button. "Don't like it rough? That's okay. I'll be gentle with you."

He rubs his neck where I can see a little redness start to bloom. A light smile emerges, and he shakes his head a little. I don't know why he's the one smiling, but I don't like it and step back towards him. My hands angle his face as I kiss him, pulling his lips down towards mine. I'm not soft or kind, but rough and punishing, and he meets my force with his own, but it heats in seconds, burning hot and fast.

Finally, his hands come into play, and he holds my shoulders as he moves us towards the nearest wall – pinning me against it. I wrangle in his grasp before he can press his weight against me, not wanting to be at his mercy, and we begin an awkward and fierce tango of moves to assert dominance.

The kiss continues, but it grows in aggression as we're pressing and pulling. Our arms explore, looking to command and hold the other, and it just sends the need simmering inside me to the next level.

He uses his weight and shoves me harder into the wall, so my teeth press down and bite his lip until I can taste the copper tang. There's no complaint from him, but he pulls back and wipes the blood from his mouth.

"Sorry. I know you don't like red on my lips."

I lick the blood from them as I take a moment to catch my breath. I know this is all foreplay. It's fun, and exciting, but I feel like we're simply saying hello, perhaps in the most truthful way since we met.

"That was fucking stupid of you."

"Well, you made it difficult to get any reaction. Are you hard yet?" I reach out my hand and trace the ridge in his pants. His hand wraps around my wrist, and he grips, but it's not just to keep my hand in place.

The pressure grows and grows until I can't move my hand, and the pain makes my whole body tense. The smile that began to emerge disappears, and he pulls me along and through to the bedroom. I try to slow him down, but he's far stronger than me.

He hauls me around, and I fall onto the bed. I kneel up and turn to face him, swiping my hand across his cheek to show displeasure at his force. It barely registers on his face, and he looks at me with coldness in his beautiful eyes.

The slap to my cheek I don't see coming, but I feel it. It lands sharply, and pain explodes down one side of my face. My hands reach to cover the spot, but I hide the shock and pain as all they'll do is show weakness.

"Make no mistake, Alexia, I'm the one in control here." His hands knock me off balance, and I fall back against the bed. "You said something about fucking."

"Ever the charmer." I lie back and wait, trying to re-gather my nerves. "You're a little overdressed, aren't you?"

He grabs my ankle and yanks me down the bed. "Not for what I want with you."

Using all of my weight, I fight, hitching my skirt up so I can wrap my legs around his waist and try toppling him. It works, but as I straddle him and brush my hair to one side, I can see the cold rush across his face again.

He moves his arms to rest behind his neck, and I stare. His lips are still red, as is the bite mark on his neck. I'm sure I look a little messed up, and I can still feel the skin on my cheek stinging with heat.

I look down at my future husband, but my confidence is a little shaken. "I'm clean and safe." My hands reach for the belt and start to undo it, pulling it free before working the button and fly. My fingers reach around his hard cock, and I finally feel just how big he is. Soft, silken skin glides through my fingers as I stroke him. A strange desire hits me, proving that I actually want him to enjoy this, and I squeeze the pressure in my fingers just a little. His eyes close for a brief moment, and that triumphant feeling floats back to the surface.

But he opens his eyes a second later and smiles.

It's a dangerous smile that makes me feel small and vulnerable, and I hate it.

In the next second, I'm on my stomach, and his hand is on my neck, holding me to the mattress, my face pressed against the cotton sheets.

"This has been amusing, but you should listen carefully. You have no control here. None. The quicker you get that through your head, the better."

I don't answer right away as I'm too busy swallowing down the panic rising inside of me.

His free hand runs up my leg from my ankle, over my calf and up to my knee. The pause is pregnant with so many thoughts and emotions, but he doesn't move his hand under my dress.

"Let go, Abel. Please." I hate that it sounds like he's won so easily, but this certainly isn't as fun as it was a few minutes ago.

"I'll let you go when I'm ready and done with you."

"Don't do this."

"Don't fuck you? You were the one asking to be satisfied."

I've manipulated and won over plenty of men in my past. It was easy with them. Played their game, while all the time, they didn't know they were falling into mine. I made myself a promise a long time ago never to give up my control. But now, he's shattering that, just like I smashed the bowl earlier today.

"Please," I beg. "You can tell me what you like, just don't hold me down."

"I'll do whatever the hell I like to you. Holding you down and putting you in your place will be a certainty."

With that, he yanks my body, draping me over the edge of the bed. His grip on my neck is still tight, and he tears at the zipper on my dress with his other hand. He doesn't stop where the zip finishes and simply tears the material from me.

In that moment, all the fun and games dissolve around me, and I'm back to being a scared girl, and my indifference for Abel Cortez crystallises into hate.

CHAPTER FIVE

ABEL

This is probably the best position I've seen her in since we met. Face down. Frightened. Real.

I stare down at the skin exposed to me and take some time appreciating it – back, ass, legs. It's all as fine as it should be, considering the number of years she's spent perfecting it. Irrespective, it means nothing to me but a vessel.

The underwear gets torn, and I sling it to the side so I can get this done. There's no care in me about her feelings, nor is there the first thought about making it pleasurable for her. The only thing that's in my head is making sure she understands the balance of power between us. There isn't a woman, nor man, on this planet that will ever control me again. I do whatever I do with only three ideals in mind – profit, power or family.

"Please, Abel," she says quietly. "No … don't … don't hold me down."

"I warned you. I made it very clear what I expect. This has not been it." More pressure increases on her neck, and my fingers spread over her cheek and chin to hold her face flat to the sheets. I'll do whatever the fuck I want to her. In whatever position I choose. Frankly, this near sobbing coming from her mouth is both stimulating and irritating. She might not be letting those tears fall, but I can feel the tremor in her body, see the glistening in her eyes.

I'm more interested in seeing them come out of her than I am the rest of this shit. It's the only thing real about her.

Still, I push my hand downwards until it's between her thighs and I'm straining them apart. She fights me at first, trying to use strength against me one last time. It doesn't work. All it does is make me increase my own pressure until I can hear her gasping for breath.

"You'll lose this fight, Alexia. Whichever way you try playing it. This is what you asked me for." She twists, trying to get her head out from beneath my hand. Four of my fingers go inside her at the same time, knuckles putting enough force behind them that she startles and tries moving away.

"Please. No!" she shouts.

"Yes." The pressure on her cunt increases, and both my hands do their worst to hold her still and force my way in. "This is the way I fuck women like you." Her ass moves, struggling and shifting to try evading what's happening, and then her hands try reaching back at me. She's got nothing anymore. She's pinned, in pain, and beginning to understand what being with me means.

"You're hurting me," she cries.

"Hmm. Maybe you should have thought about who you agreed to marry, Alexia." I pull my fingers out of her a little and twist my hand, pushing back in at a different angle to get my knuckles where they're going. "This belongs to me now. As does the rest of you. Questioning what we did for a living before committing to one of us would have been sensible."

She doesn't answer. She pushes her face into the sheets and tries biting at them to contain the scream she wants to let out. "But I suppose you thought you'd get one of the younger ones. One of the ones who you could manipulate." I shove and turn my hand, grating my knuckles around inside her until I'm in and fingering all around everything I own. She stills immediately. "You feel that? That's me making a point. This is my cunt now. You screw with me and I'll make your life hell for the fun of it. I hope, for your sake, you heed the warning."

She does whimper and choke at that.

And then the light, muffled sobs start coming.

I pull my hand out slowly, dragging my nails so she feels every inch of me invading her, and grab hold of her leg to bring her down the bed. Her hips get lifted until she's got her ass flush to me, and I grab hold of my dick. She's slack in my hold now, as if she's given up fighting. That's probably wise, considering the argument that's happening. Not that I'm all that wound up yet, but I still smear liquid from her cunt up to her ass, pushing my thumb straight inside that to make sure she understands that everything is on my terms. If she thought this was going to be enjoyable, she was wrong.

My dick gets pushed in her ass with little to no thought. It goes in hard and deep, and I listen to the sounds she makes. Gasps, squeals, panting. She scrapes at the sheets, tries grabbing hold of the edge of the bed for leverage to get away.

"Please, no." I've heard it all before. Seen it all before. Held them all before. She's no different, and her attempt at escape won't work either.

My fingers dig in sharply, gripped tight to her hip bones to make sure she stays exactly how I want her. She's tight inside, and that does at least satisfy my want to come. So I keep the drives in slow and steady, letting it build inside me so we can get this finished.

I grab hold of some hair and tilt her head back, becoming more desperate to see those tears falling. She trembles as I turn her back to me, tries sniffing them back and reaches for my hand in her hair to stop it tugging so hard. I pull harder. In fact, it gets wrapped around my hand until she's got her shoulders up to me and her mouth inches from mine.

"Let them come, Alexia. I want to see them. I might believe

that." Her face hardens instantly, regardless of her lips trying to stutter around mine. Her tongue snakes out, as if, even now, she's still trying to control my desire. "Your mouth means nothing to me."

So I force her back down to the bed and shove her face back on it. And then I fuck harder. I fuck hard enough that she can't contain the screams and shouts she's been trying to hide. They won't stop me at all.

My weight gets used to overwhelm what's left of this fight in her. I doubt it'll work completely this time, but her ass gets used as much as I deem fit for this session. It's raided and ravaged in ways she's never felt before, because this is what she needs to understand about me. I'll brutalise her. I'll treat her like a whore. I'll even cage her to get her how I need her to be if it comes to that. There is no limit I won't cross to get what I want, and fighting the inevitable will only cause her pain.

By the time I'm done and coming, I don't even know if she's breathing under me. I grunt and close my eyes for a second, pulling my own ragged breathing back to steady again. She whimpers some more. Chokes out on her still–hidden sobs and crawls herself up into a ball as I start pulling out of her. The vision makes me sneer and move to stand. She's far from done yet.

And this lesson is far from over.

I look down at my spent dick and wrap a hand around it to ease the last of my cum out. It seeps gently, enough of it left that I smear it onto her face and harshly hook some fingers into her mouth. She squeals as I start pulling her towards me and tries moving her exhausted limbs to keep up with me. "You're not done yet. You'll undress and clean me now."

The tattered dress slips from her skin as she moves, and I keep looking at her face for any form of disrespect. She doesn't show any. She gets up on shaky legs and starts undoing the buttons on my shirt. Everything about her shakes her way through the process.

47

Still, no real tears falling, though. Not even when I make her suck me dry of her ass and remove my pants and shoes like a maid.

"Fold them. Neatly."

She seems blank, as she does as I ask and drapes my clothes carefully on the back of a chair. Void of anything. And for a moment, I consider what she's been through in her life previous to me.

"Shower," I murmur, once I'm fully naked.

She nods, keeps her head lowered, and holds the wall for support on the way. The shower's switched on, and she goes about washing down my body. There's nothing seductive about it. There's nothing remotely intimate about it, either. It's a chore, just like this marriage is. But what it also is, for me at least, is a schooling in manners and obligations. So I don't let her clean herself when she tries. I switch the shower off and stare at her waiting there. Mainly because I want my cum in her ass, and I want her to keep feeling my knuckles inside her. Perhaps if she keeps hold of that sensation for a while, we might find a balance I can deal with.

"On the floor by the bed," I mutter, as I grab a towel and step out.

She looks up at me. It's the first time she's dared since this started. "What?"

"You heard."

"You can't make me—" I stop towelling down my hair and bring my stare back to her.

"I think you know I can. Keep trying my patience and you'll find out how bad this might get for you." My gaze drops down to her open mouth, and my own lips tip up at the potential that offers me. "You've been relatively good, Alexia. I suggest you remain that way unless you'd like to join one of our training camps. Women seem to learn quickly enough while they're there."

We're eye to eye. Both naked. And both trying to come to

terms with our situation. The silence carries on while she thinks about the possibility I could force on her. Good. She should think hard because the facts are very real. They're cruel and savage and barbaric, especially with the women that fight.

Eventually, her eyes dip back to the floor. "You're enjoying this."

I walk out of the room and point to a spot where I want her. "You don't get enough thought for me to enjoy you. Get on the floor."

I look back as I'm pulling my pants on, and watch as she slowly, painfully lowers her ass to the floor. "On your knees." She grimaces, winces, and turns her body, shifting herself until she's perched there like a common whore.

I pull my shirt on, tucking it in and then doing up my belt. "Is this what you wanted from me? Are you satisfied?" She frowns and keeps looking at the floor. I sit and reach for my shoes. "I suppose you're right. We've got it out of the way now." Her eyes look up at me, nothing but hate shining from them suddenly. I thread my cufflinks into place, then reach for my jacket with a sigh. "Hate is good. It makes you strong, which makes you useful as a Cortez." I don't mind her hating me at all. What else did either of us think this would be? I'd rather the reality of that than this pretence we're in. "But use it wisely, Alexia, because if respect doesn't come with it, your life here will be miserable."

She doesn't even flinch at the sound of that. She just dips her head back to the floor again and stares at it. I'd like to think she's learnt a lesson, but she's too arrogant for that just yet.

I walk to her, picking up her chin so I can stare into those eyes. I like her fight, in all honesty. I find it provocative and stimulating, and perhaps, later down the line, we will find a balance in that. Until then, she has to be at heel. She has to toe the line and act like I need her to if I'm to bend for her at all.

Her chin gets dropped away, and my fingers run lightly over her silken cheek as I move for the door. "I'll be back to pick you up tomorrow. Remember what happened here. You forced this on yourself. You asked me for this."

I leave with nothing more. I have work to do, and whatever this has been, and wherever it goes from here, we'll probably have this argument again at some point soon.

She won't win that one, either.

CHAPTER SIX

ALEXIA

I'm left, and for a split second, I'm grateful for the reprieve. My limbs ache, and my body screams, but it's the noise in my head that shouts the loudest. The vows I gave myself – the promises I made are all lying in tatters, like my dress on the floor.

It's been years, and after all this time, my future husband is the one to bring me to my knees. Up until tonight, we were in a game – a dangerous one – but still a game. We both knew this, and I, as I've done so many times before, won.

But not tonight.

I drag myself up and tread softly across to the bathroom. I keep the lights off and run a washcloth under the faucet. False illumination won't show me anything I've not seen before, and I need to keep the memories blurred and fuzzy in my mind. Because no matter how much I hurt or how humiliated I feel, this is only the beginning.

With gentle hands, I wash the cloth over my skin and between my legs. I rinse it out and enjoy the relief of the water on my skin. As I place it back in the sink, I notice two torn-off fingernails.

I take a glass and fill it with water to quench my dry throat. Tears sting my eyes and burn my chest as I fight to keep them in. I've been so strong – so controlled – against the likes of men like

Abel Cortez that I've forgotten how this feels. I've proudly hung words like powerful, independent and confident around my neck and worn them like armour, each year adding to the protection against the sharks in this world. Sharks my father swam with and even baited the water for. And now, confident in seeking our revenge and being able to manipulate and coerce as I've done for years, I'm at a disadvantage because Abel isn't like other men. He's not a shark.

He's far more deadly.

Hate.

There aren't many in this world I'd describe as hating. It's always felt like an ugly, vengeful word – unsophisticated and raw. Not an emotion associated with my actions. But after tonight, it infects me like poison and flows through my veins. It crystalises, straightening my spine and hardening me for what I now see coming.

I hate Abel Cortez – the man I'm meant to marry. He's the man whom I'm supposed to seek my revenge from, but as I lie on the sofa – I can't face the bed yet – all I can think of is how deep this well of coldness inside me can grow.

~

The morning arrives, and my body is stiff from remaining still for much of the night. I couldn't sleep – my mind raced with regrets and sorrow, and now, it's hard to recognise the woman who marched into this place with her own plans.

Last night Abel saw me at my weakest, and while I'm still licking my wounds, I don't want him to see me as defeated. I'm not. I'll never be that. But I do need some time to form a new plan.

The schedule for today involves wedding dress shopping. A delight for many a bride, but alas, I can't count myself amongst them. Before I can face any member of the Cortez family, I have to make some adjustments to my appearance.

The light of the morning shows the true damage Abel inflicted last night, not that he'll care to see it, but I don't want others to see my weakness. I cut all of my nails, file and re-apply some polish. It's a temporary fix, but one I can rectify with Jamie's visit. I'll ask her to bring her nail technician with her, too. Next, I fix the dark shadows under my eyes, hide the finger bruising on my neck, and choose an appropriately dressy outfit that makes me look as tempting as I know I am but also shows less skin than I've done so far.

An hour later, I go downstairs for breakfast.

The house rules are a little vague, but I head to the veranda, and as soon as I take a seat gently, a buttoned-up staff member appears.

"I'd like French toast with berries and whip cream." It's an indulgence I haven't afforded myself in a long time, but I need to fortify my strength with something good.

The house staff doesn't say a word but nods and disappears, and there's no sign of Melena, which is a bonus. I'm not up to sparring with the woman today, and I fear I'd say something too far.

Fifteen minutes later, a platter of juice, coffee and my order of breakfast is delivered. My spot in the shade affords a little comfort from the already too-hot temperature, but my woes are lessened by the delicious food before me.

When I'm alone, I cut into the soft, fragrant toast and spear several of the ruby-coloured gems. It's perfect. A succulent, sweet filling with a bite of tartness to cut through the generous sweetness. I finish the plate, lapping up every morsel as if this food can stitch my broken pieces back together. And in a way, it can. Or at least begin to.

Once finished, I check my lipstick and sit sipping my coffee.

The plates are cleared without a word, and I'm left in peace. It doesn't last long. Voices intrude on my solace, and, like it or not, I must fortify myself for today.

Abel's low baritone travels and meets my ears. My body stiffens with tension, but I force myself to relax. With him is Wren. She looks happy and chatty, and I observe their body language while I can for a moment. She's comfortable around him, relaxed even with her partner nowhere to be seen.

They arrive at the veranda but don't stop their conversation or show any indication they've noticed me. It's rude and infuriating, and I add the slight to the list of other annoyances as they huddle, looking over at the pool. I stay sheltered in the shade, but I can hear what they're discussing. My wedding. Wren has her little tablet out again and is writing notes over the screen. My wedding.

Just as I feel the anger surface at their lack of mind to include me in this conversation, they pause. Abel turns and, with a hand shadowing Wren's back, leads her towards the driveway. Perhaps they think they can go wedding dress shopping without me? But Abel turns, his eyes cast an inspecting glance over me before he simply calls my name as if I were a dog.

And to my horror, I stand and follow.

My jaw aches from clenching my teeth together for the entire journey downtown. Like the show at the house, I'm not involved in the conversation. Instead, I'm relegated to the back of the car while Wren and Abel talk. My mind shuts the conversation off, and I drift to a place where I might feel real emotions, real connections with people. It's a fantasy I have, or rather a dream that I had when I was a girl, being passed around to whomever Father needed to impress. And now here I am, repeating that same behaviour.

The wedding shop is gorgeous. Wren greets the shop manager animatedly.

"The place is ours – we have two hours of exclusive use, Abel." She doesn't address me.

"Let's get to it. Do they have the dresses ready?" Abel asks Wren, but the manager, an older woman who's aged gracefully and with sophistication about her neat and understated hair and makeup, responds.

"Yes, they are ready in the changing area." She looks at Wren and then to me as if waiting for something to happen.

"Oh, I'm a part of this, am I?" I mock. "I was beginning to think you'd be trying on my dresses yourself, Wren. A shame we don't quite have the same figure."

My venom isn't only aimed at her but at Abel, too. But I can barely look at him.

The shop manager directs me further into the store and towards the changing rooms. As with many bridal boutiques, I imagine, there's a central raised platform with half a dozen changing rooms around it. A plush white couch and a dozen mirrors.

"I'm Margaret," she whispers to me as she holds one of the curtains open for me.

"A pleasure, Margaret. I'm Alexia." I step inside and, indeed, see a wall of white dresses.

"Shall we get started?" she smiles. "Now, Wren sent me your size, but anything can be altered."

I place my purse on the chair in the small room and begin to undress. Margaret helps me step into the first dress and then buttons me up.

A simple but indeed elegant fitted silk dress with a small train. I glance in the mirror before Margaret opens the curtain and all but pushes me out for my entourage to critique.

With my head as high as I can lift it, I walk towards the centre dial and stand before my husband-to-be. My eyes don't look for his; I seek no approval or look of love that might announce the dress as 'the one'.

"Um, it's a little plain." Wren pipes up. "You'll be able to wear whatever style with your figure."

"What about the rest of them? What would you suggest?" Abel addresses his question solely to Wren.

"We have a few selected. Let's see them all and then make a call."

I step down and back into the changing room.

The hate stirs inside me like a sleeping serpent but not ready to strike.

"Not the one?" Margaret asks.

"Apparently not."

We continue through the next few dresses. Margaret buttoning, tying and pulling me into each of the chosen gowns. My body feels like it's on autopilot – going through the motions.

There's been little or no reaction from Abel. And even Wren looks fairly bored with the parade of white. Until the final dress.

"This is my favourite," Margaret whispers to me, and I finally look at the narrow mirror in front of me.

It's beautiful.

Elegant, classic and looks like it's made to fit me and me alone. Emotion chokes in my throat, and I have to grasp my chest.

Lace and pearl embellishments decorate the fitted dress that hugs my curves and sets off my figure and my skin tone. I twist to look at the back, laced up to perfection by Margaret's experienced hand.

"This is the one." She pats my hand and moves to the curtain, opening it for me.

This time, I glide to the centre stage, and I have to suppress a glimmer of a smile that's threatening to break free across my face. As I stand and wait, I'm embarrassed that a part of me hopes they like this dress as much as I do, and internally I scold myself for such a reaction. Hope is dangerous, especially in a situation like this.

Abel and Wren are in conversation when I come out, and Abel barely gives me a passing glance. Wren looks more closely, and her smile has a softness that wasn't there previously.

"This is my favourite," she proclaims, but addresses her comment to Abel.

He takes a second glance, but he doesn't look me in the eye. "Whatever you say. You're in charge, Wren."

It's on the tip of my tongue to scream at them – if I'm to have any say in the dress I'm to wear to my own wedding, regardless of it being a sham or a fake wedding. But after last night, everything has shifted. It's become a wedding of hate over family responsibility or loyalty, and I'm weary of Abel and what he's capable of now. That doesn't diminish the fact that I still want this dress and not something that Abel or Wren decide I should wear.

Wren looks at me.

"This one," I say, careful not to put any enthusiasm in my tone. It'll probably ensure this small thing is taken away simply out of spite.

"Oh, I'm so pleased," Margaret announces from the sidelines.

"It is a beautiful dress." Wren's musing makes me want to scratch her eyes out, but I know she's only playing her own part in this fucked-up affair.

I step down to change before anything further can alter. I'm also at the limit of what I feel I can endure without saying something. The goodness of this morning's breakfast is wearing off, and the urge to be alone – to draw in on myself – is growing by the second.

As the dress fits perfectly already, few alterations are required, but we still leave it with Margaret for a final fitting a week before the wedding. Wren speaks to her directly, and I adopt the position of the dutiful bystander. Abel is more interested in something on his phone and takes a phone call away from us before we leave the boutique.

The conversation back home is as it was before – Wren runs over vendor details, plans, confirmations and the plans that are already in place with no second thought or consideration that I'm the bride, while Abel nods and agrees at particular points.

He seems distracted, though, and I wonder if I'm to endure another night like the last one this evening.

My eyes look to the vista we pass, and I search for strength I know I have – one that saw me through the abuse I suffered at the hands of my father's 'friends'. I was a child then, and knowing I've survived my past gives me courage.

After all, I'm not doing this for my father. I'm doing this for me. My plan. My ambition. And my revenge.

CHAPTER SEVEN

ABEL

Weeks have gone by. They've been the same as they've always been. Days and weekends have disappeared into the mire of cruelty we've chosen as our life. People have been disposed of. Women have been taken. Profit has rolled in. It's all as unsurprising as the previous months. We're a formula. A barbaric formula of necessity mixed with greed. Elias being six feet under proves that.

Staring at the ground, I picture him in my head as I've done since he died. It never would have happened if I'd been sharper. I wasn't, though. I was distant and distracted because of problems back here. And now the only thing I have left of that brother is dirt and bones. Shame. He would have been good for this marriage. Evil.

Vengeance is coming, though. In time.

The only thing that has swayed the monotony of normality is Dante and his newfound love. I stand and look over the view spread out across the valley. He deserves that feeling. He took the brunt of everything for years before I came back out. He did well at it, too, apart from the Mariana screw—up. Although, much as I hate the thought of it, the brutality of that night probably did her some good in the long run.

The mass of noise behind me is quietening down now. I can

only assume everyone's being ushered to their seats so this farce can begin. I check my watch and turn back to the building, taking a long breath inwards. I've spent little time with Alexia over the past weeks other than necessity. I haven't had the time, nor did I see the point. We're not in love, and I'll never pretend to be, either. She's just been at the house, and Mother has fed back information to me about her movements or attitude. Nail and beauty appointments seem to have been high on her agenda. Yet more fake–ass bullshit. She doesn't need any of it.

Dante stands up by the fountain in the garden. He nods his head upwards at me and flicks his smoke on the ground, twisting his neck around to get that collar and bow tie off his damn neck. It's time.

The strides seem endless towards him, and for the first time in years, I want a smoke of my own. It's not that I care that I'm marrying her; it's that I despise being tied to something I don't trust. Everything in this family is about trust. We've all earned it, and we've all paid our dues when we've screwed up. Every single one of us knows we'll be there for each other, and every single one of us knows we'll die for each other if we have to.

"You ready for this bullshit?" he asks. My brow arches at the question, and I keep moving past him. Ready? Doesn't matter how ready I am or not. It's just some words and a piece of paper. "You know we could–"

My hand goes to his shoulder, and I look forward towards the crowd all taking their seats. "We're not doing anything other than this."

Knox and Shaw are already up at the archway of flowers acting as an altar, and I smile my way down the run of chairs until I'm up beside them. There isn't any talk of congratulations, nor will there be. This is a business transaction as far as we all know, and, as I survey the line of Ortega's sitting and smiling, I know it's the same for them. Maybe the other two hundred guests think differently, or maybe they don't. I don't give a damn about their thoughts. After today, not one family name will be able to come up against us. We'll be stronger than we've ever been, with a reach that outstrips most of our potential enemies.

There isn't a priest here to service us. I chose a celebrant rather than tarnish the name of God with the likes of this sham. He'll never forgive me most of my sins anyway, but the thought of asking for repentance at the same time as living a damned lie wasn't a choice in my eyes.

"She's here," Dante says.

I look back at him as he puts his phone away and slowly turn my head the way everyone expects. Wren moves through the crowd until she's sat next to Mother. She looks up at me and nods as if everything is as perfect as she can make this charade seem. It is from her perspective. Bellini's grounds look beautiful. The decorations – extravagant. The timing and order – excellent. She couldn't have done a better job of making it as it should be.

Violins start their wedding march within a minute, and I watch all heads lean back to look the way I've looked. Little Lolita Ortega comes first – Alexia's cousin's daughter. She throws her white lilac petals and skips her way through the aisle without a care in the world. Her life will change in time. She'll be as barbaric in nature one day as we all are, given her family. She'll learn to hate and loathe, and eventually, she'll either fuck to survive or be fucked for not being good enough at it. She'll turn from this sweet–natured human and become filled with the necessity of callousness that we've all become.

Mariana trails her in a long, lilac gown. Tall, beautiful. Elegant. The chiffon flutters over her skin in the light breeze, bouncing off the deeply dark skin we've all been born with. She smiles at me and catches hold of Lolita's hand to tow her sideways. It's as insincere in nature as mine is, but she's a good actress. Always has been.

And then there she is – Alexia Ortega.

A snatched breath rips through me. She looks every bit the queen she's been bred to be. She did when she tried the dress on, too, but here, now, in this setting and with all the embellishments, she looks ready to rule the world if she gets the chance.

I keep my features flat and look over the full length of her as her father, Miguel, steps up beside her. She's exquisite, no matter how much I loathe the thought. She's everything a man could ask for. Poised. Perfect. Striking. And for one moment in time, I imagine this being real. I stare at her and focus on her hazel eyes lightly covered in makeup, and then at her lips barely laced with lipstick, and then at her high angled cheekbones that could cut glass, and I wonder what we both might have been before we became who we are.

She's in front of me and Miguel is handing her over before I've finished imagining that. She smiles, takes my hand, and gives her flowers to Lolita, who blushes as I look down at her and runs behind Mariana for support. A frown crosses my features as I look away. It's been a long damn time since anyone's blushed in front of me. A long time since anything was as real as that reaction would be.

"Welcome, everyone," the celebrant says.

We both turn to look at him, and I drop Alexia's hand so it falls at her side.

It's just words then.

Words and promises.

~

Late afternoon turns into evening, and I keep trailing guests with Mother at my side after dinner. She introduces me to people I don't know, and keeps me apprised of anything I need to know regarding who those people are. It's nothing but business again.

There's no one here that I consider relevant for care because only my family hold that position in my head. The food's been eaten and Champagne drunk until a haze of raucousness douses the air.

I drift my gaze in search of my family. Dante's with Wren out at the side of the room, and Knox is talking with one of the many politicians that are here. He catches my eye and swings his head to the left of the room, where I eventually see Alexia surrounded by several of my kind. In any other circumstance, jealousy might swarm through a man in my position. She's drunk, laughing, flirting, and sending coy glances at the men she sees as important. This isn't any other circumstance, though. It's mine, and for that, she should have been more intelligent than she currently is doing.

I back away from the conversation I'm in, rip my bow tie off and flick the button, and turn on my heel for Alexia. She's still laughing about something by the time I get to her, and for a brief second or two, that laughter carries over the music. It seems real for once, and the sound of it hits parts of me I wasn't ready for, causing something like possessiveness to guide me.

The irritation makes me cut straight across the guy who's making her laugh, and grab hold of her arm harshly. She braces instantly and swings her body into me to make damn sure the world understands who her husband is. One hand drapes over my shoulder, and the other snakes across my waist in the perfect show of happiness and marriage. A fucking lie, but at least she's understood I'm pissed and she needs to get with the program.

"Gentlemen. I need my wife."

The word hangs bitterly on my tongue as I guide her away, and the fact that she continues the charade better than I'm managing, regardless of being trashed, irritates me further. People cheer us as we walk towards the exit of the room. Women drool at the insanity of marriage, and men throw shouts of innuendo as we pass. I'm not insane, nor am I remotely interested in the sanctity of marriage on my part. But what I do need to make fucking clear is that there is only one person she will ever flirt with. And there is only one person who will ever fuck her again.

The low, quiet energy of the night air hits me, and I shrug her body from mine, nearly pushing it away from me. She balances and looks back at me, shoulders rolling to square her back into the perfection she's been all day.

"You're acting like a slut."

Her face morphs from boredom to surprise, and then she laughs. "You're jealous?"

"I'm offended."

"Because I was enjoying another man's company?"

"Because you were behaving like a whore."

She walks away from me towards a table full of Champagne and lifts a full glass, swilling it down with apparent little care for etiquette. "Well, maybe that's because you treat me like one. And I suppose if we're being honest, husband, I am one in some ways, aren't I? Although, I've yet to receive any form of payment in kind, beside the name I get the pleasure of using." She walks off again, no sign of the drunk woman of a moment ago. She barely gives me a backwards glance. "Perhaps if you showed any reaction to me at all, I wouldn't have to go looking for it elsewhere."

I follow. "That isn't what this is."

She looks at the ring on her finger as she wanders to the terrace and view, and then glances at my hand for the mirroring image of gold. "Maybe not, but you could try to show me you're interested. There's barely any makeup on my face, at your request. No red to stain my lips. And everything else here has been at your request." She takes another sip and glares at me. "I'm wearing my wedding dress, for God's sake. I don't even know if you like that."

"Why would you care if I like it or not?"

"I don't, but at least here, with all these people, I get a chance to say what I want without having to catch my tongue." A few people walk by, enjoying their time, so I wait for more to leave her mouth. "I thought things would improve, but you've been like a block of fucking ice all day, Abel. Is there nothing I do that pleases you?"

"Lower your voice."

"Why?" she looks around at the guests, barely containing whatever fury she's harbouring. "Maybe I should shout loud enough so that everyone knows what you're really like. Even you wouldn't dare hit me in front of my father."

"I would. Be careful." I grab hold of her arm and lead her further away from the noise, ducking us under a veil of roses until we're in a dark, secluded area. "This isn't the kind of behaviour I welcome."

"Can't you do anything without hurting me!" she spits, attempting to snatch her arm away. "You're an animal." I hold tighter and pull her closer, pushing one arm up behind her back until she's face to face with a tree. "Can't you behave like a gentleman for one day!"

"Yes, I'm perfectly capable of acting like a gentleman when someone deserves it." I press onto her back, holding her square against the surface of the bark. She pants and tries fighting her way out again, waving her free hand around to get to my face. "But you're right, I am an animal, Alexia. And you keep goading me." My free hand reaches down and grabs the bottom of the dress, fingers trailing up her leg until I've got a handful of ass in my grip. "Do you need to be satisfied again?" Because, annoyingly, my dick does.

"What? No. Not here. I—"

"I think it's time for my conjugal rights." She stills instantly and shivers, trembling in wait. "You are my wife, after all. Put your hand on the tree. Now." It wavers in my view for a few seconds. "Put it on the fucking tree and I might go easy on you." I pull off her pinned arm the second she does, and reach down to get more of the dress out of the way. "Is this what you want? My dick inside you?" She stays perfectly still, but slowly rounds her neck so she's looking at me. "You don't get my face as well. Turn away and stay quiet."

I rub on her ass, pushing the material of the dress out of the way so I can get past it and the lingerie. She moans the moment my dick lands on her skin and starts behaving like she should. I watch her hand flex as I run my dick down to her cunt, watch the nails dig into the tree. Gold fucking rings. My own hand crawls up her arm until it's covering hers, and before I know it, I'm sinking inside her and groaning at the sensation.

It's a haze of fucking after that. I can barely find my way through enjoying it. I'm rough, and without sentiment, but something about the feel of her in my hands and the taste of her neck on my lips is tantalising me past sense. My drives get deeper, and the pressure in my dick grows. At some point, I feel her fingers gripping mine as I grate on her with my teeth. She's angling up for me, trying to give me deeper access, and I take it with every next drive inwards.

My hand grips her hip and then moves up to her breasts to push one out of the corset. She can't contain the pants and moans then, and she keeps her face staring at the tree as I asked for. Everything's manic. Nothing's stayed or controlled like I normally am. I fuck like I've not fucked for years, and I make sure to pull every last second of it out until I'm done and she's whimpering.

Cum pours out of me into her, and I bite down hard on her shoulder to give her a piece of that feeling back. I pull her hand in the same breath and push them down between her legs. The rings tangle and clink, reminding us both of what's happened today. "Remember who this belongs to now," I snarl. Her legs widen, and I swallow at the sensation it all creates. It's the first time I've felt connected to a woman in years. Maybe it is full of hate and cruelty, but it's something to feel. And that, together with these damn rings on our fingers, sends me straight back to the cold-hearted animal I am.

I pull out of her without any other thought and leave her standing there against the tree. Ass exposed in the dark. Cunt on display. Fine dress, all crumpled and covered in dirt and cum. I snort at the vision and put my dick away as she turns to look back at me. That gaze could be filled with venom, or regret, or perhaps surprise. I don't know, but whichever sentiment it is, I still reach for my wallet the moment I'm back to calm and controlled.

The new black AMEX gets flicked at the ground next to her feet. "Payment." She looks at it in the scuffed-up ground, then back up at me. "For the fucking, Alexia. You're right, you are a whore. I suppose you need paying for your position from now on. Perhaps you can earn my face next time."

CHAPTER EIGHT

ALEXIA

I stare down at the plastic he thinks I'm worth, cross my arms over my chest and wait.

"Pick it up." Abel's command is clear, but I refuse.

This is not who I am. I won't grovel on the floor for handouts. He might have bullied me and left me questioning my position in this plan – in this relationship – but I am an Ortega, married to a Cortez, and I won't cower any longer. Certainly not after it's clear that he isn't as unaffected by me as he plays out.

"No."

"What?"

"You heard. I don't need your money despite you treating me like your little whore. You know, I didn't expect that from you, and it caught me off guard, but I won't be your plaything. You can't pick me up when you want, get off on me and then lock me away. This is a relationship, if only in a business sense, and while I don't expect you to treat me as a real wife, I fucking deserve some respect. Especially after all the fucked-up shit you've given me."

I ignore the cum seeping through the lace panties and down my leg and pull my dress back into position the best I can. I'm sure the bite mark will be noticeable, but I can either laugh it off or hide. Not that I'm not doing that on my wedding day. I'm done being pushed around, especially in front of my father.

"I thought that finding a way to please you might help us both tolerate the situation. Well, I'm through playing nice."

"I warned you." He snatches my arm. "This isn't behaviour I tolerate."

It might be my weaker arm, but I can still plant a slap across his cheek. He barely moves, but I still made a damn point. "I don't care. I won't tolerate your behaviour either."

Placing my stilettoed heel right through his precious card, I crunch it into the ground before making my way back to my celebrations. I fluff my hair, pinch my lips and slide back into the too-tipsy bride character that seemed to get him so riled in the first place. My smile is bold across my face, but I know if people watch closely – if they knew me – they'd see the act. I've gotten so good at it over the years, I wonder if anyone would be able to tell.

Abel's sure to be behind me. He won't want to let me think I've gotten away with the last word, so I head for the throws of the party, getting lost amongst the revellers for a moment or two.

As I'm looking behind me, I bump into Wren.

"Oh, I'm sorry." She apologises but manages to look me up and down at the same time.

I snatch her wrist and pull her through the hall and out towards the restrooms.

"Alexia, what the—"

"Look." I cut her off, shutting the door and throwing the lock. "I get that we don't like each other, but you're my wedding planner. Have you anything to cover this?" I point to the place on my shoulder where I felt Abel's teeth score my skin – setting my whole body alight. That part wasn't particularly welcome, especially after our track record, but it was different this time, and a part of me liked it. Maybe because I knew he felt it, too.

"What—"

"Please don't act all innocent and wide-eyed. You're dating The Dragon. You know what being with these men means. Now, can you help me?" The words sour on my tongue. Asking for help is a sign of weakness, and I can't often afford that luxury.

She holds my eyes as if assessing if she really wants to help or not, but I can tell she'll cave. There's a shared past between us before we even met. My brother saw to that, but in a way, she is the reason he's dead. Seeing her dictate and arrange today was bad enough, but, as I'm fast beginning to realise, I'm not going to win this battle on my own.

When you go to war, you need allies. That's why I married Abel – so our family will be strong. It's time I start playing for the long game.

"I've … maybe … I think I have something. We'll have to go upstairs to the suite." She tries to smile, but it comes off like she's nervous.

"Lead the way." I stand aside and let her unlock the door. We head up to the room I got ready in, and Wren flaps around, pulling at several garment bags and then joyously holds up an airy sheath of fabric. It floats in the air as she brings it over to me.

"Here. We can cover it with some makeup, and then if you wear this." She starts with the cover-up job, places the fabric over my abused shoulder and then discreetly pins a few folds to the dress, forming a sort of sash. "There."

It spoils the line of the dress, but that's better than the alternative. "Thank you."

"Okay then. I've got a few things to go and check on. And I believe the dances are long overdue." She signals to the door and backs towards it. I take a moment to clean myself up in the bathroom, and with a last glance and a deep breath, I follow her down, digging deep to find the glowing-bride mask I need to show everyone.

At the bottom of the staircase, Abel is waiting, surveying the area and no doubt looking for me. His eyes hit Wren first and then travel to me. I watch as the anger and frustration cloud his features

– only for a second – before it's gone again.

Wren slips past him, and he waits for me.

Smiling at him, I take the last step down to close the distance between us and imagine that this man is the light of my soul and the keeper of my heart.

My hands rest on his chest, and I lean towards his neck. "You look like you have something to say to me, husband?"

"I have plenty to say, wife, but I doubt you'll listen. We're overdue on the dance floor."

"And whose fault is that? You're the one who wanted to fuck me into submission." I kiss his neck and turn to make my way into the main hall area, but he catches my wrist. I immediately freeze, expecting pain or a struggle, but he threads my arms through his and escorts me, as any gentleman – and certainly a husband – would.

As we enter, cheers and applause ripple through the guests, and he leads us to the centre of the dance floor. He pulls me into a hold, and the band music changes as someone announces, "Mr and Mrs Cortez."

We both smile and nod to the crowd around us, and then he begins leading me in some kind of waltz-like dance.

"Why?" I ask.

"Why, what?"

"Why did you go through with this when it clearly causes you such frustrations?"

We're not looking at each other. I'm peering over his shoulder with a fake smile on my lips, but maybe here, with all eyes on us, we can have an honest conversation.

"The marriage was arranged. This is a business partnership."

"So romantic."

"I thought I'd explained that already, or do you need another lesson." His hiss imparts all the threat I need, but something has shifted between us, and I won't allow that kind of treatment again.

"No. And I won't allow another episode like our first time. Never again. It's a vow I made to myself before, and you made me break that. But not for a second time." I move my position to look at him, hoping he can see past the vengeance and hate and see the seriousness behind my words. "I mean it, Abel."

My brilliant smile is an act for onlookers, but for a second, I think I see interest in his eyes. Words cease, and we continue the show of our happy first dance. Abel's mask is less than perfect. The crease in his brow is a near-constant feature, showing me he's at least thinking, but he doesn't miss a step.

Finally, the music ends, and I slide from his grip, but instead of heading to the sidelines, I catch Dante with Wren amongst the guests. It might be time for a little fun. I walk over to him and extend my arm. He just looks at it and then back at me. Wren nudges him with her elbow, which earns her a scowl.

"Come on, Dante. You can't deny the bride a dance on her wedding day," I tease.

"Like fuck I can't."

"Dante!" Wren steps in, and there's a silent conversation between them as they look at each other.

He doesn't say a word but does eventually lead me onto the dance floor and proceeds to dance. It's not as formal as with Abel. His body might be stiff with tension, but I can't deny he can move.

"A dancer. I wouldn't have expected that." I try, hoping for conversation, but he doesn't respond. "You know, out of the two of us, it's me who should have the issue with you."

"Don't fucking start. I don't care if you're Abel's wife."

"Relax, I'm not here to make enemies. Isn't that the purpose of this fucked-up wedding? Allegiances?" Again, no answer, and as we move across the floor I see Abel dancing with his mother, but he's frowning in my direction. Maybe he doesn't trust me with his brother, either.

"I think I'm done." Dante finishes moving, but just as he's

about to let me go, he pulls me back so he can whisper in my ear. "I don't trust you. And if I had my way, I'd gut you like I did your brother. Don't ever touch me again."

"May I cut in?" My father's timing, for once in his life, is impeccable. I smile at him and nod as he takes my hand and I watch Dante stalk off.

"Are you enjoying the wedding?" I ask.

"This isn't a party, Alexia. This is an opportunity, and so far, Melena has held up her end of the bargain." We sway to the music, and I bite my tongue and smile. "I see he's not immune to you, Daughter. He's been watching you since the two of you finished dancing. I trust you've been treating him right." He glides us around the dance floor in an attempt to show some poise and skill but fails.

"Don't concern yourself with how I do my job, Father. Just know there was never any doubt about my role in this. Yet you still doubt me, even as we dance in the middle of the wedding between our families. I'm now Alexia Cortez, and thus securing the alliance we need."

"We, is it?" he chuckles.

"Well, Daddy, it is we. I just wish you could see that." I stop moving and drop my arms from around his neck, stepping back and away from him. After everything I've endured today, I know my limits, and a screaming match with my father in the middle of the dance floor is on the cards unless I walk away.

I push past a few other dances and grab a flute of Champagne from a server on the way out to the lobby area. There isn't enough alcohol to drown my emotions as of this moment, and playing pretend – keeping my mask in place is fucking hard. But at least, having had little input to the guest list, I'm not overwhelmed with people now. Frankly, I'm grateful that the few people around show no interest in striking up a conversation with me or having anything to say to the new Cortez bride. The few families that were here from my side are all distant relations, and Lolita's family left hours ago.

I take a large gulp of the extra-dry bubbles, and my attention is drawn to voices. Looking over, I think I recognise Melena with a younger woman. They're in a heated discussion about something, but I can't see who she's arguing with. And then her dark hair spins out, and I see it's Mariana.

"Come on. I'm done. I'm taking you home," Abel's voice rumbles from behind me.

"Home, well, how lovely." I turn and bat my eyes, even though I know it won't affect him.

"Your home. And I want you ready at ten tomorrow morning. We have plans."

"Oh, a honeymoon?" I know it's not, but I can still point out all the shortcomings of this wedding union.

"No. Work. So put down the Champagne, smile, and maybe we can escape this charade."

CHAPTER NINE

ABEL

The silence of this quiet area eases me awake, and I drop my feet to the floor and stare at my own walls. Dark grey surfaces stare back at me, all of them lined with equally dark, modern furniture and paintings that I didn't choose. They suit me, though. She knows me well like that. I suppose she would. Carmen. She was the person I chose to match my own cruelty, and she's good at it regardless of living in that life herself before I elevated her out of it.

I walk for the shower to get ready for the day ahead. It's the same routine I follow each morning. Come, clean, dress. I might be married now, but nothing has changed for me. I didn't stay with my wife last night, nor did I treat her with anything other than the spite she got earlier in the night. I watched her behave impeccably for the rest of the evening, and I drove her back to Terrell Hills so that the whole charade fit the guise it should have done.

And then I came here.

Gentlemanly behaviour is for those who deserve it.

She doesn't. In any way.

Sitting for a while in the silence after I'm ready, I stare out at the sleek modernity of the outside gardens and pool. I can't imagine a woman being here. It's all mine. My space. My solace. My independence from a family that consumes my every moment.

And in any case, Alexia would hate it. She'd say it was too small, regardless of its size, and then complain that the area didn't live up to the reputation her name was used to. It doesn't, nor mine in reality, but this is where I chose. It's quiet, not overlooked, and hard to get to without my own security system seeing everything coming for me.

The phone rings as I'm drinking the last of my coffee, and I swipe it before heading to my car and setting the alarms with my palm.

"They're here. What time will you arrive?" Carmen asks.

"In about two hours."

"And Dante for the others?"

I check my watch, as I slide into the car. "He should be there in thirty minutes."

"Is the asshole joining him?" I chuckle, mildly amused at her irritation with Shaw.

"No. I'll hold them if you can't manage it."

"Fine."

She ends the call with nothing else to say, and I start the engine and head back to Terrell Hills, inputting Knox's number. He answers on the third ring, sounding like he's barely awake yet. Not surprising at this time of day.

"What?" he snaps.

"I want that money by the end of the day."

"Yeah, yeah. It's covered." It wasn't two days ago, which is when it should have been in our accounts. "It's not my fault Wren got pissy with Dante and made him help her with shit for your wedding." My brow arches as I speed up onto the freeway. "You should've stopped that crap before it began. He'll turn soft. How is marriage?"

"I wouldn't know. Where are you with Reed?"

He walks somewhere, probably heading for the whisky he's about to sink. A glass clinks, proving my point, and then he starts up with his lie. "There's some intel, but he's hard to track. Seems like he was seen in Miami at some point, but some of the guys back in Europe that survived the bomb say they've seen him in London."

My sneer drops, as does my patience level with him. This has been going on for months, and whilst I was relatively alright letting him find his way with whatever he's been hiding for a while, I'm done with being lied to now.

"Meet me at the holding room at noon."

"Why? I'm supposed to be meeting Dante uptown and–"

"Be there, Knox." He's got one more chance for honesty.

I end the call and keep driving until the entrance to the main house comes into view. Phillipe Moinez, one of the guards who walks the grounds, nods as I drive through and stands firm at the gates behind me. None of them are really needed anymore. We're pretty safe up here in this district, but it makes Mother feel safer. Whatever she is to me, or has been, she deserves that. The others won't understand, but I remember those early years. I was part of it on the streets when we first got here. She ran, with me in tow as a child, and we ended up here.

Parking up, I walk around the back of the mansion and down towards the pool to meet her. She smiles as I get to her, and waves me towards a seat.

"Good morning," she says.

I nod and pull out a chair. "Is my wife ready?"

She chuckles and stares out at the pool, sipping her orange juice. "I believe she's getting dressed. Seems odd saying that word and relating it to you. Wife." I turn to look at the pool rather than her. "I'm still amused that you chose yourself. But I suppose, with Dante becoming useless, it was inevitable and–"

"Be careful, Mother. You know I don't appreciate your tone about that. Without him, we'd be nothing. Offer him a little more respect in the future or I'll get frustrated with you."

She frowns and lowers her sunglasses. "Get a check of yourself, Abel. You are my firstborn, and I will not be tempered by your attitude."

I stand before this becomes difficult to the point of no return. "You, Mother, will learn to heed a warning. I am not your plaything anymore." That was a long time ago. If it could be called play. She made me good at dispassionate response, though. I can't deny that.

Checking my watch, I look towards the house. I'm already frustrated that my wife isn't where she'd supposed to be at the time I requested. Add in Mother's attitude and this day is going downhill. "You neither control nor govern me any longer. Don't push me past my limit."

"Abel, I wish you wouldn't get like this. What is wrong with you lately? Have I not given you everything? My whole life has been for your existence and survival."

I look back at her perfectly manicured body and hair, then up at the place she calls home. "Your life has been for your own survival and wealth. Don't forget that wealth is now mine and, if pissed, I might become more aligned to my own agenda than yours."

Walking off without giving her any more room to talk, I scour the grounds for my wife. I have work to do, and if she doesn't get here within the next few minutes, she won't be getting the guided tour I've decided to introduce her to. Hate or not, and lie or not, she needs to begin understanding what we do. Not because she'll be involved in it, but because she needs to learn how to be deceitful about it if needed. Our families are now working together in some respects. My side of that deal is something she's never seen before.

I wait at the entrance lobby, pacing the floor for her arrival. I'm about to just damn well leave when she turns into the corridor and sways towards me. Blonde hair sits neatly in a low bun at her neck, and a fitted blue trouser suit screams class and money. Heels finalise the look, adding that edge of sex appeal I'm beginning to appreciate.

No matter how much my breathing wants to catch at the vision or flawless simplicity, I frown and turn away from her towards the car.

"Good morning, husband," she says, as she gets in the car beside me and slides her sunglasses on. "What delights do we have in store today?"

I side–eye her cheerful attitude and pull us out down the drive. "You'll be learning today."

"About what?"

"Who I am and what I do."

"Well, isn't that exciting," she drawls, looking out the side window. "Perhaps getting to know each other a little better will help."

"With what?"

"Our marriage."

I keep driving. In reality, she's right – it might, because after today she will understand my ability to be as cruel as I am. It took time to build up layers of savagery for my brothers, but for me, treating women like property has always been embedded. They've always been that way. My mother belonged to my father, and the rest of the women I knew at an early age either belonged to him, or then her when she finally broke free of him.

The journey continues in silence, as I think about that part of my life. A mother who's turned from a whore to a madam is a confusing state of being for her son. Respect women, but only certain ones. Treat them like a queen, but only if they deserve it. Hold your family as close as you can, but never let them break free of the villains you've pushed them into becoming. And in the middle of that change, my father came back. He found her and wanted to take it all from her, citing that he was her owner – her pimp – and so everything she'd created was his. It was the first time I watched a woman take revenge by way of a bullet. And the first time I realised that a man touching her with anything but respect would die at my hands one day. Several have. One got me a long stretch in Huntsville.

"Abel?" I look over at Alexia. "Where are you?"

"What?"

"In your head?"

"I'm driving."

"No, you're thinking. We might not be the perfect match, but I'm well versed in the crease in your brow. It's currently uncomfortable with your thoughts."

I keep frowning and pull over towards the exit we're approaching, shifting gears to ease down the slip road. Prison does that to a man. It makes him uncomfortable with what he did back then to survive. Fighting every day. Killing, often, without being caught. Banding together a gang to do as I ask by making others fear just the thought of me. I even had to back down on occasion so the guards got their playtime with me.

"It's good that you can see that, Alexia. Don't play with it, though."

She doesn't say anything else for a while as we head through back roads and dirt tracks. She looks at the view, or the car, or anything but me and my thoughts. We're close to the old airstrip near San Marcos when she sits sideways and does look straight at me.

"This car surprises me." I glance sideways at her, then back at the road. "Dodge Challenger. Hellcat. Latest model. The black I get, but I would have thought you'd have an older version."

"Why?"

"I don't know. Moodier perhaps. They're aged like fine wine and full of grunt. Grating gears and all that."

"Are you flirting with me?" Her mouth stops as if that just rattled something inside her, and then she dares one of those smiles she uses to get what she wants. "Don't do that, Alexia. There was a minute's worth of reality there. Use it." She frowns and keeps looking at me, shifting a little in her seat. "Talk to me about how you know cars."

"My father. He's obsessed with them. I suppose I did anything I could when I was young to be noticed – be his perfect little girl. He and Nicolas were always so close, though. I never had a chance." She looks back out the window, probably thinking about her own version of life before this time we're in. "Do you like it?"

"The car?" She nods. "Yes. I especially like the bulletproof windows."

"I guess this is the safest place to be then."

"That depends on what mood I'm in when you're in it with me."

I pull along the gravel track and down to the warehouses, watching the two guards at the entrance as I park. They keep their stare fixed on me, knowing all too well what wandering eyes get them regarding the merchandise. Not that Alexia is that, but they wouldn't know what she is to me yet.

Intense heat hits me as I get out of the car and walk us over to the building, and the minute we're inside the room the usual noise and smell of sweat and smoke starts infecting my system. I look around and glance at Alexia, gaging her reaction in these morally inept confines of iniquity. She's as poised as she usually is, with a face that seems as blank as she can make it.

Carmen's voice shouts over the darkness and music, and I follow the sound until we're into the middle of a training room and watching four women walking the same steps I've seen a thousand times before. One of them trips over her heels, near falling to the floor in the process. Carmen's on her like the bitch she is, dragging her up by her hair until she's standing and trying to walk again.

"Ah, there you are," she says, coming over to me. "And this must be your new wife." She leans in and kisses me on the cheek.

"Hello, Mrs Cortez," she continues, offering her hand. Alexia takes it and nods, no other response than that. "I'm Carmen Bennett." She's not. That's a name she chose when she became this new version of herself that hides in shadows and destroys women's lives for the healthy profit she makes. "Dante has managed reasonably successfully without Shaw being here. Would you like to see the new intake first or the ones he's been dealing with?"

"The new ones. When will these four be ready?"

"Next week. They're tabled for the Bourbon Lounge, but I was thinking they might be better for sale to the market. None of them are particularly special. Especially not that one," she says, flicking her head to the one that fell. "It might be better falling into a canyon somewhere, to be frank." Hmm. "Keep moving, girls," she shouts. "Remember who's in the wings waiting for you."

"Who is in the wings?" Alexia asks.

"Ratchet," Carmen replies.

"Ratchet?"

"Yes. Ratchet. RATCHET? SHOW YOURSELF!" Ratchet, the man we use to keep this formula rolling the way it should in the form of fear, or entertainment, appears in the corner with his black leather mask strapped in place. He lifts his chin at me and nods, then retreats to the black shadow he came from. "He's quite sweet under that uniform," she continues. "Well, sometimes anyway."

Dante walks around the corner just as we're turning it, shirtless and drenched in sweat. "Keep going, Carmen. I'll meet you there." She leaves, and I turn back to Dante.

"Brother," he says, wiping the back of his neck with a rag.

"Knox will be here in fifteen minutes."

"Why?"

"I want to see him before you leave."

"Alright."

"How many done?"

"Eighteen. They're heading out for Mexico tomorrow. I'll get the next load from the border when I've got them bedded in at the new houses." He looks at Alexia for the first time and frowns. "Ten to Carrera's, and the other eight to Elena Cruz's place. I'll go wait for Knox."

"I don't think your brother likes me," Alexia drawls, as he leaves.

"Like has nothing to do with it. He doesn't trust you. None of us do. You haven't earned it."

I start moving again, winding corners I barely know and not caring how welcome she feels. This is a relatively new building for us. We change them constantly. Not necessarily because of the law — we have that dealt with — but because of people and the media. The last thing we need at our door is the wider—world interfering with our profit margins.

Racks of large, tall cells come into view as I round the next corner. They're mostly empty at the moment. We shipped thirty out three days ago, another twenty the week before that, but I glance in the far room as we keep moving. Dante's work shines back at me as I look over the women hobbling around in there.

"Why are they all limping?" Alexia asks.

"They've been marked." She looks confused. "Branded. On the base of their foot."

"Well, that's barbaric."

"We are barbaric. And it's necessary. We make a cut of everything they make. Either by selling or loaning them out. Sometimes to houses, other times to private buyers."

"All over the States?"

"Mainly, but Europe is being worked on. We had a problem a while back."

"Was it something to do with Elias's death?" I look back at her. "I know he was killed. My father didn't know or care to share the details."

"Yes."

"I don't have all day, Abel!" gets shouted down the corridor.

A half–smile lifts my face at her cutting tone, and I turn sideways to make my way down the next hall of metal.

"You like her," Alexia asks, catching up with me. "Carmen? You've never smiled like that for me."

"I do. She has earned it. In varying ways."

The grating sound of fingernails runs along the bars of a window as Alexia passes it. "You've fucked her."

"Yes."

"Still?"

I don't answer, mainly because it's none of her goddamn business who I fuck or when I fuck them. But no, not for a long time now. She was one of the few that interested me years ago. It was her vindictiveness that earned her my respect. She stood there in a room full of sex and men waiting to buy her, and then, once bought, she stabbed her new owner in the heart. Covered in blood, and perhaps waiting for her own death, she looked up at me and smiled. It intrigued me enough to give her a chance.

"How long has she worked for you?"

"Long enough to understand me."

We get to the room and turn into it, and I watch as Carmen opens up the back wall of doors. The truck gets reversed, and the haulage doors are opened to block off all exits other than straight into here. It's the first look at the new intake either of us has had.

The dark confines of the truck move as the women shuffle and jostle inside.

"Most of these are already working girls. Some were picked up from the streets. Others were pulled out of raided houses and cells upstate," Carmen says. "Come!" she shouts, waving them down. "You're safe enough here." For now, at least. "We have food and clean clothes."

They slowly start emerging one by one and drop to the dusty floor. I look over each one as they make their way out, taking in their shape, looks, hair and features. All good enough, apart from one of them. And that's nothing to do with what I've been examining.

"Line up," I mutter, watching them hover around.

They do, barely looking at me. I move straight to the girl at the back, reaching for her face through the others. She squeals and tries backing away from me, so I grab tighter and stare down at her. "How old are you?" No answer. Just fear and trembling features.

The two new finders come in from the front of the truck, both of whom should have known better than to bring an adolescent into my space. I look at one of them, raising a brow for clarification.

"She was on the streets when we were travelling back." He shrugs and looks at the other one for help. Help is gone now they've fucked this up.

"She's underage," I say, flicking her face away from me. Probably fourteen at a push, regardless of her curves. "You should both be able to see that. And now she's seen me."

"Man, what does a few years matter?" he says, flustering words.

I move at him, pissed that he'd dare talk back about this, but just as I do, one of the other girls makes a run for the open door. I catch hold of her hair as she goes and push her straight to the ground. My boot goes over the back of her neck, crushed in hard to make sure she stays down. "I made it crystal fucking clear about the sixteen–year–old policy."

He looks over the young one and sneers as the bitch under me struggles. "A whore's a whore. And it's not like they've got identity cards on them. They've all got pussy between their legs." Carmen moves backwards in my eyeline, pulling Alexia with her. "Just another profit, right? What's the fucking problem? You need to chill the fu–"

My gun is out and he's shot straight in his forehead before he finishes his words. All the women scream and run in my periphery as the spray of blood sweeps back at me. I don't move from it. I watch him drop like a stone, keep my pressure hard on the girl under me, and slowly look sideways at the other finder. We're not that organisation. We might be cruel, and we might be savage, but kids get their chance at life before we make them rot. Maybe they get caught again a few years later, but until then, it's my only hard limit on profit.

"Do you understand that?" I ask, tilting my head. "This is what happens when you contravene a direct order." He backs up some steps, putting himself near Carmen and Alexia. I can't make up my mind if it's for defence or aggression, so wait for a move of some kind. Dante chooses that moment to come into the room, slight panic on his face considering the gunshot. He's in front of Alexia before I even have to ask, pushing the guy back out into the centre of the space so he's nowhere near her. Hate or not, he'll do exactly what he needs to to protect what's mine unless I say different.

"Talk to me about giving you a second chance."

Little fuck nods and looks back at the girls. "Fuck, man. I didn't … think. I don't know. I'll get it right next time." He moves away from the women on his own, backing himself up to a wall and raising his hands. "The others are good, yeah? I got them all. Just don't …"

I watch him swallow his fear, then wonder if he's pissed himself yet. "No one under sixteen. Ever. Carmen?" She walks out towards me. "Get rid of her."

There aren't any words of response. She just walks for the girl and starts pulling her from the space. I keep square with the guy I'm thinking about trusting again, wondering if this was enough or if he needs more encouragement to follow the fucking rules successfully. He looks at the girls again, and something about that moment riles me. Fucking up and now looking at the merchandise?

I loosen my weight off the girl on the floor and watch her run back into the mob of new intakes. "Dante, my wife needs a drink while I deal with this."

Not that I care if she sees my violent nature or not.

I just don't want her tainted with his blood.

CHAPTER TEN

ALEXIA

D ante all but drags me back through the dark corridors
we came through and eventually turns into a room
that feels less like the bowels of the operation.
There's a window in this room, and it's set up as an office.
Although, I'd bet there are no papers or documents associated with
the real business here.

He lets go of my arm and heads to the corner of the room,
grabbing a bottle of something and pouring. Without a word
between us, he thrusts the tumbler of golden liquid towards me.

"A little early to drink, don't you think?" I offer.

"No." He takes the glass in his hand, drains it, and heads back
to the table to pour a chaser. In this gloomy light, I can see the
tattoo snaking out from beneath a shirt he wasn't wearing earlier.
The material creases as he moves, smudged and dirtied up with
sweat and grime. He looks every bit the vengeful killer I know he is
and a mile away from the man I danced with yesterday at my
wedding. The lack of shirt and appearance earlier, plus the
conversations before Abel blew that man's brains out, make me
think he must be the one to mark the girls. Or should I say
merchandise. Especially as he seems to be wearing his own kind of
brand in the shape of a W. Interesting that a man like him would
be that committed to a girl like her.

The way they treat the girls, the way Abel manhandled the girl earlier, brings a sour taste of bile to my mouth, but I control it and swallow my nausea down, and with it, my memories away. The flip of my stomach is a warning, but I force a deep breath.

I perch on the arm of the leather chesterfield positioned in front of the desk while Dante stays in the corner, watching me like a hawk. Abel said his brother doesn't trust me – with good measure, I suppose – but I have to wonder what act or deed I'll be required to perform in order to earn that trust. Or maybe it's simply a matter of time because regardless of him trusting me or not, he would have protected me up there. His movement towards me didn't go unnoticed, and it makes me want to question why. Like so many things in this family I've seen, I can't seem to guess or predict anything.

And that puts me at a disadvantage.

"Does Wren know what you do?" I don't expect she does, and I don't expect him to answer, either. His eyes narrow, turning his features menacing and violent.

My question isn't answered, and after a while, Carmen, followed by Abel, walk into the office. There's still blood flecked over his face and shirt, not that it bothers me, but it is a new version of my husband to imagine. Carmen motions to Dante, and he follows her back out. Her eyes linger on me a fraction too long at the door, and the urge to slap her cocky little grin courses in my veins. She believes she's better than me, and that is an opinion that I won't tolerate going forward. I just need to figure out how to get that message across. Especially considering she's clearly in Abel's inner circle. A position that I assumed would be for family only.

"I haven't got long. Knox is due shortly," Abel murmurs from the corner.

"And I'm assuming I'm not invited to that particular conversation."

He picks up a glass, pours and drains the contents before turning back towards me. "No."

I bounce my leg, crossed at the knee. What I imagine in my mind – what I saw Carmen do to those girls – is like poison to me. It seeps through my blood, wiping away the armour and resolve I've built over the years.

"Can I ask you something, Abel? Why did you bring me here?" My father expected unthinkable things from me. I was a tool for his ambition, and the scars will never heal. And now here I am, face to face with another monster who profits from the same pain and humiliation I endured.

"I've told you that. It's time you understood what Cortez business is built on."

"I think it's more than that." I stay sitting on the edge of the couch, my body vibrating with an urgency to escape. But then I consider how that will look. I need Abel to trust me – to know that a little blood and honesty isn't going to affect me. More than that, I need him to see that I'm beginning to understand his games. "I think you wanted to shock me. To frighten me and to show me why I should be afraid of you."

He's the one to move first. He steps towards me and looks down, his eyes landing on the pink blush on my lips. "Are you?"

"No," I answer confidently, and it's the truth.

He scoffs, and I see this as another sign of control – controlling my behaviour with passive threats. Ironic, as he's quite good at the physical ones.

"Everything you do, Abel, is calculated and for a reason, and ultimately, for your family. We're a living statement to that truth. There are no missteps with you."

"I agree."

"So, why did you bring me here?" I stand and walk past him, making sure to brush my shoulder against his – the briefest of touches – and pour myself a drink.

"Seeing what we do is a very different reality to hearing about it. It was a test."

"And do I pass? Watching your new husband kill a man the day after your wedding is quite a honeymoon."

He grabs my jaw and turns my face to his. "See, that fake mouth of yours trying to be clever is only going to piss me off. You've been warned." He shoves me back, but all he's done is tear off the mask of indifference I've been fighting to keep in place.

"You want me honest?" I shout. "Fine. You sell women as property – even mark them as yours. Of all the things I've done in my life, marrying a man that thinks that's okay only gives me another reason to hate you."

"And selling drugs up and down the country is more respectable?"

"Choosing to take drugs is a very different line of work."

"Choosing? That's an interesting take."

The hatred I harbour for my father, for the position he put me in, and the fact that I'm now married to the family that killed my brother and yet still treated like nothing more than a plaything, builds the emotions swirling around my head and chest.

I step closer, making sure our bodies are touching, and look him in the eye. "My father used me as a reward for his criminal partners and to garner favour with others to build his empire – the empire he doesn't see fit to share with me. I continue to be his pawn. I know how those women feel. And it's certainly not the same as choosing to get high on coke." I let him take in my words. I doubt they will be too much of a shock. "The only redeemable difference between you and my father is that you have a moral conscience to ensure at least the girls are older. My father didn't care."

The pain that lances through my chest at that admission is greater than I thought, but he wanted honesty. I can't be more honest. And if this strategy is the wrong one to make any type of headway with him, then so be it.

I hold his gaze, unwavering in my truth.

"Honest is much better on you," he says.

"Funny, it doesn't always work out for the better." Our proximity is heated, and I know that despite our animosity there's chemistry. It's becoming a constant push and pull that's as hate-filled as it is deadly. "Why is it alright for a seventeen-year-old girl to be down in your dungeon and not a sixteen-year-old? What is that moral compass?" I tilt my head and wait. "Surely, your profit would be greater for underaged girls. I know men would pay for that," I spit, as anger flares through me and I remember when I was first given to a man.

"That's the rule. One of the only ones."

"That's not an answer," I seethe.

"The rules of my business aren't for you to question."

"That's not going to stop me. And you know what, you make me sick. Although, at least now I know why you treat me with so little respect. You view women as property."

His hand runs up my neck and tangles in my hair. The grip starts gentle, like a caress, but grows, sparking my nerves from the top of my head down my spine. "Careful, Alexia. I've indulged in your little show to satisfy my own curiosity. Don't spoil it."

"Uhh humm."

Abel doesn't acknowledge the interruption behind us immediately, keeping me in his hold. And still his dark eyes don't move from holding mine captive. "You're late, Knox."

"You're otherwise engaged."

At that, he drops his hold of me and straightens his suit.

"I'm excused now, I take it?" I ask, looking between Knox and my husband.

"Yes. I'll have someone take you home."

"I'll take your car. I can handle it." I hold out my hand for the keys. After our little heart-to-heart, this will be an interesting test of my own. I've only been alone within the confines of his mother's house since I arrived. Every trip or visit I've been escorted. Every move accounted for.

"And if I don't trust you?"

"Well, that's too bad. How is anyone meant to earn your trust without an opportunity?" I smile at him – one of the smiles I know he hates because I've used it a thousand times before him.

He's hard to read. The crease on his forehead when he's thinking is his only discernible tell. Of course, he doesn't try to hide his feeling of distaste towards me well. But now, standing in this room after everything he's done and shown me – everything I've confessed – he's a giant question mark wrapped up in a damned, sexy suit.

"Abel, we have business," Knox states.

It doesn't rush Abel's decision. It's like he's inspecting me for the first time. Perhaps analysing what this moment, or maybe my confession, means to him.

I hold my nerve and stand tall.

"Don't make me regret this," he murmurs, as he pulls the keys from his pocket and drops them into my hand. My instinct is to wear my smile with pride, but I know that's not what he wants. So, I nod and glide out of the room.

I take a deep breath when the door closes behind me, and I swear the oxygen sets the adrenaline pumping. Then, walking out of the building, I head straight for the car. It's been a while since I've driven one, but I'll enjoy this joy ride.

The door closes, I turn the ignition, and the car rumbles to life, vibrating through my entire body. My foot hits the gas, and I floor the car out of the parking lot. The rush is my first taste of freedom in months. It's a wave of possibility and relief, all mixed up into a heady cocktail, so much so that I can't contain the smile that beams across my lips.

Part of me wants to gun the car and never turn back. I've

manipulated and worked my way into and out of every situation I've wanted to in the past, but Abel Cortez is different, and whilst a part of me wants to put him and the rest of my life in the rearview, making that choice will be running away. If I do that now I'll always be running. I'll never forgive myself for it. The fourteen-year-old me will never forgive myself.

My fingers grip the leather of the steering wheel, and the simple gold band glints at me in the sunlight. I married into the Cortez family. It might be a fake relationship built on mutual hate but marrying and falling in love isn't in my plan. My plan is sculpted in revenge, and I can't rush it. Now, I have another facet to add to the plan.

If I can just hold my nerve a little longer. If I can bury my feelings and wear the dutiful wife mask until the time is right, it'll work. I've paid my dues, and it's time to show everyone why I should have been in the same position as Nicolas was and that I'd never make a mistake like he did.

For a few more miles, I enjoy the strength and space the Challenger offers. And then I turn the car around and head for Terrell Hills.

CHAPTER ELEVEN

ABEL

Wandering in halfway through Dante's idea of hellfire, I look around the old place and watch the flames beginning to lick up the side walls. Bottles of liquor get tossed at surfaces, as he drags the owner of this establishment over to a seat in the middle of the room. The guy – Saul Goldmann – looks about ready to die, but that's not stopping Dante elongate his death. A few months ago Saul said he wouldn't piss around with his obligations. He was warned.

He chose to ignore that warning.

His brother – Liam Goldmann – stands on the side wall away from the flames with Shaw holding him. I walk closer and stare into his eyes, watching as he struggles for freedom to reach his brother. He won't. He'll watch him burn, and then perhaps he'll think twice when we let him carry on living. "I know. It hurts," I murmur. He glares back at me and tries shaking Shaw off again, then looks back at his brother. "But he knew, Liam. Dragon's breath had already been shown."

I twist back to look at Dante, smiling as he gets invested in his work and pours gas at Saul's feet. It takes me back to my younger years. They were times when I'd use my feelings rather than sense. I was like him then. I took all those sensations and visions I'd grown from, and I poured hatred into everything.

One heavy punch lands on Saul's face, just enough to knock him partially out. He'll still feel the burning as he dies, though. And he'll still scream his way through his death so this fuck hears it.

"To the table," I tell Shaw. Liam gets hauled backwards and turned until he's pushed over it, and I pull my blade out. "What shall I take to make sure you understand?" I ask Liam. "Dick?" He looks at me under the pressure of Shaw's grip against his head, then tries struggling. "But then there'd be nothing to fuck that pretty wife of yours with. I could help with that, though." That hits home. Women always do. His eyes widen, jaw slackening at the thought of me on her.

I keep staring, making sure he appreciates the thought, because I mean every word of it, and he knows exactly what that means. I'm nearly invested in the thought of her ass, anyway, when Dante laughs behind me, breaking my mood. "Hand then." Shaw drags it into place, covering his wrist to keep it still. "Are you listening, Liam? Do you hear what's coming for you? Regular payments on the twenty eighth of each month. No straying outside the rules we've set for you. Zero fucking drugs. You're not a cartel we allow space to."

My blade positions over his thumb, and I hit down on the top of the blade, forcing it to crunch through bone. He bellows out his pain, still trying to shrug Shaw off. Pointless. No one gets around his kind of pressure when he means it. "Don't fuck around with me again. Next time it *will* be your dick, then head." I pick it up and slam it down a few times to make the point felt. "Remember what's happening here and you'll be fine."

The smell of burning leather breaches the air, and then the shouting starts in the background. I listen to it and Liam as he tries to call for mercy, and slowly turn away from the death unfolding to find Knox. My part here is done, and there isn't any mercy. I don't have any to give, and I barely remember a time when I did. But in these shouts and pleas, Kayla springs to mind – still crying and bruised. Still saying no.

Two corridors later, I find Knox in the back room used as a counting house for laundered income. I watch as he heaves the last bag of money out of a safe and starts counting. He's meticulous, as always, regardless of the smoke beginning to engulf the building. He cuts through the notes with the precision of a banker, licking his finger to dampen it with each next pile processed.

He flicks a look towards some folders on the table. "Title deeds to this place and the restaurant on Broadway. I'll get them to Grasby." Charles Grasby Junior. Our attorney. A nasty piece of money–bred asshole. I like him. "How long do I have?" he asks.

"Five minutes." He nods and loads another bundle of money into one of our bags before picking up the next. "How much longer does this lying go on?" His hand hovers on the money for a fraction of a second, and then he carries on counting. "My patience is wearing thin, Knox."

He frowns and throws another bundle in the bag. "Just let me do this first."

I do, whilst I listen to the continued screams of suffering coming along the corridors. Not only because he needs to work out how much money we're still owed, but because any lesson in manners he might need isn't going to happen in a building that's about to fall into itself. At least he hasn't lied about his lying. Which is more than can be said for Liam out there. He lied about Saul hiding things from me, and all that after Dante had already sent a message through these hallways.

Picking at my nails, I clean them out and try not to think about Kayla's face underneath me. It doesn't work. She was fourteen, a virgin – purposely so – and the daughter of one of Mother's whores. Nothing but property, Mother said, as she brought me in the room and told me she had a treat for me. It was a treat in her eyes because underage virgins were worth a lot of money. My wife was right yesterday – they still are. But regardless of profit, I can't get the look of fear on Kayla's face out of my head sometimes. I still fucked her as I was expected to, while Mother stood in the room and watched. I rutted like a hormonal adolescent and took what was offered. Under duress, maybe, but I did as I was told. I obeyed.

Sneering, I look back up at Knox, still counting. It was my fifteenth birthday that day. And whilst she wasn't my first, she was the first I held in place. A week later, Kayla was pushed into the main whore house and used by anything that wanted her. I'd broken her in. I'd been given a gift.

At least I never hurt her physically other than tearing a slither of skin in two.

And I did eventually atone for my part in her life after me.

A low sigh drains out of me, as I think back on Alexia's confession and the look of disgust in her eyes. It didn't surprise me that much. That's the kind of man Miguel Ortega is, and no doubt she was an asset he could use at that age – or even now considering this marriage I'm part of. It riled me to hear it out loud, though. It took me straight back to Kayla, and then to watching all the other girls Mother used and degraded for profit at that point. I'm no different from her now in reality, but perhaps, for the first time, I found some respect for my wife. Or at least some sympathy.

I don't know what to do with either of those feelings. We're nothing but hatred bound with gold rings. And yet that fire she brought at me – real fire that ached inside her to get out, to find vengeance – I liked it. More than I want to admit.

Shaw and the sound of dragging feet and shouts eventually stops in the doorway. He looks in at us and nods his way towards the back exit. "It's time," he says. "Dante's on his way."

I nod and watch him haul Liam away, before picking up some of the bags Knox has spread around his feet. He gets up after the last bundle of money has been counted and loads several bags up on his own shoulders, swinging the last one over his head.

"I'm done."

I watch him go and wait for Dante to show, then step in behind him as he tosses a few more bottles of liquor along the hall. One last glance back and I see flames creeping around the corner towards us, an inferno building behind it. Wood starts creaking and groaning under the pressure he's created, and then the smoke thickens to near opaque around us. None of it means anything other than an enforcement of the rules. The Goldmann family are lucky there was only one dead man and one building destroyed tonight, because if it happens again – if Liam dares bring drugs into our area again – I'll gut his wife in front of him before he feels my wrath himself.

By the time I'm out into the night air and pulling in clear breaths, Liam is getting a reminder of the manners he should have acknowledged while his brother was still alive. I chuckle lightly and pull Dante off him, pushing him towards the car. We're done here for now, and I have more important things on my mind than debtors, infringing cartels, or Alexia's past. Namely, why they've both been hiding things from me for too long.

The drive back towards Knox's place is slow and winding, and I stay quiet and wait for him to speak. He doesn't. He stays fixed on the road and nothing else until we finally pull into the long driveway that leads up to his place in the woods. I'm alright with that. I'm neither wound up nor angered at the moment. But I'll be both if there hasn't been a damn good reason for the deceit.

They all get out and head into the house, and I give them time to deal with whatever shit they've got to deal with together. They'll be getting their stories straight, and Dante will be trying to knock sense into Knox about why this was ever hidden from me in the first place. Shaw won't know a thing about anything. I know my brothers well – all of them. They're loyal. No disputing that, but they're individuals too. Knox – the thinker. Dante – the muscle. Shaw – the questioner.

Unsurprisingly, when I walk into the house, there's an argument in full swing shaking the fabric of the building. "Sit your ass down," Dante shouts. I listen, wondering how much longer this will go on before Dante finally loses his cool. "I told you how this would end."

The sound of knuckles meeting bone lands hard, as I keep moving towards them, and by the time I'm around the corner into the main lounge area, Knox is pinned on the wall.

"Get the hell off me," Knox shouts, jostling for space. Dante doesn't.

I get it, he's pissed he's been asked to hide something from me, but I need the truth now. Whatever this has been, it's done. "Let him go," I command, as I head for the bar. Knox rips at his jacket the second Dante does, and then starts pacing like he might just get pissy with shit that was his own making. So I watch that, too, ready to knock some damn sense into both of them if need be. "Calm down."

Finally, the air starts settling into neutral. Dante stands in the open doors onto the deck, his back on display as he stares out at the dark of the woods. And Knox does eventually sit his ass down, shrugging his body like a kid who just got caught doing something he shouldn't.

"Talk to me, Knox."

He huffs and looks away. "I know where he is. Reed."

I pour my drink, filling the next three shot glasses alongside it. "And?"

"He's in New York with Logan Cane. At least, he's under his protection."

Leaving one glass on the counter for Shaw, I walk for Dante and hand him his. He scowls and takes it from me, downing it with nothing to say about anything. "Why?" I ask, turning for Knox.

"I don't know, but I've been trying to work out the connection. There isn't one that I can find." I offer up his drink and walk backwards until I'm leaning on the side wall. "But you know Logan, Abel. There's no point going in there like a bunch of banshees. We'll lose, and someone will probably get killed. We're not doing that." I keep looking at him, waiting for more. "We've got to be tactful or at least have something to barter with."

I down my own drink. "Do we have anything to barter with?"

He nods. "Yeah. A priest."

"Priest?"

"Yeah."

"How do we barter with a priest?"

"He's fucking him."

Dante spins around at that information, seemingly surprised. "Logan Cane is fucking a priest?"

Knox looks over at him. "Yeah."

"Just fucking, or involved?" Shaw asks. Good question.

"The latter. I think but—"

"You didn't tell me that?" Dante snarls. "Why all the goddamn waiting if it's that simple? We go in there, get the priest and use him as bait." Knox gets up and paces again. "Don't know why we haven't just gone for the wife or kids anyway."

I glare at Dante, making my point felt.

We don't touch kids.

"Don't bring that bullshit at me," he growls. "Elias is six feet under and you're more bothered about a couple of Cane fucks? Maybe if you both stopped acting like mothafucking politicians we'd—"

My hand goes up. "Calm down before I turn hostile."

He throws his arms up in the air, turning his back so he can cling onto the doorframe rather than use his aggression. "He's been wasting my goddamn time. All this could be over and finished and—"

"No one's saying anything concrete," Knox cuts in. He comes to a stop, looking at me. "But there are whispers. A lot of them.

Going for the wife or kids brings all-out war. You both know that as well as me. We've got a chance with the priest. Especially now that you've got Alexia's family in tow. Logan might think reasonably."

Reasonably. One thing most of our world knows is that nothing about that man is reasonable. "Why didn't you tell me?"

"Because …" He turns away and walks over to the bags of money from earlier, lifting a few to take them out to his safe.

"Knox?"

"Because I can't read you these days. You're like a goddamn explosion waiting to detonate, Abel. Cold as ice one day and then ready to annihilate everything the next, and we all know how you feel about our reach. You want more. But we'll lose if you go in like that and we're not prepared." He lifts another bag and starts walking.

"Get your ass back here. Now."

He hovers and sighs, shifting the bags around on his back before looking back at me. "There's no sense in it, Abel. None. You're a wrecking ball about that city. Fuck knows why. We don't need New York. Isn't what we do have enough for you?" No. And everything I'm doing, I'm doing for this family. To keep us surviving and safe and untouchable. If I want to take on Logan Cane, I will. "See? You're already thinking it. And that shit is nothing to do with Elias being dead or Reed. That's just plain fucking greed. As usual."

"You're beginning to piss me off."

"Yeah, but someone needs to say it and I'm not a kid anymore. Dante thinks with his fist or dick most of the time, and Shaw's not even worth talking about." He drops the bags to the floor and looks over at Dante, practically begging him for a fight he'll lose. "It's time we had this said. What is the plan now you've got Ortega's backing? Swarm across the country until you're knocking on Logan's door with attitude and nothing else? Give him a reason to come get Mariana and have some fun? Yeah, let's put her through that again, shall we?" He looks at Dante. "Because we were just fucking great at protecting her the last time, weren't we?"

Dante moves sideways and passes me, probably as ready as I am to have a discussion about manners. "Motha fucker—"

"Leave him," I snarl.

He stops about three feet away and waits, vibrating with resentment and hatred. It gives me the time I need to make my way in front of Knox and glare.

"Jesus. We're not enough, Abel," Knox shouts. "We'll fucking lose! What the hell is wrong with you? Why can't you just be okay with what we are? We just need the priest as a threat. And then we leave with Reed and deal with him."

I'm not battling the same rage as Dante, not entirely. Mine's based in animosity about who sits at the top of this goddamn tree. Truth or not, Knox doesn't get any decisions about who does what or when. He delivers what I ask for, when I ask for it, and he should be doing both with the same sense of loyalty that every other fucker around me wears.

"For an intelligent guy, you're a dumb fuck sometimes." My hands grab at his shirt, authority sending him straight back to a wall until he's backed up with no way around me. "This is my goddamned family, Knox. My fucking decisions. You don't get to make a choice about anything unless it's what I've agreed to." He tries keeping that stare fixed on mine but buckles as I keep glaring in response. "You remember what happens when you go out on your own?" He swallows and turns his head sideways, no doubt remembering the time I beat him senseless for screwing up a deal because he thought he knew better. "Yeah. Nothing's changed. You hide shit from me one more time and I'll make a point of reminding you how that felt."

I keep staring, keep threatening, and slowly begin to lose my own cool under the thought of damage. Family or not, I don't like being lied to. Add in standing up to me about shit that no one understands but me, and I'm back inside fighting for my goddamned life. Maybe if he'd had half his time taken from him inside that cell he'd understand why reach and power is everything to me.

Dante's hand lands on my shoulder softly. "He gets it, Brother."

I frown and keep gripping, nowhere near ready to let this little asshole get away with his attitude problem. The hand crawls down my chest and around it to start pulling. "Abel. I get it, too. Back off, now." I do. Not because I want to, but because I'm being made to. That's a pretty dangerous place for me to be in, as the look of panic on Knox's face proves when he gets free space around him. "Knox. Go," Dante says quietly, still with his arm holding me.

I watch him walking out, then spin on Shaw for something to glare at. He looks straight at the floor, nothing but platitudes all over his features. Yeah, he knows too. He's been beaten for the same kind of crap.

"You cool?" Dante asks. No, I'm not cool. I'm a furnace that wants to vent somewhere. Anywhere. "Fucking asshole." My brow arches and I aim my hostility at him instead. "Not you. Him. Little shit always did know us like the back of his hand."

He stares and waits for me to say something, or maybe offers himself up for the beating he knows I want to give to someone. I've got nothing to say other than anger and still building fury. And he doesn't deserve what's going on inside me.

A drink slides across the counter top, the sound making me check out whatever the fuck it was. Shaw nods and holds up his own, attempting to stare me down or cool me down. I don't know which one, but I take it and drink. The burn barely touches the sides and before I can snatch the bottle and sink some more, I spin for the door to get myself the hell out of here. Nothing good will come of me staying. Rage will build. Confusion will set in. Memories of self-loathing will come. And then, when I've forgotten I love this family and do everything to protect them, I'll blow. Knox is right about that part of his tirade. I am an explosion waiting to detonate. I have been since I learnt what it's like to be cornered and without control.

I'm never being that again.

CHAPTER TWELVE

ALEXIA

The Challenger is still in the driveway.

I'd assumed that Abel would come and check on me – check that I came back like the dutiful wife I'm meant to be. Of course, he probably tracks the car.

Or worse, my phone.

All night I waited for him to come – demand his next service, perhaps, but he didn't show. Maybe our little heart-to-heart touched a nerve. Although, I suspect family business was what kept him away, and I'm yet to be convinced Abel Cortez has a heart. Even the display of morality towards the young woman yesterday didn't prove that for me, especially given his treatment of the other woman. I suppose there's no doubt that word will have reached him that I did, indeed, return home last night. So the first sign of trust has been honoured. Something I must capitalise on now when he gives me a chance.

I've shared my past, giving him a glimpse into life as an Ortega, and he's shown me the grit and reality of what Cortez has built their empire on. It's filth and misery for any of the girls who are still in that forsaken place. They're marked for life, so even if they try to escape, they won't ever be free.

I pick up the French press and pour a second cup of coffee. No sooner than I've placed the near–empty press down, one of the many house servants emerges from the shadows to clear, or in this case, replenish.

It's as if I'm watched, under scrutinising eyes, without even being aware of it much of the time. And over the weeks I've been here, I've grown used to the way they slither out and back from whatever crevice of this house they've been waiting in. Melena doesn't need to be present with me; her spies will report back to the lady of the house my every move.

By the time I've drained another caffeine hit, I'm bored, so I take a little stroll around the house. Refusing to stay in my assigned 'rooms', I peruse the main room, or the big room, where I first met my fate.

Cut crystal decanters, a tiffany lamp, all the hallmarks you'd expect to find in a house like this. Except now I know exactly how they paid for all of this splendour. Surprisingly I've never had a problem with what my family do for a living. Maybe because I've never been included in any of the inner workings of Ortega dealings, I can be naïve about the damage drugs can do to a life, or perhaps, it just isn't as personal as human trafficking.

"Mother!" I stop still, recognising the voice calling from the hallway. It's Mariana.

I tread carefully around the outskirts of the room and head for the exit on the other side, listening at every footstep.

"Mother!" She sounds pissed at something, or maybe just at her mother. The memory of them both at the wedding, arguing perhaps, springs back to mind. Leaving the room, I circle back towards the staircase, hoping to catch more of the show, but instead, I run into Melena.

"Good morning," I offer. I look past her and see Mariana at the end of the hall with a look to rival her mother's.

"Family business, Alexia." Melena nods, and with that, a server-come-guard ushers me towards the stairs and up to my suite, sequestering me safely out of earshot. The man even shuts the doors on me.

My eyes look skyward before I count to ten and then try the door. They haven't been locked so far, but I wouldn't put it past anyone in the house, especially Melena, or Abel, to keep me locked away if there was something they didn't want me to hear about.

It opens, and I walk straight back out and immediately hear raised voices. I keep my distance and listen for any words of information to help me better understand what's causing the issues at the heart of the family. Any crack is an opportunity for me to apply pressure and splinter it further.

Maybe it's time to get to know my sister-in-law a little better.

My steps are slow and purposeful as I descend the stairs and listen more carefully.

There's a lot of shouting, and they both switch in and out of Spanish as their tempers flare. Age, interfering, and something about making decisions on her own. I try to keep up and can fill in the blanks that perhaps Mariana isn't as free as she makes out she is.

I take the opportunity and head down the stairs to intervene.

"Mariana, nice to see you. I was just going to have lunch if you're interested? Abel seems to have forgotten he has a wife already." I shrug and smile, hoping she might take me up on my offer.

It's obvious I've interrupted, and Melena's glare punctuates that observation.

"It's funny. I thought I made myself clear this was family business," she seethes.

I turn to her and flick my wedding finger. "You see, it's funny. I thought I was a Cortez now?"

"You are, Alexia," Mariana says, smiling.

"You don't get to speak for this house." The snap on Melena's tongue is scolding and reminds me of how I've been treated time and time again by my father. "You have a lot to do before we call you real family, girl. Don't forget that. Now go." Melena steps in front of Mariana.

I hold her stare before I retreat, but not to my room. Despite the heat I hated when I first arrived, it's something that offers at least some form of dependability. My view of the gardens and pool is at least appealing, and I don't feel like I might trash the space at any given moment if I'm there.

I unbutton my dress and lounge in one of the sunbeds, resigned to a boring afternoon.

~

I'm left on my own for the rest of the day, and there are no interruptions of shouts or screams from inside, so my amusement is non-existent. Until Abel's shadow of a figure blocks my evening sun.

"Husband. How nice of you to make the time. Your car was getting lonely."

His lack of response is out of character at best. He doesn't say anything else but heads inside. And I follow.

We end up in the big room, as I like to call it now, and he's pacing. The crease on his forehead is firmly in place, and he's certainly not displaying his usual behaviour.

"Your mother declared I'm not part of this family today. I found it quite irritating."

He picks up one of the decanters and sloshes a large measure of drink into a glass and downs it, but no words fall to contradict what I was told.

"Okay then," I muse, standing next to him. "Pour me a drink." He does. "I'd like to talk about what I can do because, frankly, I'm going out of my mind being locked away here. I couldn't even persuade Mariana to go for lunch."

He nods, but it's clear he didn't hear a word I said because he would have an opinion as to what I'm allowed or not allowed to do – he all but declared that when I arrived. But it's been weeks now, and we're married, and I need to be smarter when it comes to our relationship.

"Why don't you take me to dinner? We're not on a honeymoon, but we can still have a civilised dinner as husband and wife? I'll even drive you." I smile, and a part of me has a genuine interest as to what's on his mind to make him act so differently. I made the effort yesterday, and I got my first step in any kind of positive direction.

"Fine. Bellini's."

I hide my eye roll. After getting married at the place, I'd hoped we might eat somewhere else. "Great. I'll go and change. You can help if you like?" I run my fingertips over his shoulders as I step past him.

"Don't. Just get dressed." He looks me up and down, the first glimpse that he's even seen me today.

"Are you tempted? Isn't that a job of a wife?" I bite my lower lip.

"Your job is to do as I say. And every time you pull this sexy fake shit, you remind me of who you really are. Go before I change my mind."

After using my looks as my only real form of attack for so long, it's hard not to fall back and rely on them, but Abel's right, and I could scream at myself for the mistake as I walk upstairs.

I pull out a dress and heels, refresh my face and pull my hair back into a sleek ponytail. Understated but still with an edge of glamour. He might not want me to look or dress the way I'm used to, but I have my limits.

Arriving back downstairs, I find him waiting in the hall. So, without another word, I take the keys from the side table and walk out to the car, not giving him the chance to change his mind about me driving. Surprisingly, he lets me with no complaint, so I slide into the seat and start the engine.

Maybe cars can be our level ground.

"Do I need to warn you to be careful with my car?"

"Abel, I know more about your car than you do. Relax." For the first time today, he actually smiles. It's soft, almost resigned in some ways, but it's there. No scowl, no temper. And I like it.

We arrive in one piece, and being behind the wheel helped improve both our moods. My smile is still genuine as I pull up to the restaurant and hand the keys to the valet.

"I'll be the one taking those back."

"Spoilsport," I pout at him but let him lead me inside. "So, if I'm not allowed to keep driving your car, what about one of my own?"

He looks at me. "The same?"

"Well, beggars can't be choosers. You can call it a wedding gift. I'll even allow you to choose it for me, but I do like yours."

We enter, and I glance around the familiar surroundings, now back to the usual restaurant setup. Despite it being early, it's still busy, but there's no problem finding a table, it seems.

"Champagne?" Abel asks. It's on the tip of my tongue to smile and agree, all happy and showy, but that's not what I want.

"Actually, I'll have sparkling water and a Mojito, please."

"Whisky. Neat." The waiter nods and turns. "Are you going to surprise me by what you pick on the menu as well?"

"You asked for honesty. Champagne is too dry for my taste. And I don't think we've eaten together enough for you to know what I'd enjoy on the menu."

"You were insistent on Champagne last time."

"I was, wasn't I. But now, I'd like to understand the parameters better."

"Parameters?" he questions.

"Yes, I think it will help us both." And I know it will help me understand the inner workings of Abel Cortez, and, despite our start, the thought he might open up to me is appealing. Sexy, even. This powerful, unapologetic man is sexy as hell when he's brooding. Less so when he's taking it out on me, though.

"Okay. You asked what you could do earlier."

"Oh, so you were listening." His eyes narrow, and I offer a sly grin. "See, parameters. How much I can say without you reacting as I've experienced in the past. What you're happy for me to say and not. It's like a tightrope, and it isn't a skill I've mastered yet."

"You want a guide? Don't fucking lie or hide things from me. I'll know, and I hate it. Save the bullshit for someone else."

"Fine. But then I want the same back in return." I lean forward and interlock my fingers. "And considering we're in a fake marriage, I'd wager it's going to be harder than you think."

He scrutinises me. "Considering there isn't anything fake about me, I don't see how."

I'm struggling not to feel this as a trap. "And if I win, what do I get?" I ask.

"My car."

"And what will you want if you win?"

"Peace."

"What?"

He sighs and picks up a napkin, seeming exhausted about something. "An end to this, Alexia. We settle, and you attempt to show me exactly what you are without your past dominating you."

Well, that surprises me. I think it over. He wouldn't go into this without knowing he's a sure bet, but I like the idea of winning his car from under him too much. "Deal."

Our drinks arrive, and we order. I choose the ravioli in tomato consommé and return my gaze to Abel. He picks up his drink, having ordered himself, and another sigh drops out of him.

"Did you even like the beef last time?" he asks.

"It was adequate, but you said you didn't want any lies. So no, I wasn't a fan, and I don't want to eat red meat again. It was on the menu at the wedding, which was out of my control. I'm not eating it again."

"Fine."

"You know," I study Abel's face and see the crease in his forehead begin to show. "Mariana and your mother aren't seeing eye to eye."

His face clears and he looks quizzically at me. "You're spying?"

"Call it entertainment. I'm in that house alone all day, every day, unless you've sent for me or made plans, or I have my scheduled visit from Jamie. It's why I asked about what I could do. I'm going out of my mind."

"And you want me to fix that?"

"Well, offer a suggestion, at least. Or lift the ban on being escorted everywhere I go."

He lifts his hand, and a waiter comes scurrying over. Seems he wants another drink. "Trust, Alexia. It doesn't come quickly in this family."

"Something you've made quite clear, but you've made me think that there's a possibility of trust in the future. Like with the car." I sip my ice-cold sparkling water. "Although, I'm still confused over the whole business."

"What don't you understand?"

"Well, you. And your family. You clearly don't respect women, yet Mariana is included in all family meetings around business that I can see. Your mother is the head of the family." I watch his reaction to that needle. "And Wren is clearly the new princess of everything."

"What don't you understand?" he repeats.

"How can it be both? How can you include Mariana, trust her and involve her in your business, and Wren, although I know she doesn't know everything, while paying so little respect to us?"

"Us?" The waiter uses that moment to bring another whisky and set it down. "You mean you."

113

"Yes."

He smiles like I've asked a stupid question that needs breaking down for me, only he doesn't. The food arrives, and he sets about his meal.

"Well?" I prompt, feeling on the outside, like so many times in my life.

"Mariana is our sister. She's as much a part of the business as everyone else. She's also proved herself on more than one occasion. My mother built this business, and we now run it. She should be respected because she's earned it. And Wren is the woman Dante loves."

"But why does that grant her an automatic pass to the family?" I don't see why one equals the other.

He sets down his knife and takes a drink, looking up at me after. "Dante trusts her. We trust her."

"But it's more than that. It's respect, too. You listened to Wren, took her advice and respected her decisions."

"Why wouldn't I listen to her? She's good at what she does. Our arrangement is different. You're a business decision. You'll only be seen as part of this family when you've shown me who you really are."

I take a few bites of the soft ravioli while I gather my frustrations.

"And Alexia, you mention a word about the full extent of this business to Wren, and I'll come down so hard on you you'll wish you were never born."

I frown but nod at yet another show of respect to a woman other than me. Maybe it's because this conversation just highlights the disappointments I've always felt with my own family. They showed me so little respect in comparison to what these women seem to get. I've never known it any other way.

"I've always been shut out from decisions my father and brother made. The Ortega's don't view women favourably. Neither do you, or you wouldn't be trading in girls. Maybe I'm just trying to understand why Mariana would want anything to do with it."

"I suppose you should ask her yourself, but don't be fooled by her appearance. She's a Cortez through and through."

CHAPTER THIRTEEN

ABEL

"**B**ut she's not, is she? A Cortez, I mean," she says.

"We're all Cortezes."

She finishes her third bite of food. "No. Dante and Knox are, Elias, too, before he was killed, but neither you nor Mariana or Shaw are."

"Is there a point?"

"Well, again, there seems to be this bond between you all, and it all comes down to your mother – the feared matriarch, I suppose." She runs her finger around the top of her Mojito glass, dipping it into the drink and sucking her finger dry. "See? Women. Respect. It's such a contradiction. You sell women and yet some seem to be treated as if they're revered."

I don't offer up an opinion on that. It's just the way I'm built, and because of that, all my brothers have been built the same way, with me guiding them. The fact that Mariana came along, giving us a sister to deal with, helped tame even Elias' behaviour.

"Why did she choose to keep that name and not your father's, or maybe Mariana and Shaw's father?"

"I chose to keep that name for us all. Richard Harris was a dick."

"Was Emilio Cortez a dick too?"

"No. He was the kind of man I admired. Ruthless. Aggressive.

Merciless."

"And yet you killed him."

"Yes."

"Openly. In a restaurant full of people. Rather stupid for someone like you."

I take my time and watch her eating the last of her meal. It's not like it's hard knowledge to know about. It was all over the news for long enough, but the fact that she's brought it up now, probably to try dissecting me, is irritating my bad enough mood.

"You've been researching the past."

She leans back and laughs, taking her drink with her so she can suck on the straw. "Of course. I'd hardly be a sensible wife if I didn't know about my husband. You never told anyone why, though. Just admitted guilt and went to Huntsville for it. That was a long term inside that you could have avoided had you been less passionate about it."

"Passionate?"

"Openly like that? That's the sign of an emotional killing. It tells me you're less heartless than you seem. So why? Why so reckless?"

I close my cutlery, down my drink, and look around the restaurant under a sigh. If she thinks I'm talking about that with her, here or anywhere else, she's wrong. "Time to go."

Her hand comes across the table, fingers closing over mine. "Abel, don't. I think this is one of the first real conversation we've had. You liked hearing something about me. And I'm not trying to pry, just understand you. It must have been hard for you. Confusing. Different fathers, let alone a Madam for a mother." She pauses. "What about your real father? Who was he?"

"He's dead."

"I know that but–" I tune the rest out and look at her mouth moving. Some part of me wants to smile at her attempt to wheedle her way in, but that's not happening. Certainly not tonight after a hard day and all that shit with Knox about Logan Cane. She'll get nothing sentimental or emotional from me unless I can trust her not to use it against me. At the moment, trust is wearing thin with my own family, let alone her.

"What do you do, Alexia?"

"What?"

I stand and point to the bar, crooking my finger at her to follow me over to the private area behind it. "You asked earlier if you could do something. What, exactly, are you capable of doing?" I signal Mike – the barkeep – on the way past the bar, two fingers up in the air for another round of drinks.

She falls in behind me and waits for me to find a table in the Club area. "Well, I can do a lot of things."

"Really? What?"

"You want my resume? You know, none of you make it easy to be involved in family business, but I'm more than just my body and my looks."

I pull a chair out for her and take my own seat. "Believe it or not, I'm well aware of the capabilities that body gives you. You're not unlike Mariana or Mother in that respect, but what I can't stand is the fact that someone I don't trust is in the middle of my life."

"You could try a little faith?"

"Faith?" A chuckle rumbles through me. "Faith and I parted ways long ago." The drinks arrive and I down mine, glass up in the air immediately so Mike will get me another. Damn, I needed that. Feels like life's a constant fucking battleground lately. Still, it's never been any different. Brothers fighting. Mother scheming. Mariana pushing. Day after day of business and death and girls and problems chasing my ass. And now a wife to deal with.

I sigh again and stare at the look of her perched over there all pretty and perfect – my wife. "You really are stunning, aren't you?" Her eyebrows shoot upwards, surprise evident.

"Why, thank you. It's nice of you to say."

"It's not a fucking compliment. Do you know how many pretty women I've looked at over the years? Thousands. Redheads. Blondes. Brunettes. Row after row of pussy. Most of them begged and pleaded. Some tried this same kind of bullshit you're pulling. None of it worked on me. Maybe if you'd had a mother to guide you, you would have learnt that not all men bow to sex appeal. She ran off though, didn't she? Left you with your father knowing exactly what would happen to you. Weak-ass bitch."

"I see you've done some research of your own."

I nod, as my next drink arrives in front of me. I down that one, too, and look back at the bar for Mike again. He nods and brings me the bottle. "I think I'm about to get real fucking drunk."

"Wow. Not the Abel I thought would join us tonight. This is interesting," she says.

"You think? I'd run if I was you." No one likes me much in this mood, and she sure as hell isn't gonna like me if I get my hands on her scheming ass. I pour a healthy double and pick it up. "Go home, Alexia."

"Oh no, I think I'll stay for whatever this is. Could be fun."

My eyes roll and I stare out at the view. "You don't get it, do you? But why should you? You've never been anything but a bartering chip passed around to anyone who wanted you. No real responsibility. No fucking point in reality." My gaze comes back to her, and I watch as her face starts taking offence. I knock the drink back and pour again. "You don't know anything about respect, or loyalty, or love, or any other fucking emotion that should be relevant in life."

She doesn't. Maybe she was never taught it. She should have been. That's what family is.

Another drink slips past my lips, and I keep staring into the night sky around me through the window. I feel alone even though she's here. Always do, regardless of family.

"Perhaps if you gave me half a chance to prove myself, you'd

119

find more than you're giving me credit for," she says.

A bitter chuckle ebbs through me, and I sink another drink. She wants a chance. I don't have any space inside me for chances. My life is hassle and never-ending problems. I need certainty. Especially from someone who is supposed to be by my side rather than plotting my fucking downfall. "If you're here for vengeance, you should think again. Your father is a piece of shit and your brother deserved to die, Alexia. He took something that wasn't his to take. He touched something that wasn't his to touch. He violated a part of me so deeply ingrained that he lost his chance for life the second he did it. If Dante hadn't gutted him for daring, I would have."

I look back at her, not caring a damn about her reaction to anything. Or maybe I do. Maybe that's why I've bothered saying anything at all. Maybe I'm tired of yet another goddamn battleground and trying to navigate it. Either way, I'm done talking. Maybe I'm done with her too. I don't know anything at the moment. I just want to drink until I can't see straight. Maybe clarity will come tomorrow. Maybe some goddamn peace will follow it. "Take the fucking car. Go home."

Because I need to wallow in my own space.

I need to be alone.

~

Hangover from hell annoying the fuck out of me, and I pull up and get out of the car. Not my usual one, because Alexia took it home and left me as requested. I look up at the building and sink some soda, trying to get sugar flowing through me in an attempt to get this headache gone. It doesn't work, and by the time I'm up to the door I'm aiming at, my body is telling me to sit the fuck down for a while and relax.

"Hello, Brother." I walk past Mariana and look around the large penthouse apartment she's in. The door closes behind me, and I keep moving around the luxury space. Elegance and finery drips from every surface, with only the most lavish finish put to everything she's created. "Will it do?"

I keep walking, checking every detail and corner. A large bar nestles on the far side of the open-plan space, with several leather couches close by to corner a modern fire. A single gold pole dominates the other side of the room for dancers, bolted tight into the floor and ceiling. I head off through the hall, opening doors to the bedrooms, and then make my way to the master suite. A king-size bed dominates on a stepped platform, with gold sheets and dark blue accessories and yet more luxury. Marble lines the bathroom, and more gold embellishments finish the look. Effective. And hopefully, considering the spend, profitable.

"Is there any food here?"

She giggles and turns on her heels, leading us out of the other end of the bedroom. "All this work to create the correct ambience and you're talking about food. Do you ever think of romance?"

"No. And I doubt it'll be thought about here either."

She points at a doorway in the hall. "That's the private elevator for clients by the way. They can park underground and access this without anyone knowing." Clever. I watch her walking in front of me, a smile on my face that she won't see. She gets better at being one of us year by year. More astute. More demanding. More persuasive in nature. "It's ready as soon as you want to begin using it. There's a list of suitable men who are more than ready to get their money out."

"How much have you told them they'll have to pay?"

"Five thousand an hour." I chuckle.

"And what kind of uptown dick pays that much for an hour?"

"The kind of dick that likes what he sees when I offer class to the service." She spins to look at me, as she opens the refrigerator in the kitchen area. "Unless you haven't noticed, you're a little like them the last few years." She looks over my suit, smirking to herself. "Quite refined these days really." No, I'm not. This is just a pretty outlook. "Anyway, I told you it would work. They're from all over the States. I've already expressed interest in other apartments in Austin and Dallas."

"How many clients do you have lined up?"

She nods at a couple of black notebooks on the countertop. "See for yourself. The small one first."

I pick it up while she begins making us some lunch, and flick through the pages. They're all filled with photos of clients and their names and addresses, even bank account details for some. Knox helped with that, no doubt. Not that we'll be taking anything but cold, hard cash from them, but access is always useful. "A little black book. Amusing."

"Hmm. And now look at the other one."

I drop the first and pick up the next. It's as meticulous and in depth as Knox's would be if it was his notes. Cost of purchase. Cost of refurbishment. Any associated monies needed or used. Planning consent from the city for alternations. I keep scanning the information. Not necessarily because I need to, but because I want to make sure she knows I'm always at her shoulder when it comes to anything she does for us. She hasn't let me down yet, but this is her new venture, one that apparently elevates us out of the trash.

"This isn't the purchase cost we discussed, Mariana."

"No, but I needed the floor underneath this one."

"Why?"

She motions me to the dining table and places a plate of food down, pushing it in my direction. "The elevator? The original structure made that difficult so I had to move things around."

My brow arches. "You needed another eight hundred thousand dollars for an elevator?"

"Kind of." I keep staring and pick up a sandwich to eat. "And there could be two more apartments fitted into the space now I've put the elevator in so it's not a bad investment, certainly not in this part of the city. One large one would be even better. Probably worth double what we paid. Knox was okay with it when I asked for the money." I chew and swallow. That isn't the reason she's bought the floor underneath this one. "And it's got really nice views over the city."

"No."

"Oh, Abel, please. I can keep an eye on this side of the business and be on call for the girls."

"No."

She stands and starts aggravating herself with my stance on this. "Why are you being such an ass about this? I can't live with her any longer!" Yes, she can. "You don't know what it's like. Every damn day she's in my face and making my life hell. God, she's such a bitch."

"Careful, Mariana. I'm in no mood for this shit this morning."

"No. I'm done. Everyone else gets their own place. Even Shaw, and he can barely shave his goddamn face without slitting his throat. Which I wish he fucking would on most days." I lean back and keep eating, watching her storm around the place. "Look at what I've done here! It's immaculate, and I'm perfectly capable of dealing with this side of the business if you let me."

"I know that."

"Then why not let me move in? I can get the place downstairs refurbished and deal with it all from here."

"You're not safe here on your own."

"Oh, that's bullshit. I'm a grown woman, Abel. I can't stay at home all my life, and she hates me as much as I hate her so I'm doing this. In fact, I don't need your permission anyway. I don't even know why I'm asking because I bought this in my own name."

"Sit down."

"Do you know what? I'm beginning to understand why Dante

gets so pissed with that tone of yours. I have a right to leave, Abel. A right to make my own choices and–" My chair scrapes the floor as I get up, cutting her tirade off and silencing her tongue.

"Sit, the fuck, down." Her head drops to look at the floor, and she frowns away her temper tantrum. I huff and take my time looking at her, getting a check of my anger. She's glowing in her rage. Just as any one of us should be when we're being bullied. "Please. Sit, Mariana."

She does after a few seconds, and eventually looks up at me. "Abel, I–"

My hand goes up. "I understand why you want to leave, but we can't protect you here."

"What about if I make two apartments and we have a guard or something living in the other one?"

"No."

"Dante has something similar with Wren and that works."

"No."

"Why?"

I sit again, sigh, and push the half-eaten plate of food away. "Because you'll just wrap any guard around your finger and then not listen when he tries to contain you."

"Contain me? See? That's exactly what I mean. I'm like a prisoner sometimes. Knox isn't contained. Even my own twin isn't and I'm far more capable than him. Why do I have to be?"

"Contained is the wrong word."

"You're right, it is wrong. It's wrong on so many levels I don't even understand why you'd use it. In fact, explain this to me. You were thinking about me marrying Nicolas before that whole thing went south. And don't tell me you weren't because I know you were even if Dante didn't like it. But I'm not allowed to live on my own?"

"That was different. You would have been protected there."

"Like you're protecting Alexia? She's as much a prisoner as me.

Is that what you would have preferred for me – on Nicolas' leash and being fucked under his direction? You won't give a goddamn inch, will you? On anything."

"Cool down."

She leans in, ready to make a direct point, no doubt. "Oh, you'd like that, wouldn't you? You'd like me to be servile and do as I'm told without challenging you, but guess what? Not going to happen. I'm not your wife. You don't get to threaten me with brutality and pin me down because you don't trust me."

"Mariana–"

"I don't even know why you bothered marrying her, considering she spends all her time doing nothing for us. In fact, why not just kill her and end her misery? It's not like you're even trying to use her for something other than fucking." My palm tightens into a fist on the table, and fury starts building. "Either way, I've earned trust in this family, Abel. I've earned my rights, and I will not be treated like a fucking prisoner!"

"Shut the hell up about being a prisoner. You're not one. You have a car, freedom, and money to do whatever the fuck you want whenever you want to. No one stops you from going out or living your life. The only thing I restrict you from is this, and that is to keep you safe. Tread carefully with your words. I'm getting pissed with your attitude, and this is about to turn offensive."

She crosses her arms and glares at me for a while, letting all Mother's spite and wrath settle on her features. I understand it. I even admire her for it, but nothing changes, as far as I'm concerned, when it comes to this.

"So that's it, is it?" she spits. "Even after I've done all this and proved myself with responsibility and business, I'm to live my life at that house until some man screws me into marriage? Perhaps then I can go live with him if you agree he's okay for the family? God, you're an asshole, Abel. Truly."

Swallowing down the anger that wants to surface, I slowly push my chair out again and stand. This is going nowhere other than arguments and dead ends, but I suppose she is right on most of that last attack because that is the plan. Until I know there's someone who cares about her the way we do, she's not living out here without us wrapped around her.

I turn and head for the entrance lobby. "I'm glad you understand the way this works. And I'll tell you right now, before you get any stupid ideas in your head, that dick you're fucking around with comes nowhere near us. He's trash. Don't make me deal with him." I open the door and sigh, half looking back at her. "You've done well here, though. Let me know when you open. We'll need to pick the right women."

There isn't any response as I leave, and I don't expect one. I'm sure she'll sulk on this for a few days yet. Or maybe try getting Dante to make me think differently. She won't change his mind either.

CHAPTER FOURTEEN

ALEXIA

Despite our evening meal as husband and wife and telling Abel that I needed something to occupy my mind, I'm again left in this mansion, which is no more than a glorified prison.

Sure, there are signs that things might get better, and it's only really been a short time since our nuptials, but it's getting harder to remain patient with so much time on my hands.

Especially after my dismissal. Abel's like an infuriating puzzle. He opens up just enough to tempt you and then shuts you down. In my case, sending me away so he could get drunk. Because, of course, he couldn't just be open with me for a fucking change. He demands so much but gives nothing in return. Frustrating and irritating that he hasn't changed. Part of me hates him. I'm in this situation where he's controlled and taken advantage of, but I can't say what I really feel because, well, that isn't the game. I'm just not sure what's the best way to play it anymore.

The big room is empty, and the heat from outside has surpassed my tolerance today. However, my skin will thank me later for saving it from sun damage. And besides, out of spite, I refuse to stay locked in my rooms.

"Urghhh!" Mariana storms in and slams the door behind her.

"Oh, sorry. I didn't think anyone would be in here."

"Please, don't mind me. But I'm not moving just because you've waltzed in."

"Relax. I'm not my mother, thankfully." She heads for the liquor and pours herself a drink. Maybe this is where they serve all the good stuff. Mariana's idea of a drink is a hefty one, three fingers of amber liquid, which she knocks back like I'd expect Dante or Abel to do. Her, not so much.

"Bad day?" I offer.

"Something like that."

"Care to share?" I'm not the overly talkative type. I don't have sisters, and most of my girlfriends were superficial, at best – another element of my fake life – so I'm not sure how to talk to other women without being a bitch. Having people be afraid of you or hate you has its uses.

She looks at me as if she can't quite make out if I'm being genuine. "Family business. The only thing we ever discuss or argue about."

"The same family business Abel took me to see the other day?" Maybe if she knew what I know, she'd be less secretive.

"No. This is my own venture, but it's more than that."

"Does my beloved husband have anything to do with this?" It's a fair gamble he'll have some involvement considering he seems to run the family. Something I'm sure Melena disagrees with.

"Your husband," she pauses, "is an ass. But I'm sure you know that already."

"Well, I am abandoned once again with nothing to do. At least back home, I knew my place in the business and could do what I wanted from day to day."

"Well, the Cortez family certainly want to keep their women safe." She pours another drink and sits on the over-stuffed sofa opposite me.

"I'd substitute safe for controlled." Mariana and I could be allies if I play this right, and I need more of those.

"Well, maybe for you. You are, after all, an Ortega. You will be controlled until you can prove yourself." Seems Little Miss Cortez has some spine.

"Okay, what is with this proving myself shit? I married my family's enemy. Don't I get any credit for that? I came here openly into your home after you killed my brother, and you're all acting like I'm some evil witch needing to be locked up. This marriage was in good faith to both our families."

She looks at me, and for the first time, I can see the venom in her. The same look her brother has on occasion. "Our family isn't like others, Alexia. It's stronger than each and every one of us. Stronger than blood, and you're fucking right you need to prove your allegiance to us. And, as you already know, you're not the one who can give us access to the rest of your business. Your father is. So, you might want to stop your complaining."

"I see. Nice speech. Your big brother pushed you around, so you're trying to flex your status with me." My smile is a little much, but I want her to realise that she can't mess with me. I might not be trusted by either family, but that has meant I've had to hone other skills, and I'm extremely good at reading people. Abel, not so much, but this little one is an open book. It's a shame. We have a lot in common. If she could get off her pedestal, no doubt elevated by all of her brothers, it would help. "Remember that no matter your opinion of me, or if I do someday become trusted by Abel or not, it doesn't matter. You'll always be the baby of the family. The one they will all wrap in cotton wool and keep at arm's length. You're part of the business, but not on your terms, and I doubt they let you get your own way like you do in everything else in your life. Because, well, family is everything to them, right?" I stand and leave Mariana thinking over my truth.

Plus, I don't want to give her the opportunity of a comeback.

I make sure I stay out of everyone's way and have dinner in my suite. The conversation has got me thinking, though, and it's time to call my father. We've not spoken since the wedding, and while I'm quite happy about that, there is a purpose to all of this. And he needs to hold up his side of the plan.

The call connects after several rings.

"Alexia."

"Father. I thought we could catch up."

"Not the impression I had from your wedding."

"You were rude enough to question my role on my wedding day. Anyway, I thought you could share the advancements you've been making now that we are all one big happy family." The sarcasm is heavy, but he'll understand what I'm asking.

"I have several new contacts that Melena has initiated."

"And the logistics?" I press.

"Not yet. However, I'm told that a meeting with the wider family will be forthcoming. That's when we'll negotiate."

"Forgive me, I know I don't know the full details of the operation, but wasn't logistics and moving our product wider the one goal we needed in this plan?"

"Careful, Alexia." There was a time I'd dread hearing that tone from him. Not anymore.

"No. I'm here, locked in a room and married to a Cortez in order to progress our business, and there's no progress."

"These things take time. You don't simply barge in and demand."

"Well, we fucking should," I seethe. "If you don't show our strength, they will dictate and walk all over you. Do you need me to set up a meeting between you and my husband? Do you need me to push our own agenda with the Cortezes?"

"Alexia, I don't need you to dictate how I do business. I've warned you before."

"And I've warned you not to underestimate me. I told you that we could have everything we've ever wanted, but you seem unable to grasp that. Clearly, you admire and respect Melena Cortez. She and you put this whole thing together, even at the expense of Nicolas. Why is it such a stretch for you to have the same faith in your own blood?"

The silence on the other end of the call tells me everything I need to know. If I'd uttered those words face to face, he'd have back-handed me and beat the rudeness out of me. Now he can't do that. He has no control over me or what I do because, like it or not, he needs me in his game of power, and maybe he's realising this for himself. For the first time in my life, I feel powerful over my father. "I'll take your silence as a good sign that you're finding the words to show me that you trust me to make this work in Ortega's favour. You can carry on believing you're in control, Daddy. I'll be in touch when the rest of my plan is in place – the plan that sees us exact the revenge we deserve, or have you forgotten all about that, too?"

"Alexia–"

"Don't. You can't say anything to me right now. You can wait for the meeting with my husband and see what they're prepared to support you with. If you don't need me, then prove it."

I end the call, my heartbeat pounding in my chest and anger bubbling through me. Between him, my fake husband and the little show down with Mariana, I'm ready to explode. Or break something.

I leave the room and head towards the formal dining room. Luckily, there's a member of staff heading towards what I presume is the kitchen; I've still not set foot inside it. "Excuse me!" I shout. They stop dead and turn. "Is there a gym here? I've only seen part of the house and could really do with a workout." The startled look on her face tells me she's not sure what to say. "Tell me!" I shout, and she jumps a little.

The little nod is amusing, but she scurries off in the direction of

Melena's wing, so I follow down a staircase, through a door and into a small studio space.

"Thank you." I smile, then turn around and head back to my room to peel off my clothes. They get dropped to the floor as I rummage in my drawer for yoga pants. I don't usually work out at home. Back in Miami, I'd go out for yoga or Pilates and have my list of appointments at numerous spas and beauticians – all part of the package of Alexia Ortega, but here? I'm barely allowed out of the grounds.

Pulling my hair back and securing myself in a workout top, I head back downstairs. Being tall meant I was good at running at school. Of course, I never tried very hard at sports, but every now and then, it still gives me an outlet. Every time my father thought he could use me and control me for his gain, I'd run. Like my own brand of therapy – exercising the memory or experience.

Setting the controls on the runner, I start off on a gentle walk, increasing the tempo until I'm jogging and pushing it further until I'm flat out. My lungs start to protest as heat spreads up to my face. It's been a while since I've needed to run like this, and I'm out of practice. My feet are sure as they pound down on the rubber track, and after a couple of minutes, I settle into a rhythm. My mind begins to clear, and the anger dissipates with every breath I take.

"What the fuck are you doing in here?" Melena's witchy voice screeches.

And my peace is shattered.

I don't stop right away but bring down the pace gently until I'm walking. I'm not turning around to look at her either, assuming she's still waiting for my explanation. When I finally stop, my legs feel a little unsteady underfoot, and I curse that Melena will see me in this state – red-faced and sweaty – but maybe it's time.

"Melena. I was having a workout. I asked about a gym and was shown here. It didn't seem to crop up on my earlier tours."

"Because this is my space. Not yours."

"So, there's another gym I should have been shown to?"

"Don't be ridiculous," she scoffs.

"Well then." I pause and take a few deep breaths. In my haste to get my frustrations out, I forgot to bring water or a towel with me. "What did you expect? And you know, it would be nice if you didn't see me as the enemy that has to be locked away in a particular room of the house. We've not spent much time together, but we're living together. Let's not be bitchy."

Her eyes narrow at me, and I think I might have pushed her too far for a second.

"Bitchy. I see." She stalks towards me. "I thought that was your trait. Don't think we've not done our research on you, Alexia."

"I was a bitch, and I can certainly be one when I need to be, but you, of all people, must understand that in a man's world, we can't look weak."

"I was never weak." The toxicity in her voice is there for a reason.

"No. You've just built this family up, and now your children are taking it right out from under you." It's a fair assumption and one she'll hate.

"And what would you know about our business? You're just a pawn to us." Her deflection is quick, but I know a woman like her must be aware of what's happening.

"Interesting you only see that. It's disappointing, frankly. I thought you'd understand the sacrifice I've made for my family. Something that your daughter might want to learn." I push a little further and wait for her to bite, but she doesn't, regardless of my provoking her. I need to, though; otherwise, understanding how to take this family apart from the inside is going to take a lot longer than I want. A few comments to stir the volatility will work in my favour.

"I see my son hasn't taught you where your place is."

"Oh, he's been clear, and perhaps if I were just another one of your 'merchandise', then I'd have fallen into line like a good little girl. But, like it or not, I'm here and can be an asset. And I'm sure I'm more, should we say, dispensable than poor, young Mariana."

I feel her presence – her scrutiny – more than anything. It's overbearing in the small room. "Some of my children are yet to understand the meaning of the sacrifices we make for our family. That alone doesn't offer you an advantage. But, I can see that you might be more useful than the ring on your finger has provided us." Her eyes drop to my hand, and she does a very good job of making me feel inferior as she slides her gaze over me. "We're done." She pushes past me, and I let out a sigh of relief.

"I'll make sure I let you know next time I want to use your little gym space." I leave Melena, hopefully, with something to think about.

Coming into this house, I knew I'd have to watch for her, but I didn't realise there could be an understanding between us, or something that could work in my favour, at least.

By the time I get back to my room, I'm exhausted and grab a bottle of water out of the mini-fridge and down it. Checking my phone, there's a message from Abel.

Taking you to dinner. Dress up. Be ready at 7.

Plenty of time to get ready. Although I'm already mentally reviewing my wardrobe. So far, there's nothing that's pleased Abel, and while most of my decisions have an ulterior motive, there's something about a man's gaze to boost your ego that nothing else can compensate for.

I pick a skin-tight skirt and silk top that's alluring and sexy but not in the obvious way some of my choices have been in the past. No red lipstick, but I ensure every other part of my makeup is beautiful yet understated, and then I top it all off with my favourite heels.

I'm waiting for Abel with ten minutes to spare. Even though my shoes deserve better, I pace the lobby area, waiting. If I'm honest with myself, I'm looking forward to what this evening might mean, even though I still feel in the dark as to Abel Cortez.

The door opens, and I already have a smile creeping over my face. But it's not Abel.

"Dante? Not the brother I was expecting."

He looks at me and gives me a wicked grin. A grin that doesn't show any frustration or suspicion of me, and it sends ice through my veins.

"No. Don't worry, though. You'll see him soon enough."

CHAPTER FIFTEEN

ABEL

Mariana's words cut deep the other day. She called herself a prisoner, and then called my wife one. She's right about Alexia. She is until I can trust her. I can't trust anyone until I know them – every inch of them. I need to know their fears, their problems, their hatred and malice. I need to know how they tick – why they tick.

I've deflected the only option I have to find that until now. Perhaps I've been giving myself room to breathe rather than deal with the inevitability that will cause should she find sense. But either way, I need her onside and looking at what she's got in front of her rather than what's behind, because having an enemy in my space isn't carrying on any longer.

Another round of men come past me in the dirty, old room, this time carrying a dead body wrapped up in plastic. It'll be taken out to the desert soon and buried, perhaps to be dug up by scavengers at some point in the future. Doesn't matter. It was just another whore from the streets, and snuff films make a lot of money. We facilitate that, whether that world around us likes it or not. It's just business. Nothing but business.

I come here to watch, occasionally. It's the need for something more than I'm used to, something to titillate my unresponsive detachment. But that's not why I'm here now. I've made a choice based on instinct because I can't go on knowing my wife is scheming behind my back. I knew it would be part of this deal long before I agreed to it. It's the way that family is wired – the way she's wired. That's why I took her on myself, to shield my brothers from having to deal with it all. Add in the email from Mariana an hour ago about Alexia trying to wheedle her way in, and Mother's spiteful tongue about her, and I'm ready to finish what I was about to start anyway.

The damp air and smell of sweat and blood drift around my senses, bringing my mood further down with every passing minute. She'll be here soon, and then maybe after we've finished, she'll start being honest with me about who she is under that life she's lived. It's the only version of a wife I'm interested in. And the only one that might get to meet a husband she'll enjoy rather than hate.

"Abel." I look at Chance Pierson, as another guy walks past him, and nod. "Good to see you." He offers his hand and we shake. It's not overly friendly, more business-like. We've made a lot of money off each other over the years, and, like or not, we're on the same wavelength about life. He happens to be a whole lot more sadistic than me, but that's a useful trait given his profession and this venture he runs. "Why are you here? Carmen booked the room."

I cast my gaze at the door Dante will come through. "Training."

"But the fact that you're here implies you're doing it yourself." I chuckle at the thought. Who else trains their own wife? "I expected Carmen. I did wonder why she bothered leaving my place this morning."

"Different kind of training."

"Ah." He looks at another couple of women being dragged past, and then a half-dead guy. "Well, studio four is as clean as it gets. Send me the film."

"I didn't come here for clean. And you can't have this one. No filming."

His smile broadens and he stares for a few moments, seemingly transfixed by me withholding something from him. I'm not surprised. I wouldn't usually. "Why not?"

"It's not for sharing."

"Possessive? You?" He laughs and starts walking away after the women, hands in his suit pockets. "Rude now I think about it. Although, I guess I owe you favours." He stops and turns back, spinning on one heel in that smooth way of his. "I hear you're married now."

"Yes."

"How's that going for you?"

I don't answer. Just stare as some kind of reply. Fundamentally because I'm not sure yet, but other than that my marriage is not up for discussion.

"Right, well, have fun in there," he says, carrying on away from me. Nothing about this will be fun.

More minutes pass by before the door eventually opens. A mass of limbs gets shoved into the room, with Dante helping contain its ferocity. She still manages to get a slap to his face somehow, regardless of not being able to see through the hood he's put over her head.

"Fucking bitch," he growls, backing away.

"Be careful, Brother."

Her body spins around at the sound of my voice, her hands ripping the hood off at the same time. All that blonde hair tumbles free, and I watch as she glares at everything around her. I give her a minute to take in the visions and smells and keep staring until she eventually finds my eyes again.

"What the hell is this? And why the fucking hood?"

"You aren't allowed to know where this is. As I've said, no one trusts you yet." I keep staring at her perfection – her manicured and expensive disposition – until I get to her feet. "Take your heels off. Dante, give me a cigarette." He offers the pack and I pull one.

"And the lighter." He lights one of his own before passing that to me, too. "You can go now."

He keeps staring at Alexia. "And miss the entertainment?"

I slowly look at him, a face full of disinterest in joviality. This isn't fun for me. Nothing is. This is just worn in necessity. It's the kinda way I deal with those who need to be dealt with. Marriage or not, at the moment she's a problem I need to find a route through. The fact that she's infiltrated my thoughts more than I gave credit to is escalating the need.

He smirks, nods, and walks away until it's just me and her and a dirty, used room in the bowels of an old, broken-down building. She frowns at me and looks around again, still with a pair of heels perching her off the filth she's about to get real close to.

"Well?" she says, chin up in the air.

"Take the shoes off, Alexia."

"Why?" A guy comes around the corner as she's asking, his heavy body manhandling a distressed whore who's trying her best to get away from him. Alexia steps sideways, giving them room, then tries glaring at me again. It's less of a glare this time, though. More edgy and nervous.

"I want you to feel this dirt beneath you."

"Why?"

"It's part of you now. Take them off."

She frowns and leans down, slipping them from her feet until she's barefoot and feeling the depraved world she's becoming part of. "Is that better? What are we doing?" She puts her hands on her hips in a huff – still putting on a show.

I walk away and beckon her, heading for the private space I've reserved, and watch as she walks into the darkened room. The door locks closed the second she looks at the old, bloodstained mattress in the middle of the room. She spins on me, then glances at all the cameras stationed around the walls, and backs a step away.

"There's nowhere to run, Alexia." Her gaze darts around again, taking in the rusted shackles by the mattress, and eventually landing on the only other entrance to the room. "Breathe. He'll be here in a minute."

"Who?"

"Ratchet."

"Abel? What's going on?" I don't answer. I let her fear build and her body quiver under the strain of what's coming. It's nice to watch in all honesty, because she's at her best like this. She's raw and real and full of loathing for me. I don't mind that at all. "Abel? What is this place?"

"It's a place where people profit from death. How much profit do you think that body has made your father over the years?" She looks at the other door again, then walks for the opposite side of the room. I watch her feet moving through the dirt and grime, wondering when the last time she actually touched grime was. "I'll expect more than you made for him."

"You wouldn't dare." My brow arches.

"I think you know I would."

"Why is Ratchet coming?"

"To fuck you. Or fuck you up. I haven't decided yet." She doesn't even look at me after that. She stares at the dried blood on the mattress and swallows, slowly clawing herself back to the wall. "Which would you rather?" No glare anymore. Barely any malice either. Just fear and nerves and surprise. "You won't die today, though. I'll promise you that much at least."

"I don't understand," she says quietly.

"No, I don't suppose you do."

"I thought we were …"

"What? What did you think we were?"

"I'm your wife."

"Hmm. His daughter, too. I made a million for agreeing to this marriage. Nothing in reality. A cheap price. How much more are you going to make me?" Her eyes widen, as if she didn't know that piece of information. I chuckle and go put my jacket on a stool at the side of the room. "He didn't tell you he had to bribe me to make it happen?"

The door opens, as she's trying to work through that betrayal in her head, and Ratchet walks in. It must feel that way to her. I didn't want her — didn't want the union at all. Her father bartered hard, though. Between him and Mother and the potential profit and power allowing them into our territory could bring, I relented.

I look at Ratchet, nodding at him to start the process. He moves as he usually does, stridently, and lacking any care about what he's about to participate in. Alexia skips sideways, trying to get away. That's as futile as the lie she's pretending to live with me, and I watch on as he grabs her and moves her towards the mattress.

Piercing shouts and screams start immediately, as she begins her fight. She'll lose, but I want that bite coming out strong and hard now. I want to feel it, see it, and sense who she can be when I strip this bullshit from her and find some authenticity. I walk the room as she keeps attempting to fight, flicking on the camera spotlights and pressing the button to film on one. Both of them are flooded with light, and while I frown as I watch him manhandle her to get her how I want her on the mattress, there's no denying I'm aroused by it.

Her body twists and turns, as he finally forces his weight on her shoulders, and her head whips sideways to look at me as I walk by. Venom and hatred pour off her in waves. "Let me go!" she spits. "WHY?" She looks back at Ratchet and manages to get her knee up, attempting to roll away out from under him. "FUCK OFF! Get the hell off me!"

Going back to my jacket, I pull the blade out and keep watching as he gets her left wrist into a shackle, then moves for her right foot to do the same. I walk over the second he's got her stretched out on the mattress, his one hand still pinning her right hand down. She's still trying to fight her way out as I get to her. Too late for fighting now. She shouldn't have brought scheming into my home.

He turns as I move in, giving me space, and so I get on with what needs doing. The knife shreds her skirt first, ripping the length of it until it's slashed up the middle and tattered, and then I move on to the silk blouse. By the time I'm done she's fully exposed, with torn clothes, nothing but discarded wealth on the floor around us.

"This is what you've become, Alexia. This is what you agreed to the possibility of by marrying me."

Backing off, I look down at her. Fine lingerie clings to skin, and regardless of the scenario, sweet high-end perfume fills the room and my senses. I keep looking at Ratchet's hands locked on her skin to keep her flat to the mattress rather than the flailing she's trying for. That's the one part of this I'm not comfortable with, no matter the necessity or my own arousal. In fact, Chance might have been right earlier. I am feeling possessive.

"More pressure, Ratchet." He grips tighter, causing her to wince and whimper. "Everywhere. Make it hurt. She needs to get used to it." Her arm gets pulled taut, and the rest of her strains under the force he's putting on her. She screams once, then tries arching away from what he's doing to her. She won't get away from anything he does.

"Please!" she shouts. "Stop!"

It doesn't stop and won't until she understands how far I'm prepared to go to get a wife who I trust. She's in my family's space – in their thoughts and circle. That means she either becomes a part of it that I can trust, or she'll end up treated like nothing but merchandise I can use.

Her pleading continues, and my taunting carries on. Ratchet might as well be me, because I'm damn close to inflicting the same merciless pain as he is doing at the moment. Instead, I'm watching it. I'm letting her know how close she is to becoming nothing to me.

She cries out in agony at one point. I'd like to think I'm immune to the sound by now, but eventually I nod at Ratchet as he looks up at me. He lightens his grip instantly, giving her some reprieve from the pain. She curls one leg up as best as she can and turns away from me. She's not crying, not shouting anymore either. She's just resigned to what's happening.

"Is that it, Alexia? Is that all the fight you have in you?" Her eyes blink and she keeps staring at the wall away from me, so I move into her eye line and crouch. "That's all you've got to give?" I sigh and look at her body. "It's not enough for a Cortez. Certainly not my wife. Would you give in so easily if this was an enemy?"

She doesn't offer me anything. No looking at me. No talking. No pleading. Just a tremble over her body. I put the blade down on the floor in front of her face and spin it. It glints under the arc of the spotlight touching it, clinking the ground on every rotation. "I am the enemy, though, aren't I? That's where your head's at all the damn time."

She looks at the blade spinning, and then glances at me briefly. "What do you want, Abel?"

"Want? I want you to show me some respect." She frowns and stays locked on the knife, as it slowly comes to a stop. "I want you to show your new name some respect and stop screwing around. I want you to own it because it's more than yours ever was." I get up from the crouch and stand. "But you're still playing a game with me, Alexia. Dinner the other night? A bet? Do I seem like a man who makes bets about trivial bullshit?"

She throws another glance my way. "It was just something to—"

"Shut the fuck up. I'm done with this crap. This shit you keep bringing is worthless to me. The lying, the scheming, the fakery.

It's tiring as fuck, Alexia. You're yet another burden to me like that, a constant fucking pain in my ass."

I watch her trying to figure out what's going on here, leave the knife exactly where it is, and begin pacing the room away from her. "I think I hoped you might be more than I thought you were. You're not, though, are you? The only reason you're here is to what? Get vengeance for your brother perhaps? Or steal from me for your father?" I start unbuttoning my shirt, then lever my belt undone. "And I suppose if I have to continue fucking you like an Ortega whore rather than a Cortez wife, I'm already practised at that." The leather of the belt slides out of the loops and threads into my hand, as I look down at her. "I'd rather watch you suffer, though. Disloyalty earns you nothing but my hatred. It certainly doesn't get you my face."

She looks over at me, hawk-like eyes scanning my every move. "It's not surprising really. As you said, you are a whore. You've been bred as one. It's a shame, though, because loyalty to me could give you everything you've never had. And I have plenty of whores already." I don't want another one. "This film will be worth money, though. A good profit for an afternoon's amusement. Ratchet, it's time to leave."

My stride changes, and I angle straight at her, as he lets go, ready to push as much as I've got at her to make this happen. She rolls, as my boot lands on the mattress, and grabs the knife to whirl back to me. I keep moving at her without hesitation, about damn ready to get this argument done so we can find some amount of harmony between us. The knife gets tucked up under my chin, and I keep pushing my weight into her until she's got no choice but to wrap her free leg around my waist and clamp on tight. And that's us then – her coiled around me with a blade pressed deep against my jugular, and me making damn sure she keeps it right there by laying on top of her.

"Fuck you, Abel." A smile broadens on my face as she pants

and keeps gripping tightly. I can't stop it. This is the kind of measure I like in a woman. Aggressive. Honest. Menacing. Wild. "You're not using me for goddamn profit. No one is. Never again. I'll kill you before that happens."

Her leg squeezes, either to pull me closer or to show her contempt, and I angle my head some more so she can get a clear view of what she could end if she chose to. She won't. This is the first time I've let her have a small amount of control and she knows it. I don't leave blades hanging around for someone to use against me unless I mean to.

Ratchet slams the door closed in the background, throwing the bolt to lock us in while he stands guard.

"I never wanted to use you for profit. No one's getting inside you but me anymore." She frowns as my hand travels out to the side of us. My fingers lever the shackle on her other wrist open, and she grabs at the back of my neck the moment it's free, tugging at it to make sure that knife stays true against my throat. "But I did want to see this from you."

Another tug on me. Another moment filled with venomous intentions and threats. The slow grate of the blade increases the pressure growing in my dick, making me ravenous for her.

"You played me," she says.

"It's a language you understand. And the only time I'll give you a chance to win." I shift on her, getting my arm braced by her head and pressing her back to the mattress some more. "I only ever want to see this from you in the future – this is your only warning. There's no respect for anything but this side of you." I watch her eyes, seeing my truth sink in. "I think this honesty from you deserves a new name. Lexi maybe. I'm damn sure she's more real than the bullshit you brought to my door."

She keeps frowning. No words to say about that, apparently, but it's who she'll be to me from now on if I keep feeling this about her. I push my neck down on the blade slowly, lowering my mouth towards hers. "You gonna let me fuck you like this, or are we gonna turn real hostile about it?" My hand slides down between us and finds her pussy, as I push myself off her a little. Her eyes dilate and her lips part as I find her wet enough to get on with what I want to do. Every move, every breath, I keep my eyes fixed on hers.

"How many men have you wanted to kill for touching you?" The panties get moved to the side, and I slide my aching dick in slow and easy, letting every ridge mean something other than what it has before. She swallows, arches a little and shivers – her only movements. She's all about that knife at my neck, and I get that. She can have it as long as she needs it this time around. But it's an illusion, she's still not in control of anything. I am. It's my blade that I've given her – my trust I'm showing her.

"I want you to think about how I'm fucking you now for the rest of your life. I can be real damn nice when I want to be." The ache in my dick increases as I pause to make sure she fucking understands. "We can have this. You know what you need to do." It's the authenticity of the situation – the real, raw, savage nature of it. It's not a show, nor a fucking payment plan. It's not romantic or staged or false. It's just two people fucking because they want to – because they need to. "You gonna give in, darlin'?" I groan and watch as her features begin to soften. The knife gets looser on my skin with every slow drive into her. "You gonna be real and let me look after you? Or are we gonna keep fighting?" The pressure between us builds and her leg starts relaxing, widening, so I tilt her ass up to me some more to get deeper than I already was.

And then we kiss – a real, fucking honest kiss.

I get more lost in that than I do the fucking. She tastes like hot flowers and attitude, and the bites she gently eases over my lips wind me up to a new level of intimacy. It's all need and lust. It makes my hand travel to the knife pressed between us, to her fingers wrapped around it like a vice. It gets tossed from the situation, abandoned to rattle against the ground in the background.

I don't know how long we fuck on a bloodstained mattress in the middle of a dirty, old room, nor do I care. The rest of my clothes get thrown at some point, and I stay buried deep inside her until we're both done and I'm lying with my head on her chest. She pants beneath me and rests her hand in my hair, still with nothing to say about anything. That's fine by me because this is the most honest thing we've achieved together, as far as I'm concerned. Here, in this room, drenched in death and surrounded by air thick with sin, we've been real.

My lips and teeth meander on her skin, tongue dragging the length of her until I'm back up to her face and looking into eyes I'm getting closer to. She stares quietly. Barely moving. No emotion – good or bad – that I can read. So goddamn pretty, though. Swollen lips and damp skin don't change a damn thing about her, nor should they. She is, without doubt, perfect in her desire.

"Lexi Cortez." A sigh falls from me, as I say it, and I pull back and stand for my clothes. It might be a sigh layered with years of detachment and disinterest, but for once it has an ache attached to it – a yearning that doesn't rest in hatred.

I lick my lips and run a hand through my hair because of it all, rolling my neck at the same time to get comfortable with the name. Most of my clothes get pulled on and I go retrieve my jacket, pulling the cigarette and lighter out. I sit on the stool, look over at her still chained by her ankle, and light the smoke. A long draw is pulled into my body. Barely any of the smoke leaves my lungs, as I rest my elbows on my knees and stare at her still in the spotlight. It's been a long time since I needed a hit like this. I don't know whether I should take that as a gut reaction to stupidity or not, but this is where we are and I'm running with it.

She reaches for the shackle slowly.

"Leave it on. Feel it, because that should mean everything to you." She frowns and looks over at me. Not that she'll be able to see me back here. I'll just be a dark shadow and voice.

"What does that mean?"

"I need you to listen real carefully because this is your last chance. Your life before me ends now, Lexi. There is only me. Whatever was, is over." She sits up a little taller and watches the space I'm in. "This isn't a game anymore. This is real fucking honesty coming from me, and I need you to heed the warning. All the shit you might have been up to has to stop. You need to look at me and see your future. I'm there in any version of it. How I behave is based on who you are to me. What would you rather? A slut I don't trust, or a respected wife?"

Another long draw in, this time blown back out again to create a cloud of smoke, and I stand to begin walking the room. The lights get turned off one by one until I wander past the one recording her. The smoke gets flicked away, and I reach for my belt lying discarded at the side of her to thread it back into my pants.

"I need you to understand what happened here – what I'm offering you. This is a chance to make a new life worthwhile." I crouch and pick up her chin, my eyes fixed on hers. "Learn from our time here, because other than me, no one fucks with you. Ever. No one touches you. No one hurts you either. You understand?" Gentle fingers caress her cheek, and I tilt her head to look at the sheer beauty of her. "You've been exquisite here. Keep doing that for me. Be honest. This chain holding you down? That's the Ortega still in you, not me. That's the past if you want it that way. Don't make me treat you the same as he did. Find who you want to be without your father's influence or coercion. Show me that and we have a chance."

I let go and move for her ankle, fingers making quick work of the shackle and then rubbing at the mark on her skin. "I don't expect you to love me, but I do expect loyalty. I'll protect everything about you if I know that's there, but don't make me play you like this again. Don't put me in a position where I have to show you how heartless I am. Screw up, or show me anything other than truth and respect, and a scene like this will end differently."

Straightening upwards, I offer my hand to help her up.

She looks at it and frowns, hesitant. "That still sounds a lot like a threat, Abel," she says quietly.

"No. It's a promise I intend to keep."

She nods after a few moments and looks around the room, seeming to take in the space and what's happened in it. So I wait, still with my hand outstretched and still meaning every word I've said. This is her chance for something close to togetherness. Perhaps even more than that with time.

"You ready to go home?"

She keeps staring, this time at her abandoned shoes. "We don't have a home."

Hmm. True enough.

The high-pitched shriek of fear and death suddenly reverberates through the walls from another room, and I watch as she jumps upwards and grabs for my hand. I look at them clasped together – our gold rings – then drape my jacket over her shoulders.

"Here," I say, leading us over to the camera still filming by the door Ratchet went through. I drop her hand and hammer the door twice to let him know I'm done in here. The camera gets turned off, and I take it from its housing on the stand. The light gets switched off as I pass it to her. "Keep this."

"You really filmed it all?"

"Yes. Could've been profitable if it hadn't ended the way it did." She frowns and holds it tightly. "You can watch it again if you need clarification of how serious this has been. Last chance, yes?"

I start walking us towards the door, as another scream comes from the next room over, and unbolt it. Time to leave.

CHAPTER SIXTEEN

LEXI

The woman's scream sends another volley of chills down my spine, and I clench Abel's hand even tighter. This place is disgusting, and part of me wants to wash away the filth and forget everything that's happened here.

But it's not quite that easy.

Amongst the fear and threats, there was something heartfelt. At least, that's what it felt like to me. Or that's what I took from the ordeal. This was his fucked up and twisted version of a test of strength and will. And the worst part of it? I think that I want what he's offering. To be a respected wife, a member of the family. To have responsibility and power. Not just because I have a reputation for being a bitch and have the right name, but because I'm allowed it – because I've earned it. It's a glimmer of hope that's so appealing it's dangerous.

I stand on something, and my leg buckles as I seethe, but strong hands hold me firm. I grip his jacket tighter around me, even though nobody is around to see until we make it to another door. He pushes it open, but instead of relief, I'm immediately confronted by Carmen in all her refined bitchy-beauty.

The look she covers me in is enough to push me over the edge. Everything I went through was between Abel and me, and the thought that this woman can simply walk in and be a part of that

151

makes me want to take that knife back and cut her smile from her face.

She looks towards Abel and smiles as if she's in on the joke.

"Oh, no fucking way. You don't get to look at him like that," I rage as I approach her. "Ever."

She looks bored as I block her way, and I begin to understand what those girls they use and traffic must be faced with every day.

"Abel?" She looks to him for assistance, but that's not going to work. Not tonight.

I move in front of her face again. "No. You show me the respect I fucking deserve. Don't ever look at me like I'm nothing but one of the girls you look after again. You hear me?"

Abel says nothing and doesn't come to her defence.

"I don't take my orders from you," she says.

"You'll be wise to listen to her, Carmen. She's my wife." Abel's words are what wipe the smile from her face. I see her confidence waver, and suddenly I know exactly how to topple her.

"Take your shoes off," I instruct.

Her brows pull into the worst frown, proving that at least she's not completely fake. "What?"

"You heard. Give me your fucking shoes."

Reluctantly she steps out of the sky-high stilettos. I offer her a smile and slip my feet into them. They're a little roomy, but that's not the point. This is me feeling vulnerable and like an outsider, needing to prove that I can fit into this fucked-up business as Abel wants. I can't do that with someone like Carmen thinking she'll always have the upper hand. She doesn't. She can't. And the sooner I show her that, the better.

"Thank you. Let's go."

I stride with all the confidence I can summon towards his car, his hand still in mine, and as soon as he rounds the car to reach his side, I let go of my breath and try calming my racing heart. Shaky fingers pull my door lever, and I slide inside slowly and stare out into the night.

The door slams, signalling he's inside, but I can't look at him.

"What the fuck was that about?" he mutters.

"You just put me through the worst fucking test. You wanted me real and true, and you wanted a respected wife. Well, that was me being fucking real and demanding what I want if I'm to be your respected wife." I cross my arms over his jacket and bounce my leg over my knee, letting the shoe I just stole from Carmen balance on my toes.

"I've worked with Carmen for a long time."

"And she looks at me like I'm shit. Time to show me you meant what you said in that room, Abel."

He starts the engine and races out onto the road, chuckling about whatever crap he's got going around in his head. "Not so quiet out here in the open."

"I'm sorry, I'm confused. You didn't want me docile and demure, or was that just a play again?" He doesn't answer, so I sit and simmer.

My emotions are raw, and I'm still caught between the fear of what he threatened me with and how we left that room. He showed me my past – my humiliations – but also reminded me of what has given me strength, all in that room. He's taken everything we've done, everything we've said to each other, and stripped it back. He knew what I was trying to prove – trying to do. Why wouldn't he think there's a plot against his family? They killed my brother in cold blood, yet my father still does this to me. He marries me off like a pawn in his game that he can't even win because he's such a short-sighted, greedy man. A man who doesn't value anything apart from his own status, the dollars in his bank, and what power he can buy for himself.

I grumble to myself, angry and confused. That's not what Abel values, is it? That's not what he's shown me. Although I'd be lying if I said I understood him. He's a contradiction in many ways, and that he's offering me this opportunity is still proof of that.

"Where are we going?" I ask, ready to get out of my head.

"Home."

"We've been through this already. I'm a little tired to be playing any more games."

He doesn't answer and keeps his hands on the wheel. My eyes feel sore and sting as I close them, resting them every few minutes. There's a wave of emotion trapped inside me that I kept to myself all through our little show. Angry, sad, vengeful tears. It rises up and falls back, like the waves lapping at the sand, and when I close my eyes, it rushes forward like the tide's ready to charge.

Focussing on anything other than that feeling – the threat of tears and what they will mean – I stare out the window and watch as we pass through San Antonio. Although I'm not familiar with the city, I recognise enough to know we're not heading back to the mansion in Terrell Hills.

My heart skips, and I realise I'm excited to be going back to Abel's home. Finally, after months of being locked out, he's letting me in. And, of course, I hate that I'm both excited and now confused about that. After everything I've promised myself over the years, this man has annihilated everything I've tried to build and is making me question it all. I've sacrificed for my family – for the Ortega family – yet have I ever been a part of it? I knew my doubts before Abel shackled me to them, but because of that, I have a black hole in my mind, growing with every moment about what family actually means to me.

My husband killed for his family and went to prison. He's a defender and keeper of the family name and everyone who holds it, even if they aren't technically all Cortezes. That would have been his downfall – the weakness I've been searching for to make Ortega's revenge hurt the most. But why am I doing that? And why is the possibility of being let in by him – by his family – making me feel like a stupid teenager just picked to go to Prom by the Homecoming King? I pick my date – I make the Homecoming King. What the hell has happened?

Fuck.

We're silent until he pulls up towards what I assume might be a house. I can't see past the entrance and walls surrounding it, but the car's lights illuminate a wooden gate. A few seconds later, it begins to roll to the side, revealing the driveway and, beyond it, a house. He drives through the magically opening gate and follows the driveway around, past the house and down a slight incline, straight into an underground garage. Lights spring to life as soon as we're inside, flickering as he passes two other cars parked up and swings the Challenger into the free spot.

"Quite the collection," I murmur, mostly to myself.

We exit the car, and he takes my hand, walking me back to the garage entrance. He places his thumb on a pad and the door, like the gate, rolls into place, locking the toys inside. He leads me along a path back towards the entrance of the house. Small lights recessed into the concrete light our way. Polished concrete steps lead up to the front door, and he places his hand on another pad to open it.

The door size makes me think it must be reinforced, and just before we step over the threshold, I bend to remove my shoes. I throw them out into the driveway, watching them tumble and toss over each other.

"Didn't like them?"

"I don't want her shoes here." It's a stupid thing, but it's taken a lot to be invited to see where he lives, and I feel like I've earned that tonight. I don't want to share that with anybody. Even her shoes.

The polished concrete extends inside to a reception hall floor, and the grey walls give an immediate dark and cold feel. Low lights begin to glow, but they don't light up the space. It's more like they give you enough atmosphere to appreciate the area as it opens to you. There's a glass barrier a few meters in front of us, with stairs leading down to one side and a corridor in the other direction adjacent to the barrier. Beyond that, a sitting space with more glass.

He doesn't move very fast, giving me time to take in the space around me. I'm itching to explore, searching for any indication that might help me unlock the puzzle of my husband. But I'm also still reeling from what happened tonight.

"I'd like a shower."

He puts out his arm and walks towards the corridor. We move, and I realise my feet are warm, despite walking on what looks and feels like concrete. I peer over the glass to see steps leading down into a big, shadowy room, and, as he opens the door at the end for me, I find more of the same: Greys, shadows and hard edges. The lights increase in intensity as he enters, and I watch as he unbuttons his shirt and takes it off, draping it on a chair before releasing his belt. That move, the sound as it pulls through his pants, sends me straight back to the room. Bound and vulnerable.

"No. I want to wash and clean up alone. You owe me that, Abel."

"Owe you?"

"Yeah."

His head tilts to the side as he scrutinises me.

"You can find me some clothes while I'm in there. Through here?" I point back to the only place for the en suite.

"Go ahead."

I let the jacket drop to the floor where I stand and pull the remaining scraps of material from me, followed by my ruined underwear, before walking to the bathroom. The lights activate as I open the door, warming up and bathing the space in golden light. A mini open-plan room, with a shower at one end and yet more glass, only this is frosted. And, to add to my frustrations, there are buttons on the wall to activate the water. The bastard can't have a normal shower like anyone else? He has to have a computerised system. I press the first button, and nothing happens, then another.

"Abel!" I shout. I watch him enter and look pretty fucking pleased with himself as he stares at me. "Would you mind helping me with the shower?"

His pants are undone, showing off his physique. In this light, his muscular chest and broad shoulders look even more remarkable, or maybe I'm just paying more attention. I don't know, but no sooner than I think how enticing he looks, I remember the look of him, cast in shadow and standing behind the camera as Ratchet held me down.

No.

This might be a clean slate – a new beginning for him, but it's not going to be that easy for me.

I step back against the tiled wall and wait for him to do whatever magic is needed to set the water running. He slides his thumb over the chrome panel, and the water begins to flow.

"Temperature." He brings his thumb down to the little dotted icon and slides his thumb back and forth.

"Thank you," I say through the downpour. He's getting wet from the water, and so am I.

"I could stay. You might need some more help."

A part of me wants to say yes – wants to pretend like all the bad shit and hate isn't still there so he can soothe me. It is, though. It might have been softened, and it might hold less strength than it did, but I can't see that straight yet.

I shake my head, and he seems to understand. It's another one of those moments – an honest exchange between us. They're happening more frequently now, and perhaps I can start to envisage a way through all of this.

His dark shadow leaves, and I wait before stepping into the full force of the water. It's divine, and a soft sigh escapes my throat. My eyes close, and I turn into the spray. The flashes of the warehouse, the floor, Ratchet, all flicker behind my eyes. But they intersperse with images of Abel, the intensity in his gaze, the words he spoke. The way he felt inside me.

It's a toxic mix, but the longer I stay in the comfort of the warm shower, the easier I see him. The real him. And maybe he can see the real me, too. I look down at my body and stare at the ankle that was shackled. I can still feel the cold metal cut into my skin, just as the harsh words and disappointments of my father slice through my heart. I've grown immune and hardened by time; the scar tissue now layered with years of putting myself back together.

Who am I?

It's the biggest question I need to answer. Am I a Cortez wife or an Ortega whore? And if I manage to betray Abel, trick him despite all of his warnings and deliver Cortez to my father on a platter, will I ever be anything more?

I manage to switch the shower off without breaking the damn thing and wrap a towel from the counter around me. I step out into the bedroom, but Abel isn't there. It gives me a moment to admire his room. Perhaps it could be our room? A large bed dominates the back wall, but what's shocking is the amount of glass. Floor-to-ceiling windows line the right side of the room. Knowing how protective he's been, I can't imagine he'd let people look into his space, but I can't see beyond the reflection shining back at me. The darkness versus the glass seems to oppose each other, another question for me to unlock.

There's a t-shirt and a pair of his boxers on the bed, presumably for me to wear. A smile pulls at my lips as I think about walking around his home in his clothes. It's a good thought and one I hold onto as I dress and walk back into the gloom to look for him. He's not hard to find. He's sitting in one of the chairs in the lobby area outside the bedroom, looking at the glass.

"Nice view?"

"It is." He stands, and I notice his hair is damp, and he's only wearing a towel.

"You have another shower."

"Yes. The guest bedroom. Also, in the gym."

"Can I take a look around? Grab a drink?"

"Downstairs. I'll go get dressed." He motions for me to head to the stairs and disappears into the shadows of the corridor.

Tentatively I walk around the glass barrier, looking down to see what could be part of the kitchen. Stepping down, as I go deeper, I see it actually opens up into a huge space. A kitchen area, an open-plan dining space and more glass. Past the kitchen is more living space with sectionals spaced around what I guess to be a coffee table.

Dark appliances, dark wood, polished copper. It all looks so harsh and cold together, but there's an annoying sophistication to it all as well. You can't describe it as anything other than the ultimate moody atmosphere. Although, when the Texas sun spills in, I can see it will transform, warming up to something less sinister and threatening.

There's a wet bar on the other side of the kitchen island, and I help myself to a drink. He's got an extensive collection, including Grey Goose, Absolut and Belvedere vodka, so I pour a double and add ice and a slice of lime. The drying chill of the drink is perfect, giving me a much-needed hit.

"Pour me one." Abel's voice sounds from behind me, so I oblige and hand him the tumbler. He heads to the sitting area, and once again, more lights spark to life as we move through the space.

"I'll need you to pack an overnight bag for tomorrow." He stares at the glass and not at me.

"Okay. Why don't I just have my stuff moved here? It will be easier."

He looks at me and shakes his head. "Not yet. In fact, I'm taking you home after this." And with that, he knocks back his drink.

"We're leaving?" I question, failing to hide the crestfallen note in my voice.

"Yes. I'll come and pick you up in the morning."

Anger that I'd managed to calm awakens in that second. "Still no home, then? Was it all bullshit? What was the fucking point of everything, huh?" I down my drink and then, in a rage, smash the glass on the concrete floor. It breaks into pieces, glittering over the polished floor, and I can't help but think that perhaps this is what I'm destined for – to be broken and shattered and never be whole.

"Careful, Lexi. And don't believe that we can fast-forward to a place where we automatically trust everything about each other. Tonight is day one."

"Day one should have been when we said I do. Not when you kidnapped me and locked me in a room with some maniac, shackled to a bed to prove a point."

"You're acting like a brat and not the Lexi I've come to know."

"Well, fuck you. You're acting like a jerk. Take me back."

I storm back through his pristine cave and his stuff and wait at the door. Once again, I'm barefoot, making me feel so small and insignificant. He's stripped me down and humiliated me again.

The drive 'home' is in silence, but I'm sure he can feel my temper simmering.

"I'll be back to collect you in the morning. Pack a bag, and take a look at your behaviour. Respected Cortez wife. Remember that, Lexi."

"Well, how about you take a look at what being a husband might entail." I get out of the car, slam the door, and race to the relative safety of my room.

Although I feel like tearing the place down, I can't ignore that little ache in my heart that he still didn't want me with him. After all we've been through, that doubt eats into my soul and makes me question everything all over again.

CHAPTER SEVENTEEN

ABEL

The drive to Terrell Hills is slow. I weave through traffic, letting the warmth of the sun through the window bring me back to the reality of San Antonio around me. Everything's been unfamiliar this morning; the smell of her perfume in my home, the image of her in my shower, the smashed glass still littered over my floor. Even the look of her walking around my space still flicks through my head like a movie on repeat. I'm not sure how I feel about any of it.

I pull over to a corner store and get out. She's the only woman, short of family and Carmen, to ever step foot in my home. I've been there years and kept it to myself, and now I'm thinking about sharing it? That wasn't ever part of the fucking plan, regardless of marriage.

"Marlboro Red."

The store owner turns to grab a pack and places it on the counter as I dig out some money. It's only when I've paid for them and I'm walking out the door that I truly realise what I've just done. The door slams behind me and I slide them into my inside pocket. I'm smoking again? Three damn years of being quit and she's making me smoke? "Son of a bitch," I curse.

The goddamn irony of that statement is not lost on me as I pull back into traffic and head for my wife. I am a son of a bitch. And not only that, I'm the son of a pimp. I'm reminded of that every day when I look in a mirror. I might hate the thought of him, but I'm just like him and there's no denying it. Barely any of Mother's features took hold in me, not like the others she bred. I often wonder how she feels about that when she looks at me. Must be a reminder. A sharp fucking smack around the head about who's in control around here. Still, at least I don't make her spread her legs for a living. She's damn good at doing that without needing my input.

Chuckling lightly, I pull up the drive at the house and wait. One of Mother's servants comes out carrying Lexi's bag, and I watch her walk out behind the guy. She seems looser somehow this morning, like she's shed a layer of veneer and is trying for casual, as she slides her sunglasses on. Flowing red silk skirt. Contrasting patterned top tied high over her navel. I look down at her feet. Still sharp as hell heels residing down there, though.

"Good morning, husband," she says, as she swings those long legs into the car. I smile and wait for the trunk to close, then pull off. "What is your plan for us today, then?"

"We're going home. Your home."

She turns her face to look at me, shocked. "Which one?"

"San Diego. I have a meeting with your father tomorrow." And I want to see her there with him. I want to see how she behaves, how she acts – if she acts.

She's quiet for the rest of the drive, and I don't mind that, given my frayed head this morning. It's the same damn head that keeps looking at the curve of her leg under her skirt the entire journey, perhaps wishing it wasn't as long as it is. I snort to myself, as I pull onto the rough road leading down to the hangar, and end up smiling about the thoughts running through my mind. They're filled with sin and grime. That's concerning for both me and her, because our time on that stained mattress changed my view of her a little. It's probably just the memory of that knife at my neck, and definitely the sneer she levelled at me as she held it there. Either way, though, if she screws this up now that I'm thinking about getting invested, I'll turn damn sinister on her.

"Are we staying at my father's house?" she asks, as we get out of the car and I get our bags.

"No. We're getting to know each other."

She walks beside me and wraps her arms around herself, almost protectively. "Really?"

"That's what you want, isn't it?"

"Well, yes, but after last night at yours and then me going back to the mansion, I thought …" She trails off and looks up at the jet. "You're really fucking confusing, Abel."

I nod her up the steps and laugh. "And you'd like something simple? You'd be bored within a month."

"I might not be. I might enjoy the simplicity and–"

"Cut the bullshit." I watch her legs climbing in front of me, getting a good glimpse of skin. "I don't want it anywhere near us, Lexi." She stops and looks back at me, tilting her head about. "Don't pretend you don't like that name on my tongue either. Get that pretty ass moving." She smiles lightly and turns away to keep climbing. Doesn't stop her looking back at me occasionally, though, and even I keep smiling when we reach the cabin.

The luggage is stowed, and I talk with the pilot for ten minutes before getting her buckled in and ready to fly. She watches me the entire time. Probably because she doesn't know what the hell is going on with me this morning. I'm good with that. She's getting parts of me I've kept well away from her up until now.

"Well, Abel, I have to say this is all very surprising." I get us a drink and sit ready for take-off. "I don't think I've ever been buckled in place before. Although, like this is certainly preferable to last night."

I pass her a drink. "That's because no one's given a damn about your survival before now. I do." Surprising or not, this can be her life now if she chooses it. That man she got a piece of yesterday? He lives inside me all the time. He's as direct and decent as someone in my line of work gets, and he's damn protective of anything that means something to him.

She drinks and keeps looking back at me as the engines fire and we start taxing the runway. I don't spoil it with words, and neither does she. I gaze at her high, cut-glass cheekbones and her lips, and I let her think about what I just said because underneath all this there will always be that fact chasing her and she can't deny it. No one has cared about her before. And I'm not surprised she's turned out the way she has. She's probably had to fight her whole damn life to get the slightest reaction from someone she looks up to, and then the only way she managed to get one was by opening her legs under his damn direction. For all my faults, and all my savagery and cruelty, I can't imagine doing that to your own child. I meant it when I called Miguel Ortega a piece of shit. I might even kill a man like that if his business didn't mean as much to me as it does.

~

I could have ordered a driver for us at this end of the flight, but I didn't feel like it. She wants a little control? She can have it. Might help her realise what's she's got in front of her — what she could have all around her.

The guy who's delivered a brand new, custom grey Camaro passes the keys to me and dares a glance at Lexi behind me. "That's a dumb fucking move," I mutter, signing the document he's given me. He whips his head back to me, servile in nature all of a sudden. So I pass him back the document and toss the keys over my shoulder at her. "You ready darlin'?"

I hear her heels before I see her. She smiles at me as she walks by — a wide, real smile — and slides her ass straight in the driver's seat. "Where are we going?" she asks, as I get in.

"San Diego's your city. You tell me. I don't know anything about it other than watching you in it for a while."

"What?"

I smirk. "You think I'd let someone into my family that I hadn't trailed for a while?"

"You followed me?"

"Yes."

"How often?"

"Enough to know what you did each day before me, and who you fucked and where you did that."

She frowns. "Stalkerish much?"

"Hmm."

"Right, well, which hotel?"

"We'll leave that for later. Show me what you want to do with the rest of the day first."

"What I want to do?"

"Yes, Lexi. You."

She scrutinises the empty roadway in front of her for a minute and then looks back at me again. "What's going on here?"

"Nothing. I want to know how you'll entertain me. That's what a husband and wife do, together. It isn't a trap."

"I feel like everything's a trap with you."

"It still might be." I chuckle and close my eyes, settling my shoulders back into the car. "But not today."

The car pulls away slowly, then starts speeding up, and I keep my eyes closed and let her lead me for a while. I don't care what we do, in all honesty. This is about her feeling what it's like to be trusted. I can do that out here when we're miles away from anything that means something to me. In fact, I think I'd rather fuck the rest of this day away in a bed rather than be entertained any other way. I've got nothing to do other than concentrate on her for once in my life. Dante and Knox are dealing with things back home, and short of this meeting with her father, I'm free of responsibility to an extent.

The car eventually stops. I open my eyes to see what she's chosen.

"Okay, so this is the Gaslamp District. I presume you're hungry?"

I nod and watch her get out, so I follow until we're both on the sidewalk in a crowded area full of tourists and late afternoon street life. "You chose around here to eat?" She starts leading the way along a road, dodging incomers with that arrogant attitude of hers. Not that she needs to. They move for her. "It's your turn to surprise me."

"Well, you asked for what I want to do. And this is what your Lexi probably would choose. Alexia would go someplace where she could eat half a romaine salad and be seen with the right people. I'm guessing you don't want that side of me?"

"No. Never again." She looks along the road and then back to me, a new smile emerging on her face. I'd almost consider it shy if she wasn't so good at being far from that. "Take your hair down." She pats the side of the sleek bun and frowns. "Just do it, Lexi." Her fingers take the clip out, and she slides them through the mass of blonde locks that tumble free. "Better."

"Really?"

"Yes."

She coughs and looks along the road again. "So … what kind of food do you want?" My brow arches. "Okay, alright. My choice on that as well?" I nod and follow as she starts weaving again until we end up at a small bistro. She cuts through it and signals over the mass of people, somehow managing to get the waiters attention. He points upstairs and winks at her. For some goddamn reason, I'm not one bit fucking happy about the last section of that unspoken conversation.

"I'm not sure bringing me somewhere that houses a man you've fucked is useful to our marriage."

She laughs and looks back at me as we're climbing the stairs and rounding a corner. "I haven't, but considering the Carmen thing, you've no right to be pissed at me for that anyway." She waves us out onto a small terrace area, having opened a door, and lets me get a good view of a private area with a small table and two chairs. "How's this?"

"Faultless."

Another smile beams out of her, as she takes a seat and leans over the balcony to look down below us. The guy – the waiter – arrives immediately. He looks at me and smiles, then leans towards my wife to kiss her on the cheek. Whatever the fucking conversation is between them regarding the fact that he hasn't seen her for a while gets tuned out. I'm just looking at her behaving differently as he lays the table with glasses and cutlery, and wondering why the hell she hasn't shown me any of this before.

"Abel?" I start listening again, shaking myself clear of wherever my head was. "What would you like to drink?" I shrug, because, once again, this is all her choice for the day. "Okay then. A bottle of Chablis, please. And we'll have the Carne asada fries, some burritos, and maybe the fish tacos. Enough for two."

The waiter leaves after that, and I'm still watching her and thinking about why she'd choose to keep this side of her away from me.

"What? You don't like fish?" she asks. "If you don't, I'll eat them, and you can have—"

"All good," I cut in, as I take my jacket off and drape it on the back of the chair. "Talk to me about why you like it around here."

"It's good food."

"No, that's not it. A woman like you can get good food anywhere, yet you've chosen a small, inexpensive place tucked in the bowels of a tourist trap. It's nothing to do with food."

A bottle of wine lands on the table as she's thinking about her answer. It's not poured, and the waiters gone before I've barely noticed he was here. I pick it up and pour, twisting the end of the bottle to stop it dripping down the neck.

She picks her glass up and wraps her arms over herself, leaning back away from me. "You really want to know? The truth?"

"That's what we're here for."

"Okay. It's the noise. The sound of people, the laughter. Can you hear it?" I nod and keep looking at her for more. "I used to come here sometimes. I don't even know how I found myself here that first day, but it was busy and there wasn't a table available. Thomas, the owner, that's the guy you just met, let me come up here because someone hadn't turned up for their reserved lunch." She takes a sip of her wine and sighs, closing her eyes at the sounds around us. "It's nice, that sound." Her eyes open. "I never got to hear any real laughter at my father's house, and I didn't have a place to call my own around here. So, I guess I just used this as a refuge in some ways."

"From your father?"

"Maybe. I don't know the answer to that one. And I'd rather not talk about it."

"Fine. Maybe we should discuss the length of your skirt then."

"We should?"

"Yes. It's too long."

"Really."

"Hmm. Although, I suppose you could come over here and slide yourself onto my dick and no one would ever know." Her face brightens from the seriousness of a moment ago. "I've changed my mind. It's a good length. Wear it as much as you like."

She smirks. "This flirting is very unlike you."

"How would you know? You don't know me."

"That's a good point."

She's quiet for a while. She chooses the view or the wine or anything other than me to invest herself in. I end up chuckling a little about her insecurity in all this. It's not blatantly obvious, and I doubt the wider world would ever see it on her, but I can. She's a mass of nerves under that pristine exterior. "Lexi?" She looks back at me. "Relax."

"I am relaxed."

I drink some more wine and then pour us both another glass. "No, you're not. You're a ball of tension. You're trying to work out what I'm up to, and what you need to do to keep me sweet, and why I'm doing any of this and if you can trust me. You can. Relax." She sips and keeps staring at me. "I'm not trying to play with you. I want to see the you underneath the bullshit. So, show me."

Thomas turns up while she's digesting that information and plates of food get laid on the table. Crockery and cutlery clatter about, and she laughs about something as he curses the size of the table and she catches a knife that's dropped. It's a good laugh. A nice laugh. A real fucking laugh. It's also a laugh that makes me wonder how often she's ever done it in her life.

"Okay then," she says, as he leaves us alone. "What do you want to know?"

"Everything."

"And you'll give the same in return?"

I look at the food and put a napkin in my lap. "Yes. The bet's still in play, too."

"You thought that was just a game on your part."

"Yes. Doesn't mean I don't want what you offered from it."

"Okay. Why did you choose yourself for me?" I look back up. "You could have chosen Dante or Knox. Both of them seem like they'd be able to deal with me."

I sigh. "No. That's not what I meant." She frowns, as if she doesn't understand what I've just said. I don't suppose she would. "I'm not interested in discussing where we're at, or why we're here, or what business we're in. I want to know about you." She still seems confused. I push my chair back a little. "Get around here."

"Why?" I keep staring until she gets up and walks around the small table. "Sit."

"On you?"

"Yes." She swings her skirt out of the way and perches on my knees, so I drag her ass back until she's tucked in tight to my chest and I can get my arm around her to some of the food. "Listen. We're gonna get real comfortable with each other for a while, and you're gonna learn what it's like to be treated like a queen." I pick up some fries and offer them up to her mouth. "Eat."

"From your hand?"

"Yes."

"What the hell is going on with you?"

"Eat. You could use a few more pounds." She frowns and moves her head a little, opening her mouth to take the food, so I pull it away. "Or maybe not." She stiffens instantly and whips her face back to me, indignant. Can't stop the damn laugh that comes from me. "You never had any goddamned fun in your life?" She's grabbed my hand before I stop laughing, biting the fries before shoving a taco back at my face in frustration.

I pull her in tighter as she laughs quietly and licks food off her fingers. "Well, now you're gonna have to clean this off me." She reaches for a napkin. "I know you've got better ways of cleaning me than that." So she gets the hint and leans in, using her lips and tongue tentatively to wipe the mess away. "See? We get along just fine when you relax and stop thinking. Start talking about who you are and what you like."

She tucks her hair behind her ear and gazes at me, shifting her weight around on my dick. "You're gonna be sucking me off out here in a minute if you don't stop." That seems to cause an unheard-before giggle. "I'm not joking."

"I'm well aware of that."

"Is that what you want?"

She reaches for another handful of food to push it at me again. "Not quite yet."

"Might not give you any choice."

"You know, I think today you will."

And that's how it goes for the next hour or so. We eat from each other, and she gets real comfortable on my lap and starts working out how this could be between us.

~

Late afternoon makes its way into early evening, and we end up at some bar on a back street because she doesn't think I'll like the shiny new ones on the front. She's right. I don't like anything shiny and new other than my home. I like authenticity, and I like the broken-down atmosphere of something to remind me what its life has been about.

We walked the streets for a while, and she showed me some things about San Diego I didn't know. It wasn't hard. I don't know much about this place, nor do I care in reality. All it is to me is a new part of this business we're creating and what that might offer me. But in all this time, she's still been unable to tell me anything about what she likes to do. There's been murmurs about art and museums, and talk of the sea and boat trips, but it's mainly been chatter or focused information rather than passion.

"It's strange sitting here with a man like you," she says. "Do all these women look like profit to you?"

"No. They look like people enjoying their night."

She leans in, resting her chin in her hand. "But they could be. What makes the most money? Brunettes? How about that blonde over there?" I don't bother looking.

"It's not about that. Most men will fuck anything."

"What then?"

"Usually the way they move. That's why we spend time training them. You spent your life learning to move like you do to attract men. You've honed it and made it a mission. We get months."

"You're not even apologetic about it, are you? You steal lives and profit off misery and you smile at the thought."

"I also make sure most of our girls make good money."

"And now you're trying to justify yourself."

"I don't need to justify myself. I have no one to answer to. I'm the top of my food chain, and no one's coming for me."

"Mmm." She sips her drink and leans away, scrutinising everything about me. Face. Chest. Hands. Her tongue snakes over her lips. "And do I move well enough?"

"For what?"

"You."

A smile broadens on my face. "And there you go getting all insecure and tense again. You feeling needy, darlin'?"

She stiffens. "I am not insecure, but you can give a girl whiplash, Abel."

"You're insecure and desperate for me to tell you how beautiful you are. But unless you want me to list the reasons why your daddy issues are the problem, I suggest you change the subject."

Noise erupts behind me, and I look back to see a group of guys at the bar celebrating a win they're watching on the screen. By the time I turn back she's part angling for a fight and part checking her temper. "Darlin' you're gonna ruin this by lying to me in a minute. Don't. I'll have to turn all savage on you again, and you know I'm one step away from that most of the time."

Her eyes narrow. "Fine. Do you like sports?"

I chuckle and shake my head, leaning back into the booth we're sitting in. "No. I'm not usually a betting man. Dante's the risk taker."

"I never understood the need to gamble either. It's always been about certainty for me. Control. It's easier that way. You don't risk anything if you're in control of it."

The admission makes me smile and sip my drink. "And that's how you want the rest of your life?"

"It's what I know. And you're hardly one to talk. I can't see you giving an inch on anything, ever."

"You sound like Mariana now. She's wrong too. I give plenty as long as it doesn't impact the safety of those I care about."

Something about her face softens as she takes that in. She crosses her legs and watches me, perhaps thinking about prying deeper than I'm prepared to go at the moment. "They mean everything to you, don't they? And I don't mean like everyone else's family do to them. I mean they're literally everything. You've killed for them. You'd die for them. I expect every minute of your day revolves around them and where they're at in life in some ways. That's why you didn't choose one of them to marry me. You took me on yourself to save them the potential agony of what could have been."

I swallow the rest of my drink and put the glass down, about done with sentimental thoughts. "Clever girl."

"I suppose that makes you a good man, Abel."

"I'm nowhere near a good man. Never have been and don't intend to be. But I am a good brother."

"And what about husband?"

We stare at each other. From my perspective, that's all about how she behaves from this moment on. It's in her hands to a certain extent. I'll react accordingly, and she'll get whichever version of me I see fit, depending on her actions.

Another round of cheers come from behind us, breaking the moment. "Is there anything you actually like doing?" I ask.

"Oh, we're moving on from that conversation, are we?"

"We are. How about the theatre?" I get up and head to the bar, beckoning her and sliding some cash across to the barkeep for the tab we've created.

"Movie or performance?" she asks.

"Performance."

She smiles, near laughs. "You like going to the theatre?"

"Possibly."

"What does that mean?"

I grab her hand and tow her out of the place until we're on the dirty sidewalk and watching the world go by. "It means I don't know. I've never been."

"Never?"

"No. It's not a place a man like me goes. Take me."

"Okay. What's the time?"

I check my watch. "Six."

"Have you brought a tux?" My brow arches. "Of course you haven't. And I can't go like this either. We'll need clothes."

I get my wallet out and hold out a new version of the AMEX she trashed. "You'll need this then."

Her face immediately turns suspicious, chin up in the air. "I told you I don't want or need your money."

"You think I don't know that? Stop with the bitching. This isn't an argument. This is the way I treat my wife. Accept it." She's still revving herself up for a fight, and I don't blame her after the last time we discussed money. "Lexi. Cool your tongue right down. Don't spoil this. You're not gonna like the way it turns out for you, and I was enjoying the peace."

That half sneer might still be hovering, but she relents and takes it from my fingers. "Okay," she says, looking along the street. "Fine. Let's go shopping then."

CHAPTER EIGHTEEN

LEXI

"**S**o?"

"So, what?" He looks at me as if I asked a hard question.

"You've barely talked since leaving the theatre. Did you enjoy it? I have to say, for a man like you, you fitted in quite well in your tux." He takes my arm and leads me through the hotel lobby to the elevator.

"It was … pleasant."

I don't answer and wonder, again, what the hell today is all about. Honesty, looking behind the facade, but Abel seems to pick and choose what his interpretation of that is.

We arrive back at the penthouse room he's booked, and I walk through, throwing the bejewelled clutch onto the bed. "Do you want to elaborate on pleasant?" I toss back the question, disappointed that he refuses to open up.

"Today isn't about me. It's about you." His hands grab my shoulders and push the thin straps of my dress down. His eyes are dark, swimming with desire, and that alone is enough to raise my heartbeat.

So far, sex has been a punishment or a way to put me in my place. It doesn't feel like this now, and I both hate and love the feeling simmering through me.

He twists me and crashes his lips against mine. My arms rise to wrap around him, but he keeps them down by my side with his hands. The kiss deepens and with it, the pull for this to go harder … faster.

His hands run down my arms and pull them behind my back, securing me in place. My instinct is to struggle, but I fight it back down, wanting to feel how Abel might treat me tonight.

All the talk of truth and control, of being closer together, begs the question of what side of Abel I'll see now, and my anticipation grows with every second.

His tongue licks against my mouth, sliding in and out, mimicking what I'm sure he wants to do with his cock. As I lean into him, the grip on my wrists tightens, keeping me in place like he doesn't want the contact.

"Abel," I whisper against his lips.

"Shhh." He doesn't stop kissing.

"I want to be on top. Let me please you." I twist in his grasp, but he shoves me to the bed, smothering me with his body.

His warm breath at my ear shouldn't be sexy. "Please me?" Another soft kiss lands on my neck. "You'll please me by letting me do whatever I want to you." His tongue rolls downwards, making my thighs ache to widen for him. "You'll please me by collapsing after I've fucked you raw." I gulp, nails digging into his shoulders. "Come on, darlin'. Let me see you enjoy this because, make no mistake, I'm going to make sure I do."

He pulls me back up and runs his hand down my back until he reaches the hem of my tight dress. I jolt as he tears the fabric in half, giving him access. The sound of torn material shouldn't add to the dull ache in my stomach. It should be a warning, but there's something different tonight. A shift, perhaps.

I cling onto that feeling as his hands travel over my skin, seeking every curve and secret my body has to offer. He knocks my legs wider apart and tilts my hips as he positions himself. He's barely touched me, but I know I'll be wet for him.

He shoves inside of me like he's desperate to feel me around him and pulls my body back against his. It's the closest we've been – the closest to a couple having sex. No violence, no demands, just a need between us.

His guttural moan as he pauses is satisfying, and I take the moment to catch my breath.

Before my lungs are full, he pistons into me, fucking me with a vigour that's impatient and desperate. His arms hold me up, and he uses my whole body to his advantage. Pulling me back against him, tilting me, pinching my breasts.

He's everywhere – assaulting my senses – and I love it. My body undulates against his direction. My legs inch wider so he can fuck me deeper. His hand slides up to my head and pulls my hair so I'm resting on his shoulder.

"You're so much sweeter when you bend, Lexi."

"Hmmm," I murmur.

"You can fight me all you like, but you like me fucking you."

"Yes," I admit. I do. But I want him to fuck me harder. "Harder, Abel. And touch my clit."

Teeth bite down on my neck, and I clench my muscles in response, agonising over the mix of feelings.

"Fuck! Your pussy likes pain."

"Careful, Abel."

"Why? Because you don't want me to make you come?"

"Oh, you better. You said something about collapsing on the bed." I tilt my hips back, hoping he'll get on with delivering his good time.

"Greedy."

"Yes. And if you won't let me be in control, I want you to make up for it by making me lose control."

His teeth bite back down again before he licks it away, but my clit is begging for attention. He picks up his pace before switching it up again, tilting me so he can slide deeper inside of me. As if reading my body, his hand creeps over my hip and slides over my clit, sending a wave of heat over me and pulling a pathetic moan of gratitude from my throat.

"Better?" If he wasn't making my body climb, I'd be annoyed by his mocking tone. But all I want him to do is fuck me harder, rub my clit and make me come.

"Yes, just fucking do it. Fuck me. Make me scream!" My voice grows louder, and my lack of control seems to fuel Abel's enthusiasm.

He grips my hips and thrusts back and forth harder than ever, giving me everything I want. I lean forward and brace myself against the bed. My body jolts, my arms begin to quiver and I love it. I want to fly apart; I want to feel the pulse of my orgasm through every beat of my heart.

"Yes! More!" I cry. My own hand lifts to rub at my clit, teasing the swollen bundle that will push me over.

"Fuck!"

"Yes!" The pulse explodes, my limbs hum and my body contracts around him, desperate and exhausted in equal measure.

I slump down onto the bed, pulling my legs up onto the lush fabric and let my eyes rest.

~

I wake up and look over to my right to see my husband still sleeping.

Last night was the first time we've spent the night in the same bed since we met. It was the first time sex didn't feel forced and the first time I felt myself with him. He'd been teasing it all day, and it was clear he wanted it. Sex with Abel will never be dull, and almost always pleasurable; it just depends on which Abel I have in front of me.

The one last night can stay.

The tension had been building all day with his game of 'let Lexi choose'. It was like walking a tightrope with him scrutinising each step and deciding if he'd wobble the wire and make me fall or help me across safely. He wanted to see me, understand me, and let me choose, but he's still the one in control.

I look him over as he sleeps, taking my own time to scrutinise him. Beautiful really. Savagely so, perhaps, but that hard edge he holds runs all the way through him. No pretence about it. I used to believe I was a control freak. Mainly from the positions I've been put in before. Control for me equals power, and I don't want to give mine up, but he'll never allow me any real power over him. It's clear in everything he does. He's possessive when he wants, insistent when he wants, and generous … when he wants. It all causes my frustrations to spill over, and then he chastises me and shuts down any line of questioning I have at will. Annoying isn't a good enough word.

I pull back the sheet and head through the suite to make a coffee. Of course, it's the best suite. In the best hotel. With the most perfect position and decor this city has to offer. Yet another annoying thing considering part of me wants to find fault. Perhaps so I can regain some amount of control around here, but for now, I choose not to look too hard.

He has a meeting with my father today. The last forty-eight hours have turned my world on its head, and I'm not sure how I'll feel seeing him again. I was pretty pissed at him over our last conversation. And as well as being sharp to deal with my father, I don't know what Abel's trying to do with this little getaway. Is this making up for the disappointment that I'm still not worthy of a place in his home? Or a show of strength towards my father? Something else?

Stirring the coffee, I stare out at the view. I've not asked Abel about the meeting. This could be important to ensure Ortega gets what we want from this union – something I believe my father has been slow to secure. We'll have to wait and see how it plays out, but my gut tells me that Abel will out-negotiate my father and leave him thinking he got the best out of the deal. Nicolas was better at business strategy, but Miguel Ortega isn't somebody who responds well to criticism of any kind, so that little snip of information wasn't widely shared. Of course, men talk. And they like to brag. Especially when they think they're getting something unavailable to others.

"I don't want you wearing anything you'd usually wear today," Abel says, as he walks by. "What have you got that's more understated?"

"Morning, husband. How nice it is to wake up to see you," I mock, turning around to face him.

He cocks a brow at me and heads for the espresso machine. "I see you've already had coffee. Shall we order breakfast?"

"What time are we meeting my father?"

"Not until midday."

"Great. We have time to go out for breakfast then. And, if I'm not meant to dress like me, we'll have to go shopping again."

~

We head back downtown, but instead of where we shopped for the tux and my dress for the theatre, I take him to a couple of boutique stores. They are me, but that doesn't mean I can't find something a little less seductive to wear. Understated can be classic and sophisticated.

I browse the little store, run my hand over a figure-hugging cream dress, and then move on to a respectable and boring pantsuit. There's nothing wrong with it. It's just boring, and I

180

realise that I like a little fun in my fashion. I've not been keeping up with the usual workouts, but I might have more freedom when we return. I can think about my options – the side I want to take – and how I move forward to carve out a life for myself, and, most importantly, if I can believe Abel.

"Abel, conservative isn't me. If I get something like these, I'll need a pair of heels to compensate."

He pulls his phone away from his ear and ends a call. "I don't want you to dress like you normally would when we meet your father."

"Why?" My hands shoot to my hips, pissed that he's dictating.

"Call it strategy. And, I'd like to see you in something more befitting the wife you are."

"You wanted honest yesterday. You wanted to know me, and today you don't. I've warned you about giving me whiplash before."

I trail my hands along the rack of boring pants. Fitted, alluring and traffic-stopping outfits have been what I've enjoyed wearing for years. They give me a confidence that nothing else can. An ego-boost and advantage all at once. And when men are too busy looking at what they want, they get sloppy in other areas. Something that has paid me well in the past. Abel's been one of the only men seemingly immune, much to my annoyance.

"The cream dress is fine. Just not for the meeting."

I turn and roll my eyes, grabbing a silk shirt that has a fabulous tone, the horrid pants, the cream dress, and, as I head to the changing area at the back, I swipe the highest heels.

Everything fits, and everything does look great, so I dump the garments on the cashier's desk and wait for my husband to pick up the tab.

"Happy?" I check.

"Marginally. That wasn't so hard, was it?"

"Yes. And that's me being honest."

~

If I was nervous about finding myself, as per my husband's request, being the new 'respected' Cortez wife, being that in front of my father has me feeling a little neurotic. Abel's hand in mine is clenched tightly – a united front perhaps – and irrespective of our complicated relationship, I'm glad I'm not in this alone. Even if I'm not sure what this is.

The meeting is set, apparently, at one of my father's warehouses. Meeting at a reputable establishment for either family seems to be out of the question.

"You seem on edge, Lexi."

"No. But no bullshit, remember. Or, if you'd like, I can turn back into the Ortega whore?" I snipe.

"Is that advice you're offering?"

"Just making sure we're all on the same page."

"We will be if you remember you're my wife and not an Ortega."

His eyes bore into mine as if he's challenging me, and a part of me wants to retaliate, but there's an insecurity I don't like and can't shake now.

"I don't look right, either, thanks to you." My outfit is stylish and perfect, but it just feels like I'm playing dress-up, and the confidence that comes from my clothes has vanished.

He parks and exits but doesn't open the door for me. I make my way around the car to him, and we enter one of the open doors, but he doesn't re-grasp my hand. My father, perhaps thinking this shows him in a position of power, is talking to several of his men. I only recognise one. We approach, and I have to question why my father would choose this place to conduct such an important meeting. Abel doesn't need to be convinced, nor does he have to be reassured of the product we have to sell.

Loaded trucks are visible at the other end of the warehouse, with a dozen other men around. To anyone casually taking notice, they're distributing cleaning products, but there's nothing clean about them.

"Abel. Good to see you." My father gestures towards Abel and moves to shake his hand.

Father barely acknowledges me and certainly doesn't greet me like Abel, but I do note the look of confusion running over his features at seeing me. I know him too well for him to hide that.

"It's about time we looked to put the details together of the business side of our arrangement. And, as discussed with your mother, we both believe the benefits of our alliance will be profitable." He chuckles as he gloats, but I have a stark image of the girls in that room, branded and sold like cattle.

"I'm still waiting to hear terms that demonstrate that, Miguel. Opening up your distribution options so you can expand is relatively easy for us, but do you have the people in place to potentially start a power play?"

"We have all the people ready, Abel. And you've had a sample of the product. We're yet to receive the same exchange. Right, boys?" He slaps Andreas on the back, but it's the other men around him that laugh with him, stroking his ego.

I shake my head and look away.

"Our merchandise wasn't part of the deal."

"No. My daughter was. And I'm hoping you've not brought her to give her back." They all laugh as he heckles. I feel the heat flush on my cheeks, and, dressed in this stupid outfit, I feel out of place and unarmed to let the comments roll off my back.

"You'll send the locations, revenue and product delivery schedule you want for the top three territories that you want to move into. We won't be opening up all of our supply routes. This will be a detailed and measured growth."

Abel's calm and meticulous answer irritates my father. I can see it in the tensing of his shoulders and the slip of his smile.

"All of your locations were the agreement with Melena. In good faith."

"You're not dealing with Melena. You're doing business with me."

"Listen to Abel, Father. Build the expansion, and it will grow into everything you want."

His eyes narrow on me. "And you'd know all about our business dealings? Abel, I allow Alexia here only out of courtesy because you chose to bring her." Abel's expression doesn't change, and a part of me hopes he might defend me being here. "But she needs to learn her place." He addresses me, and silence settles around us. "You've done your part. Now, run along and leave us to work out the details." He dismisses me like I'm a little child needing attention. He'd be like it when he and Nicolas started talking about products or customers, like it might offend my delicate ears. If he'd kept me out of all business, I might be more generous with my opinion of him. But, with everything in my father's life, if it suits him or benefits him, then I can be involved. He's a grotesquely selfish man, and it's times like now that I hate that I've given so much of myself to him.

I look to Abel, but he doesn't show any discernible reaction.

As I turn, my hair whips around my shoulders, and I storm out and back towards the car. Humiliating doesn't even cut it when it comes to how I feel right now.

What was the fucking point?

Abel's words from the last few days come to mind as I pace towards the car, and my decision about what family side I should take hangs in the air. It's a delicate decision in many ways because it would be my whole world – and even possibly my life – collapsing around me if I choose wrong.

The crack of the door slamming shut won't bother either of them, and it doesn't help my mood either, but I have little else to show anyone how pissed I feel. My father dismissing me isn't a surprise, but I'm disappointed that Abel didn't fight for me. He didn't stand up or counter my father. The Cortezes should be in a stronger position in this negotiation, but that's not how Abel's acting.

The meeting doesn't last much longer – a small mercy for my patience.

"I want out of these clothes," I tell him before he's even in the car. "I don't know what game you were playing with my father, but don't use me for something you keep me in the dark about. Otherwise, you're no better than him."

"Fine. We're going back to the hotel anyway."

"Was it worth it?"

"Yes."

"Good."

CHAPTER NINETEEN

ABEL

"And I suppose you're dumping me here again," she says, as we pull up the drive. "I'm getting a little fed up with that treatment, especially given the last few days."

I pull up outside the house and get out of the car, walking around it to open her door. "No." I reach my hand for her and watch her take it. "You're about to join a Cortez party."

"Excuse me?"

"It's Knox's birthday."

"Oh." She slides her hands down her cream, tight-fitting dress and looks at the portico. "Is this okay for a party? What kind of party?"

"It's just dinner for the family."

"And that's a party?"

"It is here. It won't be the kind of family party you're used to."

"Is that music?"

"Yeah." I pull her over to the door, listening to the same sounds she's hearing. Heavy Latin vibes drum through the building, and we walk straight towards Wren and Dante in the hall. He pulls his mouth away from hers and spins her away from him, towing her back into whatever dance he's playing with.

He looks directly at Lexi's hand clasped in mine. "Brother," he says, as we walk by. It might cause a frown from him, but it's all he should need to understand.

"Music and now dancing?" Lexi questions.

"Yeah. Whatever we are, we come together on birthdays. It's Mother's thing. Heritage. Drinking. Laughing. All the work and arguments get left behind, and we remember what it's all for."

"Ah, Abel!" Mother announces, as we get to the main room. She kisses me on the cheek and looks over Lexi, a smile on her face. Not surprising given the drink she's clearly already consumed. "Good, you're both here. We can get on with dinner."

For once in their life, Mariana and Shaw seem to be laughing about something in the corner. Even Knox is knocking back drinks like he's in the mood to let life run its course rather than planning it. I walk over to him and drop Lexi's hand so I can wrap both of mine around him. He pulls back after a tight hug and smiles.

"You're getting old, Brother," I offer.

"I'm still a way behind you. Check your mouth."

"Happy birthday," Lexi offers. He nods in thanks, but stares at her other than that. I'm not surprised. She probably wasn't expected at all as far as he's concerned. "I didn't know, or I would have bought you a gift."

I pick up her hand again. "We've already got him something."

"We have?"

"Hmm."

Dante and Wren walk in behind us at the same time as Mother starts ushering us towards the dining room. We all sit, which is followed by drinks getting refilled by the staff and laughter echoing around the room with no regrets about anything. This is always the way on birthdays, regardless of who we are outside of those days. Arguments are put aside, and anything to do with business gets forgotten until we've all recovered from the hangover we're about to start causing. Plates clatter and glasses clink, adding more noise to the chaos that's in store.

"So," Mother says, as the three shot glasses in front of each one of us get loaded, and flute glasses placed next to those. "Here's to who we are. Tequila for our past, and Champagne for our future." I pull the salt and lemon closer, spreading some salt on my hand and offering it up to Lexi.

"I don't like tequila," she says.

"Get used to it. We're downing all three shots, then chasing it with Champagne. And probably drinking more of it. Get your lemon ready."

She looks at me, almost stunned about what the hell is going on in here. "Okay."

"We've had some changes this year, bad and good, but we're still here. So, before anything. To Elias. You're missed. Greatly." We all raise a glass and drink. "But vengeance will come with time," Mother continues. Damn right it will. I'll do it myself. "For now, we celebrate life. Knox?" He looks over at her. "Happy birthday." She picks up her glass, licks the salt, downs the first shot, and offers him the lemon at the same time as he does.

"You ready?" I ask Lexi. She nods and licks her own salt, before getting on with the rest of it. I chuckle at the look on her face as the sour taste lands, then get real damn close to get the lemon in her lips. She swallows, visibly shakes the taste off, and picks her next glass up. "Good girl. You're going to get along just fine in this family."

She wipes her mouth with the back of her hand, frowning the taste away. "That's awful," she says. "What the hell is that?"

"It's the past."

Next shots downed, and the rest of the family laughing and sneering at the feel of cheap-ass tequila going down their throats, and we all pick up the Champagne to swill the flavour away.

"Fuck that gets nastier every damn year," Knox spits, pushing the shot glasses away. Dante laughs and picks up the bottle, more interested in that than he is in the Champagne.

"You're a goddamn pussy about this. Every fucking year you're acting like you're growing down, not up."

"Fuck you. It's not my fault you've got no palate left."

Mariana bursts out laughing and holds her Champagne glass up, toasting the air. "To Knox. My asshole of a brother who I might just like today."

Cheers of happy birthday get rallied around the table, and he nods and gives his thanks for the offer. It's all as it should be, as the food is laid down. The whole middle of the table disappears beneath plates of true, authentic food. Burritos and tacos. Mole and tamales, tostadas and sopes. It's a riot of colour and smells, all of it harping back to who mother was before us and where we came from. Same as it always is. It's poor man's food, served as traditionally as it can be in this mansion full of wealth and luxury.

Presents pass between us as we're eating and drinking. For my part, or maybe our part, that comes in the version of a set of Camaro keys tossed over the table.

He catches them and looks at the fob.

"It'll be with you tomorrow," I say, picking up a taco. "Lexi drove it around San Diego. I haven't even tried to break it."

He looks at me, clocking her name change. Add in the fact that we were hand in hand when we arrived, and everyone's making the connection without me saying a damn word about anything.

His gaze goes back to her, his smile turning warm now he's acknowledged my permission to invite her in. "How's it handle?" She glances at me and then over at him, maybe trying to work out who was asked. "Lexi?"

"Oh. Perfectly. Although, I didn't get to open her up fully so I wouldn't truly know."

"I'll take you to the track then," he replies. "You get the first test."

She stiffens beside me. Probably just as mystified about that as she is about this sense of family and happiness around her. "You would?"

"Yeah. If there's one thing this family plays with to the max, it's cars."

"And drink," Dante says, swilling down another shot and smiling at her for once. "While driving."

Wren slaps him about the head. "You need to stop that shit."

"Yeah, yeah." She giggles as he kisses her and pulls back, shoving some lemon at her face.

"We can all go," Shaw says. "It's about damn time I tried putting Abel in his place again."

I laugh and throw another shot back. "That weak-ass Charger hasn't got a chance." My own face screws up at the taste this time without salt. "Jesus, that really is nasty as hell."

"He was on your tail the whole damn way last time," Mariana drops in. "I mean, maybe with you getting so old now he's got a shot."

"Little Bella's getting ballsy all of a sudden," Dante laughs out. "Getting your witch on, sister?"

"I've got plenty of witch in me. You all need to watch your back now I've got some training in. That track gets easier every time I'm on it. Definitely now that I've got my Aston to play with."

"That British piece of shit couldn't catch a damn cold," Shaw snarls.

"You're such a dick," she snaps, looking at him. "Or would be if you had one. Shame."

We're all fucking laughing at that. Knox damn near spits his tequila out and starts snorting liquor back up and choking on it.

"That's settled then," Mariana says. "Knox. When you've finished dying, get a date down. We'll make a day of it. I've got brothers to beat. Wren, what's your driving like?"

She looks up from her food. "Erm. I don't drive."

"What the fuck?" Shaw says. "Not at all?"

"No. Never needed to and—"

"She'll wipe your ass on the way past by the time I'm done with her," Dante cuts in.

Her head whips to look at him.

"She won't if you teach her," Shaw baits. "You're as shit as you've always been. I'll teach you, baby. Don't worry. Can't have you being driven permanently like some princess without her own set of balls."

"Really?" she says.

"Yeah. You probably need some seducing anyway. God knows he doesn't know the first thing about it." She laughs at the look of fury settling on Dante's face and leans into his side. "Calm down, Brother. I'll be gentle with her. Promise."

"Little shit thinks he's Romeo all of a sudden."

"Well, maybe he will be one day," Mariana says. "When he grows a dick, that is."

We keep on like this for the next hour or two. We talk. We bait. We laugh. We drink to excess. We act like the family we are, and we involve everyone at this table in it. Mariana switches places at some point and sits next to Lexi, and whilst I don't know what they're talking about, I let it happen without any interference. This is what she needs to see and feel a part of. It might not happen a lot, but it's the backbone of who we are, regardless of the life we live outside it.

It takes a while, but Dante eventually flicks his chin at me after the conchas and borrachitos. He walks away from the table and out onto the veranda, leaving Wren discussing something with Mother. I look back as I follow him out, eyes fixed on Lexi as she tries to get involved with what's happening here. She blinks and looks up at me, smiling about something Mariana is explaining.

"So, she's in?" Dante asks, as I get to him.

"For now."

He sucks the sugar off his fingers and offers me a smoke. I don't take it. "Lexi, huh?"

"Hmm."

"And who is that? She still a devious bitch I need to worry about?"

"Probably. But she might be on our side rather than her own, so I'm giving her some room to breathe for a while."

He leans on the barrier and stares out into the night, drumming his fingers on the wood to the rhythm still pounding. "You starting to care about her?" I don't answer. Which should be enough for him to understand that I am. "That girl has got trouble written all over her, and you know it. What happened to finding vengeance?"

"I never did like them without a little trouble involved. You know that."

Turning, he leans on the railing and chuckles as he stares back inside. "You still like those spiteful little bitches, huh? You never just want some peace?" Yes. More so lately than ever. Doesn't mean I don't appreciate an attitude, though.

Laughter echoes back at us, and I end up leaning there with him and watching Lexi actually laugh — that real laugh of hers — at something Wren said. "You think she's worth trusting?" he asks, blowing out some smoke.

"I think she's never had any of this before, and she wants it. It's up to her how she takes my offer of becoming part of it. I'll go straight back to where we were if she chooses wrong."

"Carmen said she turned damn bitchy on her."

I chuckle at that. "Yeah. She deserved that moment, though. She earned it."

We both stare for a while, taking in the atmosphere and the sight of it all. Dante smokes, and we stay in the silence that's always fit us well. Never has been much need for more than that between us. We read each other without the need for conversation, and, unless he's fighting me about seniority, which he'll never damn well win, we're the tightest of us all.

"How's Shaw doing?" I ask.

"Still fighting it. Not physically. Little shit knows better than that now, but he's just not up for it. Got zero fucking bite about him when it comes to the girls." He pulls in some smoke and blows it out. "Too busy being a Romeo. Maybe it'll come with time." I doubt it. "He might need you dealing with him. We both know my tolerance for weak-ass behaviour."

I frown and think on that while Dante keeps looking into the party. Not that I should be thinking about anything other than this night, but that kid needs some guidance to get where I need him.

"Gotta admit, she's fine as hell," he says.

"Hmm."

"What's she like?"

My eyes roll. "We're not going there."

He gets off the rail. "Yeah, but Wren does this thing with her tongue and goddamn … Drives me fucking wild." I look at him, a smirk settling. "All the fucking pussy through the years and she's the only one that I want." I nod, acknowledging that with no doubt about it. "And she's got this dark side. You wouldn't think it, would you? Freaky little thing." My brow arches. "And little hands, you know? Fuck that feels good. And when she's–"

My hand goes up. "I don't want to know."

"Yeah, you do. Just like I want to know about those lips Lexi's talking with."

"Shut the hell up. That's my wife."

He laughs and turns his gaze at Wren, not remotely fucking interested in Lexi anyway. "Well, this could be fun," he chuckles out. "Never seen a jealous version of you before."

"Don't make me play with you about Wren, Brother. You won't like the game."

He literally growls at me. "You leave her the fuck alone."

"See? Don't instigate it if you can't take it."

Mother gets up in our view, taking Knox's hand and making him dance. And then Mariana's up with Shaw doing the same. I smile at it all, happy to revel in something a little less tense for a while. That's all it's about for me. Spending that time inside and missing it, perhaps being envious of Dante and what he was achieving, made me all the more focused. Years went by with them all growing and me just rotting. I suppose it made me who I am, though. And I don't regret a damn moment of killing that piece of shit.

"Go in. Be with Wren."

He looks back at me and stamps down on his smoke. "You're alright, though?"

"Yeah. I'm good. You know I like watching this. I missed too much. Go."

He smiles and walks off, a tap on my arm as he goes. Doesn't take long before he's pulling Wren away from Lexi and dragging her into the middle of the room to dance. So, I watch my wife for a while, as she takes it all in, and consider that stark, blonde hair in the middle of all our dark features. Another fake thing. Although, that face is as soft as I've ever seen it. Maybe she is trying to maintain her icy front, but she's failing. Who wouldn't in there?

She catches my eye after a few minutes and just stares out at me with one of those light smiles of hers. It's a moment for us. It's a point in time where she sees what we're all about and why, irrespective of that life we live outside of here, we're as close as it gets. Each one of us would kill if anything threatened that. Not because it would be expected, but because it's who we are.

My finger crooks at her, and I keep watching as she swerves the room to get to me. She's not hurried about it, nor does she stop herself moving to the beat as she passes Shaw and he offers her the chance to dance with him. He spins her and pulls her tight in, saying something to make her laugh some more at the same time.

Typical Shaw behaviour.

No matter him being difficult to manage sometimes, he's as much a part of us as everyone else is, and he's damn good with women. If any of us can make her feel welcome by way of flirtation – he's it. He can seduce anyone into anything. Women and men alike, if need be. Baby blue eyes from his father, with Mother's heritage colouring his frame. Handsome as fuck features. Maybe he hasn't got the savagery we older ones have, but he makes up for that in other ways. He just needs time to grow. And maybe some pushing of my own.

He winks at me eventually and turns Lexi away from him towards me, catching hold of Wren on a spin away from Dante. I watch her grab hold of a couple of drinks on the way to me and keep swaying to the beat. Her cheekbones glint in the lights as she gets to me, and she's part laughing at the show Mother and Knox have decided to engage in.

"Your mother can move," she says, as she gets to me and hands me a shot glass. I nod. No denying that. "In fact, they all can." She downs her shot and grimaces. "Not you, though, it seems."

"I move just fine."

She leans on the rail beside me and gazes back into the house. "You didn't at our wedding."

My own shot gets downed. "No. Wasn't in the mood that day."

"I don't suppose either of us were who we really are then." I turn my head to look at her, watching the light bouncing around her face. "Or maybe we just showed the side of us we know best."

"And how do you like this side of you?"

She frowns and keeps watching the dancing. I turn until I'm in front of her and push her back on the rail, blocking out the view. My hands travel to her hair, taking the clip out for her so I can smooth the wavy locks over her shoulders. "Talk to me. Real, honest talk. How's my Lexi feeling with my family around her?"

"She's probably more vulnerable. And you know that."

I smile and lean in closer, brushing my lips over hers. "You think that's a bad thing." My tongue licks across the line on her mouth, teasing it open for me. "It isn't. Not here, at least." I pull back and get my hands in behind her ass, shifting her closer to me until she's off the rail and we're free to move to the rhythm. "We're all vulnerable in our own way. Dante needs love despite his ferocity. Knox is searching for validation, constantly. Shaw doesn't know who he is yet. And Mariana is fighting for her right to be seen, to be heard. But that's what makes us real. We know each other. We accept each other. We support our faults and turn them into strengths." She slides her arms around my neck and drapes them there, smiling. "There isn't one bit of fake-ass bullshit here. Never will be. That includes you."

She moves and slides her leg between mine, getting her fine ass as comfortable as she knows we can be. "And what about you, Abel? Where's your vulnerability?"

I push her away and spin her back into me, grabbing hold to make damn sure she knows exactly how well I can move if I choose to. "Well, that might just be you, darlin'."

We grind and dance, letting the music take us away from words that don't need to happen anyway. She knows what this is. She can feel it as much as I can, whether she wants to admit it or not. There isn't a man on the planet who will give her what I can if she makes the right call and becomes one of us. She'll be as revered as my mother is, as welcome and protected as any of us are, and as valued as a wife of mine should be. That suddenly means a whole lot more to me than it's done in the past.

Dancing becomes nothing but sexually charged foreplay, and we both stop thinking about anything other than this moment we're in. We kiss, we grab, we hold. We find pieces of us we've barely found yet and we let the booze take us somewhere we need to get to. It's damn nice. Honesty, it's something I've never had, and something I never thought I'd be bringing into this home, let alone my own. She fits into me like a sweep of fine silk across my skin, damn near matching my own nature. I like it. Every goddamn second of it.

CHAPTER TWENTY

LEXI

I look at myself in the mirror, with no makeup, and wince. Partly because my head is throbbing with every inch I move. Tequila certainly isn't my friend, but there's a smile on my face all the same. Despite how awful I look and feel, there's a lightness in my chest, and I'm a little giddy about it.

I work the toothbrush and look over my shoulder at Abel in the shower. The silhouette of his wide shoulders and broad chest is a sight to behold. Despite everything, and after last night, I feel that something might have shifted – that everything he's said and shown me over the last few days might be real.

It goes against everything I've seen and experienced for the entirety of my life. That sceptical feeling and assuming the worst will be ingrained into my very DNA until I die. Yet this morning, it somehow feels like it's cracked a little. Like maybe there's a future here that doesn't need to include revenge and plotting.

My father certainly hasn't changed. And I know if I choose Ortega now, there's a risk that any type of vengeance will be short-lived and end with my life being taken.

Abel turns off the water and steps out in front of me, and he brings a smile to the corner of my lips.

"Ready for breakfast?" he asks.

"I feel like shit. Can we not just hide up here?"

"No. Family breakfast is part of the birthday celebrations."

"Fine. I'll need some time to pull myself together."

"You don't need time. You're beautiful. You have until I'm ready." He kisses my head, and I'm shocked that his simple gesture brings emotion to clog in my throat.

Him telling me what to do would usually spark my retort or annoyance, but this morning I accept it. I even feel the compliment he offered inside me, clawing at my heart.

Dressed and ready, he takes my hand in his as we leave my rooms, and we follow the sound of banter. It's a little more muted than it was last night, but it's genuine and honest – what a family should be like. We head down and join everyone at the table, and I wait for the frowning glances or suspicious looks, but they don't come.

"Why don't you look like you're suffering like I am?" Mariana whispers to me as I take a seat next to her.

"Oh, my head is pounding, believe me."

She smiles, and I see a girl I could call sister.

The food last night was delicious, but as I look at the table, I look for waffles and fruit and, instead, see dishes I have no idea about.

"Abel?" I turn my head away from the table. "Where are all the breakfast things?"

"Huevos rancheros, chorizo, chilaquiles and burritos. All breakfast."

Dante is passing around dishes and piling eggs onto his and Wren's plates.

"Does any of that go with waffles? I need something to soak up the tequila."

He chuckles and signals one of the staff, putting in an order.

I notice that Melena is quieter this morning – maybe even she's not immune – but I have a feeling she's soaking up being in the presence of her children and family.

A plate of fluffy waffles is placed in front of me, and the sugary aroma already lessens the pounding thud of my hangover.

Last night I felt accepted by everyone here – something I doubted might ever happen. Family is everything to Abel, and it's something I've never had, not like this. Suddenly, there's a path in front of me that I'd never considered. I spend time watching the interaction, knowing I'd usually be thinking about what I could use against them – what knowledge I could gain to cause damage, but this time, like last night, I'm part revelling in the genuine happiness and commitment to each other.

My phone vibrates in the back pocket of my jeans, and I ignore it, not wanting to be torn away from this.

"Mother, thank you for the hospitality." Shaw stands and is the first to leave. After him, Dante and Wren and then Knox all give their thanks, and we all stand and say goodbye.

"Test day, yes?" Knox says to me.

I smile in reply, strangely infatuated with the thought.

"Lexi," Dante says, nodding at me.

"Dante." I smile back at him, too, knowing he's the most important person in the room to win over, but my phone rings before I can make conversation.

I slip it out of my pocket to see an unwelcome name.

I glance at Abel. "I'll just be a minute." I head out through the back doors and down by the pool to call my father back.

"When I call, I expect you to answer," he starts.

I shake my head. "Well, maybe you need to consider that before you treat me like garbage in front of my husband."

"I don't know what game you were playing by turning up as you did."

"Like it or not, Father, I'm a part of this. You put me in this position for your own gain. The least you can do is acknowledge that fact, and work with me rather than against me."

"It's your lucky day then because I do need your help." The

words ring in my ear as he says them, sending a shiver tickling over my neck.

"What?" I snap.

"Don't take that tone with me. You'll listen and do as you're told."

"I'm not a child," I counter, knowing that I sound like one in my protest.

"Alexia, so help me. This is your brother's doing, and you will fix it. Now, Nicolas was making strides to expand our operation and product. He had a connection and took a large trial of drugs to test the waters."

I stare at the pool, annoyed that this is spoiling what was almost wonderful. "And." I should just hang up and leave him to his own business, but a part of me can't.

"We owe him for that deal. And the terms aren't favourable to our new venture. Mr Blackford saw that you married Cortez and is demanding more in compensation for waiting for his payment."

"So, pay him."

"We have. But he wants something else to sweeten the deal. Apparently, he doesn't like the Cortezes, and so would take this as a personal reassurance."

"Spit it out." I already know what he's going to say. He's never this talkative unless he has to be. He wants something, and he wants me to deliver by spreading my legs – something he's not asked of me for some time. There's no way I will agree after all these years. Not now.

"You need to step up and give this man what he wants, Alexia."

"I'm sorry, you're going to have to say the fucking words, Father."

"Fuck him. Tease him, do whatever he wants. I don't fucking care as long as he's happy at the end and not looking to stir trouble."

Tears sting my eyes as I hear him talk about me as some cheap whore. Abel was right – Ortega whore is who I've been – and that's all because of the asshole, Miguel Ortega.

I hang up, unable to listen to him ask this of me after everything. The phone rings again immediately, and all it does is garner more tears to cloy at my throat.

Blinking away the emotion, I take a moment before going back inside to find Abel. He's talking to Melena, so I walk up and slide my hand into his, grateful that he doesn't push it away.

"Hi."

"Everything okay?" he asks.

"Sure. Sorry, I didn't want to interrupt."

"We're finished. Thank you, Mother." He leans in and kisses her on the cheek, then pulls me towards him, and we head up towards my bedroom.

"Do we have plans for today? I could use an Advil."

"No." He's short with me, as if he's flicked a switch from before breakfast.

"Okay."

"But pack an overnight bag. I might want you to stay over tonight."

I stop on the stairs. "Overnight?"

"Yes."

"You don't want me to stay longer?"

"An overnight bag is enough."

I shake my head and storm past him and into the bedroom.

He catches the door before it slams back. "The hell was that, Lexi?"

I scoff, "Really? You don't know why I might be upset?"

"No, so cut the crap." He stares at me.

"You. You still don't trust me. And I feel like a goddamn experiment. Reward Lexi just enough, and she'll be good."

"And what do you expect? You still don't tell me everything. You took a call, you got upset, and rather than tell me, you say everything is fine and try bullshitting me."

"We were with your mother. Do we share with her now, too?"

"No, but I want you to be honest with me."

"Fine. My father called. I hung up because, for the first time, I can see a life away from him and Ortega. You showed me that, Abel. In San Diego and last night, and this morning but then you go and ruin it by only allowing me to stay over if you feel like it."

"I thought we'd been through that." He looks away and stands by the window as if my upset is invalidated.

"No. You decided. What do I need to do to prove to you? Huh?" I pace back and forth, and I can feel the emotion turning into rage. "Is it about time? Maybe on our anniversary, I can move in?" I sneer.

"This is pathetic."

"And you're being cruel. You threatened me with Ratchet in a place guaranteed to make me feel your power over me. You've pushed and pushed, and I've met every challenge and every test. You even tease me by showing me what I could have, your family. Something you know I don't have. It's the ultimate power trip for you."

I tear the t-shirt over my head, and flick through my wardrobe for a shirt.

"What are you doing?"

"Going out." I pull a low-cut top from the hanger and pull it over my head before storming to the bathroom.

"Lexi, I'm always gonna weigh up what you do to see if you're being honest. That won't change. You were the enemy. We killed your brother. You scheme and ..."

I stop and look in the mirror, tuning him out, then turn and launch the lipstick at him. "You didn't defend me to my father!" My scream pierces the air as I race towards him. He catches my arms and holds them closer to him, wrestling me so I can't hit him. "You pushed me out of my comfort zone and let him dismiss me like he always does! Where was your family loyalty then? Or is it only when it suits you? Why didn't you stand up for me?"

I twist and break my arms free. Looking around the room, all I can see is a cell – a prison of a house and a marriage and a family that could be the same. I rush towards the nightstand and swipe the keys next to his wallet.

He moves sideways, probably to try to stop me. "What the fuck are you doing?"

"Taking your fucking car and going to cool off."

"You're not leaving."

My hand slices across his face, fury overriding any sense and unable to stop myself. "Want to fucking bet?" He's said it now, which, in this mood, I'm taking as a personal challenge. Everything about his frame hardens. "And don't you dare touch me!" My back is to the door, so I back up and leave, picking up my bag on the way out.

I race down the stairs and out the main doors without looking back.

"Lexi!" he shouts after me, but I don't listen.

I click the fob, the car unlocks, and I climb in, starting the engine and shoving my foot onto the accelerator.

It lunges to life and roars down the drive, back wheels spinning out smoke.

Shit.

Too late now.

The phone in my back pocket vibrates, and I pull it out and see Abel's name on the screen. I click the icon and put it on speaker, tossing the phone into the passenger seat.

"What?"

"This isn't part of the deal, Lexi."

"Well, let's call this an amendment. After all, you've never shared the details of what's in the fucking deal."

"A month of honesty for the car."

"Well, I thought I'd skip that. What's yours is mine, right, husband?"

The line goes quiet.

"Come home."

"Umm, that's a hard one. What home would you like me to come home to? Your mother's?"

"Alexia, listen to me–"

"No. And don't think you can call me by my proper name and that will mean something to me. I'm going shopping with your fucking money. And I'm going to buy clothes that I want, and I like. And I don't care if you approve or not. I keep trying, and I don't seem to be able to change your mind for very long." My breathing is laboured, and my heart is racing.

"You're my wife, Lexi."

"I am. So why don't you let me have some fucking space from my husband, who doesn't trust me enough to move into his home." I hit the phone screen until the phone disconnects and concentrate on driving the car.

~

Three hours later, I feel at least like I have a grip on my control.

Manicure, pedicure, and a hydrating facial helped mellow my anger.

But in its wake is a sadness that's more crushing. I sit at the little bistro table and order a glass of red and lunch and watch as the world carries on.

I fire off the message, aiming to provoke him.

Thank you for the spa morning, husband. Any requests for my next spree?

But after I've sent it, I realise it's probably more to do with me wanting to show him he can trust me. We match with our fiery tempers, and sometimes that can be fun, and others, it can be painful.

Lexi, enough.

Not even close, husband.

I told you, come back.

No. You can't control everything, Abel. Accept that.

I wait for him to respond, but he doesn't.

What's wrong? Tracking me down? Going to put me under lock and key again?

Lexi, shut the fuck up

No. I said you can't control me. If that's what you want, better go and get your mother to find you some other whore.

As I hit send, I know I'm provoking him, but I can't help myself. The anger courses through me and builds into a toxic swell inside of me, and I don't want to restrain it.

What, no come back?

I keep going.

You and your family are sick and you're a fucking asshole.

I slam the phone down, cross my arms and wait for his comeback.

The red wine tastes like vinegar, and the pasta isn't much better when it arrives.

My phone vibrates on the table, and I pick it up, anticipating Abel on the other end. But it's my father.

"What?" I know my bad mood is partly down to his request this morning.

"Alexia. Listen, I understand you're mad at me, but I wouldn't ask if I didn't need you. You, of all people, know that."

"You don't get it, do you? Are you all deaf to the women in your lives?" I complain, immediately realising I've shared too much.

"Trouble for the newlyweds?" The gloat in his voice stirs the anger again.

"Goodbye, Father." I pull the phone away from my ear but can hear him still.

"No, no, don't hang up. Wait, and just hear me out."

I push the plate of food away, cross my legs and let my foot bounce with impatience. "I'm listening."

"This evening. Meet me at Grimaldi's. It's a casino on—"

"I know where it is. Why?"

"To talk. You're my only child."

"That hasn't been a concern for you in the past." In fact, according to him, I'm not even his heir.

"What you said this morning has made me reconsider. Meet me at the casino, have a drink, and you can update me on where we stand. You can even walk away if you want."

"I won't change my mind about what you asked me this morning. You need to understand that. No matter how apologetic you are." It's a hard limit.

"Understood. I'll see you at six."

I hang up, and a gnawing feeling settles in my stomach. A Cortez wouldn't be so soft, but then again, Melena Cortez would never treat her children the way my father treats me. And then I think about Abel going to prison. And wonder if maybe she would.

~

There's one thing I don't need, and that's more clothes, but I use the excuse of meeting my father to buy an outfit. I've been in fitted jeans, loafers and a silk top all day, and it's not what I'd wear to a casino. A lacey black dress, heels and a new bag are what I choose, and then I book in with the department store makeup concierge. She does an okay job, and I buy a few items to make it worth her time. All on Abel.

I'm sure he can track my purchases.

He's not messaged me back since lunchtime. I don't even know how we get over this, but that's for tomorrow.

I park in the VIP area at the front of the casino and stare down the argument waiting to come from the valet's lips. He stares at me and doesn't say a word.

"Good choice," I say as I pass.

I walk on in, unimpressed with the blaring machines and lights to the right aimed at luring customers in. The big money will be made at the back, or perhaps on a private floor for clients. There's a nice bar area I can see upstairs and, beyond that, a restaurant. I walk towards it, check the time and head to the bar. I'm a few minutes late, so already pissed off that he's not on time. The bar has a gleaming black glass top, and I order a martini from the woman behind it.

Finally, my father arrives. His large frame makes hard work of perching on the bar stool, but I'm not going to move to accommodate him.

"Alexia."

"Father." I watch him over the rim of my martini glass as I take a sip.

"So," he starts but hasn't got anything to say.

"You could start with an apology." I offer. The frown and look of disgust on his features is all I need. He's not here to make amends. It should be the final straw. I can't keep holding on to the illusion that he'll value me.

As I lean forward to get the attention of the bar woman, I look to see if I recognise any of the men around. Sure enough, Andreas is near the entrance. He gives me a very subtle shake of his head.

"Another martini and a bourbon?" I look back at Dad, and he nods. "Thanks." My nerves spike, but I battle them down with a shallow breath.

I pull my phone from my bag.

"What are you doing?"

"Checking my phone."

"I thought we were here to talk." He tries to distract me.

"And I thought you were genuine about your offer to talk. But you don't seem to have anything to say to me."

Help me. I'm sorry.

It's all the time I have to type before slipping the phone back inside my purse.

"Very well. At the start of this, you said I could have everything I wanted. I just needed to be patient." His beady eyes focus on me as if he's waiting on me to deliver this very second.

"I did. But you've only shown me that I can't trust you. You'll never think of me as a worthy daughter. So why should I work to deliver you everything you want?"

"Because you are an Ortega." His jowls shake, and his face

begins to redden. "And I've told you to." He grabs my leg, holding me in place.

"Hey." I push his shoulder, but he doesn't budge.

Dread, heavy and paralysing, seeps through my limbs as I realise the lengths he'll go to get what he wants. Perhaps Nicolas shielded me from it, but not now.

He looks over and signals with his free hand. Two men in suits walk up to us, surrounding me.

"You will never have a say in this plan or this business. You need to learn your position. And Mr Blackford will help with that."

A third man joins us, and he nods in my direction. The stir of acid in my stomach burns my throat as reality hits.

"Don't do this." A final plea, although I know it won't make any difference.

"Miguel. A pleasure." Mr Blackford shakes my father's hand. I try to leave, but the two men seize my arms, keeping me in place.

"Mrs Cortez. Shall we?"

He walks through the bar as if he owns it, and I'm dragged along behind, my weight being overpowered easily by the two men. Pushing and pulling, they wrestle me to a side door and away from the public.

I hope that Abel isn't so mad he'll ignore my message.

CHAPTER TWENTY - ONE

ABEL

That fucking mouth of hers is beginning to drive me insane, enough so that I turned my goddamn phone off an hour ago rather than deal with her spiteful tongue. I didn't defend her? She's goddamn right I didn't defend her. I wanted to see her behaviour in front of him – gauge how she reacted to the difference between what she had and what she now has with this family. She should have stood up to that crap herself. Instead, she capitulated. That isn't going to happen again by the time I'm done with her.

I stand and pace because of it all, then walk from the room to find something to take my irritation out on. Dark corridors lead me through various rooms and past cages full of whimpering women until I arrive in the main training area.

"One. Two. Three. Four." Carmen's sharp voice blasts loudly around the space, and the sound of a stick hits the ground with every number called. "Pathetic," she spits. "Again."

Waiting in the shadows, I light a cigarette and watch the round of twelve women parading their naked bodies around. They're trying to keep up with her commands, and most of them are on track. Three of them need a damn sight more work because I will not have trash leaving my premises to work. They learn to behave like a whore should. They walk well. They talk dirty well. They fuck well. And they do it with a damn smile on their face unless that's not what they're being paid for.

Smoke slowly blows out of me as I keep watching one fuck up after another. What they all need is Elias' viciousness chasing their backsides. Or maybe my own given this goddamn mood she's put me in. Trouble is, this mood ends up killing things. Fuck awful whores included.

"Brother." Dante walks past me, stripping his shirt from his skin. "Carmen? First round."

She looks over at him, as he heads towards the branding space, then begins hustling the women back to their quarters. Shaw follows them, tilting his head at every piece of ass that manages to catch his attention. Maybe if he stopped being so goddamn obsessed with his dick, he might learn to look at them like Dante and I do. They're not women to us. They're not something to fuck or enjoy or spend time with. They're cattle to be sold or used for profit.

I follow him to the cages to see how he handles the first one he'll pull through to be branded. There's too much respect going on the second he steps foot inside the cell. I look at the women around him, watching the way they try coaxing him into conversations. We don't speak to any of them. We do what needs doing and nothing more than that. They want to talk? They talk to each other. Or, if they're lucky and Carmen sees potential, they get to talk to her and she makes a call on them being groomed for the Bourbon Lounge or Berettas.

"Your sister called me the other day," Carmen says from behind me. I move out of Shaw's way as he moves the first girl out of the space towards Dante's room. "She thinks she'll need four girls on rotation. Is that okay with you? They'll need to be our finest. And tell your wife I don't appreciate her tone. I'd–" I round on her instantly, sending her five steps backwards from me with nothing but a glare. She drops her stare, choosing the floor as a good place to apologise from. "I'm sorry."

"You should be. You know me better than that."

"Yes. You're right," she says, fidgeting. "It's just that if we're to get along, I'd rather not have to fight with her."

I take her hand in mine, tilt my head, and walk us towards Dante's room. An agonised yell echoes as we walk in, and I look straight at Shaw to see his reaction. I'd like to believe the cold as stone face he's trying for. I don't.

My fingers let go of Carmen's hand, and I grip the back of her neck sharply, forcing her in front of me. "You remember that, don't you?" She keeps her head looking exactly where I want it faced as Dante pulls the branding iron off the girl's foot. He keeps his hand clamped down on her ankle, twisting his body in the next breath for cream and tape. Seamless. Pitiless. "That's still you, Carmen. Still a whore branded up and ready to work." She stiffens. "Be careful with your tone, and don't ever think you get to order me around because I fucked you." She nods against my hand, keeping her stare fixed on the smoke as the smell of burning flesh wafts over us.

Dante swings his gaze around to look at us, shoving the girl's leg away after he's done with her. "Next." Shaw pulls the crying girl off the table and walks out of the room, leaving Carmen with nothing but two Cortez brothers in here with her. "Are we about to have some fun?" he asks, looking over Carmen and standing up. He wipes his hands off on a rag. "'cause I'm real damn good at talking manners and obligations with women who don't know their place."

She steps back into me, maybe hoping the devil she knows is better than the one she doesn't. She's wrong when I'm in this mood, and my tightening fingers show her that. "No! Jesus, I'm sorry. Abel, I am. I was out of line." I push her down to her knees, neck cracking in my fingers. "I won't speak out of line. I'll behave. I will." I keep staring, a sneer firmly embedded on my face. "Abel, please."

"Who owns you?"

She looks back at Dante, then swallows whatever fight she's thinking about offering up at me. "You do."

"And what are you?"

"I'm ..." Dante takes a step closer to her. I'm damn close to letting him play. Her hands go up to try stopping him, so I push her face further down until she's eating dirt. "A whore. I'm a whore."

I'm still inclined to let him have some fun, but then I remember that she's not the woman I'm pissed with and probably doesn't deserve my wrath. I let go, watching as she crawls to get upright. "Stay the fuck down." She instantly stills on her knees. "There is no fighting with my wife. She wins. Every damn time. You understand? Everything and everyone Cortez always wins." She nods and shuffles away from Dante, flustering between me and him. "Get the fuck out of here. Go."

She's up and stumbling from the room quickly, with me watching her sorry ass, and I turn back to find a chuckling Dante staring at me. "You're such an asshole," he says. "What did she do?"

"Tried telling me to make my wife behave."

"And that got you all riled up?"

"No, my wife's got me riled up. Carmen just took a piece of it. It was either her or Shaw."

"What's she done?"

"We argued. She took my car."

He busts out laughing and turns away from me, stoking his furnace for the next girl that's about to arrive. "Well, call me old fashioned, but why aren't you just going and getting it back?" He holds his iron up, as Shaw comes in past me with the next girl in tow. "My little bird would be eating dick for a month if she pulled that move on me. Maybe you need to get more handsy with her ass." The girl breaks free of Shaw's hold and starts running for the door. "Goddamn, Shaw!"

I move sideways, blocking the exit, and stare at the floor rather than use her to go at. "You better get on that table. I'm in no mood for games today." She backs away from me, and I look back up to find her eyes, glassy with tears, looking between all three of us. Shaw grabs hold of her again. She's put where she damn well should be, Dante gets on with his job, and I'm left with nothing else to vent my frustration on.

Turning from the room, I leave them to it and head for my car. Dante's right. I'm just gonna go get my damn car and my wife. I'm done with this shit from her. She'll get in my goddamn house when I let her. Conceited little bitch is lucky I'm even offering that potential considering the family she's come from. And I'm the asshole for not offering it quicker?

The car door slams and I flick my phone on to look at the tracking on my car as I'm driving out of the warehouse.

A text sits there waiting for me. My wife.

Help me. I'm sorry.

I call her. No answer.

So I send a text asking where she is and what she's done.

No reply to that either.

With nothing else for it, I head for where the car is at full speed. I'm halfway there when I decide it's time to calm the hell down and think about what I'm going to do. Knox's number gets pulled up, and I send Lexi's number to him, press call, and pull up the ramp onto the freeway.

"Abel," he says as an answer.

"Where's Lexi's phone?"

"What?"

"You need it fucking repeated?"

"Alright. Calm your ass down. Send me her number."

"Already done."

"Right. Give me a minute then." I do, all the while listening to him working his laptop to find out where she's at. "Looks like she's at Chance's place – Grimaldi's. The casino. The phone is anyway."

I end the call without any thanks and keep driving. It's not far from the car, so I head for that and aim at ramming anything that tries getting in front of me for the rest of the journey. Roads go by in a fury of chaos. I don't know if I'm panicked or fucking outraged, but both seem to merge and cause a hate filled desperation for answers.

Eventually, I pull up and glare at the Challenger sitting there as I walk past it. With her goddamn mood I'm surprised she hasn't left it on a side street to get trashed or stolen. A bitter laugh rumbles through me. That would really improve my fucking mood, wouldn't it? Yeah, she'd be so far out of my good books she'd be tending her broken cunt for the next six weeks.

Pushing the doors into Grimaldi's casino open, I try phoning her again to get some fucking answers. Nothing happens but it ringing out, so I start searching the entrance way and formal lobby. There's nothing but other people who aren't Lexi, so I make a beeline for the tables, scouring them, too, and keep moving until I circle back to the restaurant and bar. Couples sit dotted around, and there's a table out back full of some bachelorette party in full swing. None of them contain my wife.

I walk off, knowing I've got nothing but phoning Knox again so he can track that goddamn phone down to its location in this building. I look upwards, cursing the fact that there's a hundred hotel rooms up there.

What was just building anger, turns damn vicious inside me because if she's decided to fuck someone to appease her tantrum, she's gonna feel my idea of punishment for the rest of her fucking life. My phones out again and I'm redialling Knox. He gets with the program real damn quick given my tone and starts guiding me through the masses of halls and corridors. Trouble is, when I reach the exact location, I'm in the entrance to the kitchens.

"No," I snarl, looking around me.

"Well, that's the signal. Get climbing. She'll be above you somewhere."

I swing back through the corridor until I reach the elevators. They make me wait so I head for the damn stairs and travel up to the next floor. Again, I'm met with nothing but a fucking maid's closet in the hallway.

The next floor brings me out at a hotel room. I knock. No fucking answer, so I switch Knox off and call to see if I can hear her phone coming back at me. Nothing. "FUCK!"

Redial Knox.

"Do I need to get there?" he asks.

"No. Stay on that signal."

Three more floors go by, every one of them giving me the same kind of nothing other than one with a guy and his kid answering the door. Another level and I'm so goddamn infuriated with everything that I could kill. I switch Knox off again and call Lexi's phone. This time I hear it come back at me from inside the room. Both my hands brace the frame, attempting to hold me back from what I know is coming if she is fucking someone.

Rage swells regardless, and I start kicking and barging at the door until it breaks in and gives me access. I look straight at the bed, then the lounge area in the corner, then the door to the bathroom.

"NO! Get the hell off me!" Lexi's voice shouts.

Five strides through the room and I'm turning to the bathroom. A guy stands there shielding himself with my wife, who is naked from the waist up and shaking in his grip. I take my time assessing the situation, trying to make up my mind if this was true fucking or rape, because she's clever enough to make me think what she

216

needs me to think. Torn dress, wild hair. I clock the slight mark on her neck and red print on her face, and then take in the tremble on her skin. I know that well. She's scared.

"That's my wife." She stares at me, pleading for help with her eyes without saying a word. "Let. Her. Go."

He doesn't. He tries pushing her forward into me to make me back out of the room. He isn't going anywhere. One hard shove from me into her and he loosens his grip enough to let me get around her. She gets barged aside at the same time as his hair gets grabbed, and I send four solid hits into his guts. He reels straight over the bathtub, so I slam his head at the wall a few times to make sure he feels my rage.

I climb in after him and use my knee to keep his chest down, running the faucet and using his body to stop the water draining out.

"Abel … I—"

"Shut the fuck up. Go close the door."

She leaves, and I watch the guy struggle under me as the water level rises. My hand covers his mouth to stop the shouts and mumbled calls for help, and I keep staring until the fear really kicks in. Understanding dawns for him in that moment. Nothing's going to get him out of this. Arms flail. Legs struggle. I keep fucking holding. I don't know if she watches the rest of it or not, nor do I give a damn. He touched her, and whether she wanted it or not isn't the goddamn point. No one touches her. Ever. No one flirts with her or lays a fucking hand on her, let alone fucks her – for any reason – ever again. Only me.

He splutters and coughs, gasping for air he's not gonna get and sends water splashing around. I just keep waiting for the level to rise, keep thinking about his hands on my wife and the way he dared glare at me. Maybe, in that fucked-up time while I'm watching him die, I can see her face under mine on a bed, or hear her laugh the other night. Whatever it is in my head, it's tarnished with hatred and anger and vengeance flowing through me until it's done and there's a lifeless body submerged under water.

"Abel?" I look sideways, watching her hover in the doorway. "I didn't …" She trembles and looks down at the guy, then up the wall at the smeared blood. "I …"

I slowly get myself out of the tub, switching the faucet off at the same time and pull my phone out. She hurries away from me, as I pass her, and three rings later Dante answers.

"Bring two suitcases, a heavy cutting blade, cleaning kit and some dry pants. Grimaldi's. Room six twenty-four."

"Twenty minutes."

I end the call and stare at her over by the bed.

That's twenty minutes of me in the same room as her. It's also twenty fucking minutes of me not being calm enough to deal with anything other than my own rage.

I turn for the window, shoving my hands in my pockets to contain them. "Sit your ass down. Cover yourself. And don't say a fucking word."

Her reflection moves in front of me, and she plants herself instantly.

And I wait.

CHAPTER TWENTY - TWO

LEXI

Since I've met Abel, there have been numerous times I've seen him angry. Every single time pales in insignificance compared to this. It's the first time I've ever wanted to sit and obey and the first time I'm relieved he's on my side.

He came for me.

The tatters of the dress hang from my frame, and I do my best to cover myself and be patient, banishing the shake that's set in from the mix of fear and adrenaline.

He seems unable to calm, though, pacing the room, going back towards the bathroom and staring inside before heading back out. My apology – my explanation – and the need for him to believe me build in my chest, desperate to escape and be heard, but I stay silent and watch.

He pauses outside of the bathroom door and then enters. Sloshing noises and a thud follow, and then silence.

"You. Don't. Ever. Touch. What's. Mine!"

The crack of something solid hitting repeatedly punctuates each word, making me wince in my seat. He's beating on a dead body, still furious. I can still see my husband's vicious face looking down at the drowning man from before, but now ... I don't even know what to do with that thought, so I keep staring towards the bathroom and watch as a red shadow of blood and water creeps across the carpet.

A knock from the other side of the main splintered door forces Abel from the bathroom, and Dante comes in. He looks over the situation without a word, then to his brother as he paces, and finally at me. His face is harsh and intimidating, and it keeps me from saying a word until I'm spoken to.

"What the fuck?" he cusses, as he enters the bathroom.

"Don't fucking start. Deal with it!" Abel roars in his face. "I want him gone. I want it done, and I don't want to answer a single fucking question about why!" I feel myself shrink, still unsure if Abel believes I slept with the guy or not.

The throb on the side of my face begins to lessen, but I can still feel that man's hands around my neck. The pressure's almost still building in my face from when he restricted the blood flow and my breathing in his attempt to rape me.

Dante looks between us, a question in his eyes as he starts pulling supplies from his bags. Plastic sheeting, gloves and … tools are unpacked. "Help me with this shit." He looks to Abel, who's looking out the window, his head tilted skyward. "Abel?"

"What!" he barks, storming towards Dante and squaring up to him.

"You've got to cool the hell down."

One hard shove sends Dante stumbling backwards. "You back the fuck up, or I'll keep going. Get this shit done."

"Abel, please," I interject, hating that he's screaming at his brother, who's come to help him with a dead fucking body.

He spins and points at me. "I told you to sit and be fucking quiet." I nod and drop my eyes to the ground.

I sense more than hear footsteps approaching after a while and see worn boots, not the smart style shoe Abel prefers.

"Lexi, look at me." Dante's voice is surprisingly calm. I raise my gaze and look at him. "What were you doing in a hotel room with that scum?"

My eyes flit between him and my husband standing guard, still staring at the body. Finally, I look up at Dante.

He looks me dead in the eye. "Did you sleep with him?"

"No." I shake my head vehemently and wrap my arms around myself. "This looks bad, but I didn't come here freely. And if Abel hadn't come when he did …" I don't finish the sentence and leave it up to Dante to put the pieces together.

"Has he spoken to you?"

"Abel? No. Told me to stay here and be quiet," I whisper.

He nods and looks away.

I watch him approach Abel and lay a hand on his back. He flinches, shoving it off, and Dante steps out of view.

Pulling my legs up beneath me, I block out what's happening in the room as Dante makes a phone call. I know my father has had people killed. I'm sure the Cortezes have, too. But seeing it, and hearing it, is sobering. The items Dante came in with are what they'll use to dispose of his body, but I'm not sure how they'll get rid of the blood. It's in the tub, on the floor and seeping into the carpet, tarnishing everything like a rotten stain.

I shut my eyes and breathe in through my mouth and out through my nose, blocking out the noise. Block out everything.

A man I don't know arrives a while later. He whistles as he pushes the door wide, breaking my spell of hiding in my head, then looks over the scenario laid out in front of him. Abel just stares, not trying to hide what's happened here in any way. There isn't a body to be seen anymore. But there's no hiding the remnants of blood still staining the floor.

"Someone's been having fun," he says as he closes the door and walks in. He looks me over, and I watch as Dante steps in front of me. "Who did it?"

"Me," Abel snarls. "Let's call you dealing with this room a favour owed."

The man's hands go to his pockets. "Why don't we call it you

221

giving me this one to play with, and we'll be settled."

"The last fucking man who touched my wife is in those suitcases, Chance. You still want her?"

The guy – Chance – looks back at me again as if thinking about the possibility. "So, this is the lovely Mrs Cortez. Interesting circumstances you find yourself in." I don't say anything. Don't move. Don't speak. I can barely look at him, regardless of his relaxed words. "Fine. Go. I'll deal with this. You've got fifteen minutes to get out of here. But I want three girls next week. Make them good."

Abel nods, and Dante heads out with the first bag, followed by Chance. My heart is in my throat thinking about what's in the case – what they've done – and if anyone will stop them. Taking a case out of a hotel isn't suspicious, and I doubt anyone would challenge Dante, but it's terrifying and grotesque. It leaves me alone with Abel, and I'm not sure if he's waiting to scream at me, accuse me of being an Ortega whore, or worse, just biding his time.

He still doesn't talk to me, but he does take off his jacket and toss it to me.

"You're a mess."

I pull my arms through and wrap it around me, grateful for the familiarity and comfort. "Thank you."

The time in here, staring and keeping my attention away from what Dante was doing to move the body in suitcases, has made me think of how petty I've been, demanding to be let in. If my own father can trick me, then why should Abel trust that I won't after only a few months?

Amazing how a little murder can suddenly clear your head.

After what happened tonight and my father's hand in it all, there's no doubt in my mind who my allegiances now lie with. And, if it's possible, I can understand how my brother ended up killed. He took Wren – the literal light of Dante's life. She means everything to Dante, and for the Cortez family love means everything. They defend. They protect. And Nicolas touched something that wasn't his, just like that scum did to me. My husband protected me in the most literal and brutal way imaginable. He beat the man's head into the wall and drowned him. For me. And whilst I don't believe my brother deserved to die, I can at least understand why now.

The itch for revenge over what Dante did lessens with every breath because he looked at me in this room and decided to help me, too. He looked out for me.

While I'm stuck in my own head, I don't have to face Abel and notice Dante's come back. As his eyebrows pinch together, he looks me over, nods and then leaves with the last case.

"Time to go." Abel walks out after Dante, and I grab my bag and make sure the jacket covers the fact my dress is in ruins. I can't do anything about my hair or makeup, so keep my head down and follow.

The elevator ride is suffered in silence, and then we're striding out through the lobby. Abel heads straight past his car to whatever car he used to get here. "Wait." I race to catch up to him. "Abel, I can't drive." The thought of being in control of anything right now is terrifying. "Please don't make me follow you. Take me with you? I don't want to be on my own." I want to be with you. I don't say those words, but I feel them. Despite what went on in that room after he arrived, the important part that I'm holding onto is that he showed up. He protected me.

He protected me.

"Get in."

I climb in and put my seatbelt on.

He leaves me there and walks back to one of the valets out front, then comes back and pulls his phone out while starting the engine. "Mariana, I need you to come get my car from Grimaldi's downtown. It's parked out front in the VIP section. Take it to yours, you can bring it back tomorrow."

I can't hear her response, but I'm a little surprised he called Mariana. Shaw or Knox, yes. But no, again, he offers the job to his sister – a woman.

He ends the call and shoves the car into gear, merging into the traffic with no concern for whose right of way it is.

The further we get away from the hotel, the more at ease I feel. The muscles in my shoulders begin to unwind, and then I remember I have another conflict ahead. There's no way that Abel will accept everything I say easily. He's suspicious of me every day, let alone finding me in a compromising situation. He'll see the bad before he hears anything. And I'm sure he's already run through a hundred different scenarios in his mind since he first barged into the suite. Most of them where I'm in the wrong and betraying him.

It's funny because of all the ways in which I could betray him, sleeping with another man wouldn't be one of them. Revenge and an attack on his family were at the top of my list – taking something precious to him and ripping it apart.

But after tonight, that's gone.

The air between us is stifling, thick with unsaid words and accusations as we make our way back to his place. Relief drains through me at the sight of his entrance way because he hasn't shut me out.

We park in the garage, and still, he hasn't spoken a word. Words jumble in my head as I sort through what I want him to hear first, but my overriding feeling is gratitude, and keeping my shot at being part of the family he's been shoving in my face is the only thing keeping me from speaking right now.

He has to ask. He has to give me permission to speak.

I follow him into the house, and he heads straight downstairs to the bar and pours himself a drink. He doesn't offer me one, and I don't ask. I gingerly perch on one of the chairs and wait. His pacing starts again, this time through to the kitchen and then back. He pauses a few times, seemingly in two minds about something, before carrying on

Another slosh of liquid is tipped into the glass and knocked back. "You have one chance, Lexi. Every fucking word that passes your lips needs to be the truth, or we're done." He turns and looks at me, and I see the threat in every fibre of his being. His shoulders, his crossed arms and the deep frown on his face. He's closed himself off. He's going to judge me, and if I pass, then we can maybe get another chance.

A tremor rushes over me, and I breathe in, holding my breath to try settling my nerves. In my heart, I know I shouldn't have anything to be nervous about, but dread weighs heavy in the pit of my stomach.

"Thank you." I make sure I look him straight in the eye. "I've never had someone I could count on for help before. It meant a lot that you came." My eyes begin to sting, and I blink the tears back and look away.

"Don't. I need to see you, Lexi. Every word. Every reaction. So you'll explain to me and look me in the goddamn eye while you do it. Because I'll be able to tell the minute you think about holding back or lying."

"Okay." I squeeze my hands together in my lap and hold his gaze, blinking a few times as the salty tears swim in front of me.

"My father called me earlier today. He told me I had to help him with a family problem; with a deal Nicolas set up before he died. He told me I had to sleep with him, or more accurately, do whatever he wanted to keep him happy." I watch Abel for a reaction, but there is none. "I told him no. It's been a long time since he's used me for that kind of thing, and the fact that he thinks he still can, made me angry and upset." I focus on the facts, laying out the events and keep the emotional pain inside. I thought I was immune from further hurt at the hands of my father, but the anger inside of me tells me different. The blackness that I'd clawed my way free from is as pitch as ever, and when I think about him –

my father – he's at the heart of it. "He called again after I left you, around lunchtime, and wanted to make amends and talk. I swear, I told him I wasn't interested in his plan. But I had promised him that if he was patient, he could have everything he ever wanted – expanding his business and bringing you down. It was part of my scheming, as you call it, to find your greatest weakness and exploit it."

As I confess, I expect more of a reaction. I also feel guilty for ever thinking this way, but he asked for the truth, and I want to prove that I'm capable of that. "But, things have changed, and I've been struggling with who I am, as you've been pushing me to find out. I went to meet my father with no other intention than to see if we'd ever be on amicable terms. When I got to the bar, he was late. And when he showed up with no genuine reason to talk, I started to panic. I saw Andreas there."

"Andreas?"

"He was at the meeting in San Diego. He's worked for my father for years and is loyal and trustworthy. A quality lacking in many of my father's men. He shook his head, and that's when I texted you."

"Go on."

"He introduced me to Mr Blackford. He shook my father's hand, and then his men grabbed me and hauled me to the suite in the hotel." Keeping my eyes fixed on Abel is exhausting and harder than I thought. He can see every slight reaction, every grimace play over my face. The beat of my heart has quickened, and I know my breathing has grown shallow.

"And," he prompts.

I swallow before going on. "I struggled. Nobody seemed to care, and I was behind closed doors in minutes. The men came into the room and sat me in a chair to start. Blackford seemed to like the idea of control, and he had some sort of issue with you, or your family, according to my father. He talked for a while. Only I knew that's not what I was there for. He told me about your view of drugs and that San Antonio was growing tired of your rules. He dismissed his men then. And that's when his demeanour changed." I close my eyes for a moment, and flashes of anger and pain blaze through my memory. "I tried to run first. I got to the door, but he grabbed my neck and shoved me against the door, pushing my face into it. He started to unzip my dress, so I kicked out at him until he let me go." My hands are hot as I wring them together, and despite what Abel wanted, I have to look away, so I stand and pour myself a drink shakily.

The neat liquor burns as I down it, washing away the vile taste of the words I've already spoken.

He doesn't tell me to sit back down, but I adjust so he can watch me as I continue the accounts. "I hit him and shoved him, but there weren't a lot of places for me to escape in that room. He slapped my face and knocked me to the ground. I fought and struggled more than I ever have. I didn't want this, and I wasn't going to let it happen easily. He liked to hit me. And then he got on top of me. His hands went around my neck … and he squeezed. He'd wait until I thought I was going to pass out before he'd let go. That's when he tore the rest of my dress. And, when he thought he could touch my body."

Out of nowhere, Abel springs from his stance and swipes at the nearest surface, sending everything crashing to the ground. I jump at the noise and flinch away. He looks at me, and I stare at him. Maybe this is as uncomfortable for him as it is for me.

I nod to see if I should continue. "When I stopped coughing, I'd struggle again, and he'd go back to choking me. He repeated this a few times. He never got his dick out, though. I pretended to pass out on the last time, and when he let his grip slip, I kneed him and pushed him off. I ran to the bathroom but couldn't lock him out. That's when my phone rang. He'd have been a good client for the place you took me to."

"You think this is a fucking joke?" He storms towards me, grabbing my shoulders and shaking me. "Do you think I want to hear about a man touching what's mine? About marking you?" Tears drop from my lashes onto my cheeks under his ferocity. And, a part of me wishes we could set aside the bad that's between us.

"No." I shake my head. "I'm telling you every ounce of truth I have in the hope that you believe me." My voice feels brittle as I speak – as if it might break and shatter at any point, along with my nerve.

He lets go and turns away, running his hands through his hair.

My shoulders slump. My body feels drained of all emotion and energy. It's been overwhelming, and I feel unsteady on my legs as the adrenaline fades and a chill clings to my skin. He's heard it all, as plainly as I can say, and waiting here for him to find me guilty or not is the final blow. "I think I want to go to bed."

He stares at me, giving me nothing but pent-up frustration and fury that I don't think he knows what to do with. We're locked in a stare as if waiting for something to happen. Hoping, perhaps.

"Go shower," he eventually says, walking away to his bar. I nod and turn for the stairs, unsure what anything means yet. I've told my truth and given everything I can. "Come back here when you're done."

CHAPTER TWENTY - THREE

ABEL

There isn't a sound of a door closing to the bedroom, and it's silent other than the faint sound of the shower running. I stare through the doors that lead to the pool, and down another drink. The glass gets abandoned, and I follow my view until I'm standing by the water. Rape. I'm incensed by it, no matter my own business. Not because of the potential act, but because it almost happened to someone I give a damn about. Again.

Thoughts of Mariana flick through my mind as I light a cigarette and breathe in deeply. She wasn't even born when I went inside, but I felt Dante's wrath when he told me what they did to her. She became harsher after that, less sweet-natured. And then my thoughts run to the vision of Mother and her battered body when I found her that night. Her husband had done that to her. Emilio Cortez had been kicked out for cheating, and then he came back and took a woman as strong as her and demeaned her to nothing but broken limbs, broken skin and bruises.

Three days later, she told me he threatened us all that night. He'd already taken Elias from us, and unless she yielded and took him back, he'd take Dante and Knox, too. They were his, he said. We all were, including me, regardless of me not being a Cortez at all. He was going to try taking everything so he could leave her alone and destitute. Suffer, he said.

I killed him four days after that, as incensed in nature as I currently feel. I'd never killed before that, but my time inside was, and always will be, worth the pride of seeing him bleed out on the floor in front of me. I didn't run from it or hide. I watched until the last of his heart gave in, needing to see it happen, and then sat and waited for the law to come get me. Stupid maybe considering I could have done it differently and gotten away with it, but I wasn't a thinker back then. It was all anger and pain and viciousness because no one takes my family away from me, let alone beats on the woman that brought me into this world.

No one touches something I love.

Time passes, and I end up sitting and looking at the debris on the floor from my temper. A broken vase. A glass object smashed that I didn't choose. I don't know how I feel about Lexi in totality, but I do know, without a shadow of fucking doubt, that that same feeling coursed through me when I saw her in that bathroom. It might have been mixed with distrust, but it still ravaged my bloodstream like a tornado trying to touch ground. It forced the need to destroy something that threatened me, or threatened something that was mine to protect. That's love to me, or whatever guise of it a man like me possesses.

True silence comes after a while, and I stare at the stairs to wait for her. She was truthful earlier. She looked me straight on and told it like it happened. No fakery. No bullshit. No deceit. That's all I've ever wanted her to give me. It's a shame it took her own father's violation for her to realise it, but I'm almost thankful for the behaviour.

She eventually creeps down the stairs, quiet and barely able to look at me. I follow her with my gaze the entire way until she stalls. "Come here."

She looks at me from the stairs and sighs. "I'm tired."

"I don't give a damn. We're not done."

She steps forward, slowly. She walks until she's in front of me on the couch and then just waits for my instruction. I don't know what that instruction should be. I want to argue and trash the room and prove how pissed I am, but looking at her now — at the bruises on her face and neck and the frail nature of her — means I'm not allowing another second of time together wasted without showing her that I feel, too. Never felt so much damn anger rise through me as it did when I saw his hands on her. Call it possessiveness, or protective instinct, or whatever the fuck you want, but I felt it.

I reach forward, scooping her ass to me until she's climbing on and sitting astride me. My hands travel to her hips, to her back, over her shoulders and down across her breasts. She barely moves other than to get in a little closer. I push her away again with one palm, pressing it over the length of her stomach and chest until it's behind her neck and angling her forward. We kiss quietly. No hurry about it. No anger in my hold either, irrespective of my being furious still.

Eventually, I tug at the robe she's drowning in to get it off her, and then start mouthing at her nipples to cool myself all the way down. She rests her hands in my hair, smoothing them through it cautiously. It helps. It sends me to places I haven't been for a long-ass time, if ever, considering this band of gold around my finger.

Sighing, I bite gently, letting her hands wind me down bit by bit.

"You're really that angry, aren't you?" she asks. I pull at a nipple with my teeth, sharply, testing both her and me. "I'm sorry. Let me take your anger away. Get lost in me — get lost in us." My mouth stops, and I hover my lips on her skin. That's the kind of thing a Cortez wife would say, regardless of what she's been through. She'd think of her husband before her. "That's what I'm here for, isn't it?" I grunt, as she slowly rubs herself on my dick. "That's what this marriage is." My teeth sink in, dick aching immediately.

"Just let me be part of it with you. Maybe we both need it."

Her hands slide around to my jaw, lifting it up until we're mouth to mouth again. "Use me, Abel."

My head shakes, as I look up at her. "I don't want to use you." She frowns and starts dropping her hands away to lean back again. My hands tighten on her ass. "Leave them there and look at your husband. Touch him. Understand him. I want you to."

She swallows and keeps looking me straight on. "You believe me?"

"Yes."

And that's enough. For now. There's just two inches of space between us and true, honest thoughts, until I stand up with her still in my hold and head back up the stairs. It's time to mean it and start understanding what these growing feelings really are. I've already proved I'll kill for her, now I need to recognise whether or not I'll die for her.

~

The sweet smell of syrup and waffles wakes me. I look sideways to find an empty bed, so swing my legs to the floor and stare at dark walls flecked in sunlight. Visions of yesterday come fast and thick, and I'm unsure if I'm any calmer this morning than I was last night. Good fucking doesn't change what happened. Thoughts of vengeance and death don't go away overnight. They don't settle because of one night soothing fury and hatred into a low-lying slumber. Blood still fills my visions, and my murderous hands still look the same as they always do.

Still, something did change between us here. We took it slow and easy for a while, and then I let it turn as passionate as we needed to be. Maybe we did use each other a little in the end, and maybe it was just the aftermath and me reclaiming my territory.

Doesn't change the fact that I felt every minute of it, though.

I take a shower, clean up, and grab some track pants to make my way down the stairs. The floor's been cleared of my temper last night, and music drifts softly around the space. Some old singer croons out soulful sounds, and I follow it until I find her in the kitchen at the stove.

"You cook?"

She doesn't turn round from whatever she's doing. "Barely. But a girl's gotta eat." I watch her ass moving around, maybe wishing the robe wasn't as long as it is. "You must do, though"

"What?"

"Cook. These cupboards are full to heaving."

"Well, I'm a big boy. And I don't like being denied anything I want."

She does turn around at that, smiling at something. Whatever nicety was happening disappears in a heartbeat the second I notice the marks on her neck still there. My frown drops, and she goes from seeming relaxed to on edge. "Abel?" I sneer and look away, choosing the coffee machine as a refuge from the sight. "What have I done?"

"Nothing. You want some coffee?"

She's in front of me before I get a chance to deal with the offer. "Hey? What's going on?"

"Your neck is what's going on."

Her own fingers travel to it, and then she reaches for mine to drag them up there with them. She draws them over the marks, eventually putting her hands on my face like she did last night. "But you dealt with that for me. They're nothing now, are they? They're gone. Like he is." My frown stays fixed. "Don't spoil this. Please. Let me enjoy this." I'm still not smiling about anything. "Do you need bacon?"

"What?"

"Bacon, with your waffles? You know, with you being a big boy and all. We're going to need to keep you fed up if last night was anything to go by. I'm quite sore." She kisses me briefly, lets go of my face, and sashays her way back to the stove. "Sweet coffee, please. Lexi likes a bit of sugar lately."

I get on with making coffee, and she gets on with cooking food.

We eat in amicable silence, and perhaps that's because neither of us are used to each other past the normal order of events in our life. Music keeps drifting around, though, and she keeps trying to smile her way through the fact that she was as good as raped last night. Maybe that dick wasn't inside her, but he held her down. He tried. Tie in her watching me kill him, and then Dante's carving him up like a butcher at a slaughterhouse, and she's far from fine.

Possessive, or maybe protective instinct swarms inside me. "You're sore?" I ask.

"What?"

"You said you were sore. Earlier."

"Oh, well, not really. We – you – were rough last night."

"That wasn't rough. That was passionate. Possessive even. Definitely pissed." Her hand cups her chin, and she smiles a little. "Either way, you better get your ass up on this table so I can lick you better." She smirks, stands, and picks up the plates, as if ready to take them to the sink. "I mean it, Lexi. Put the plates down."

She does, and I grab for her hip to pull her in front of me. The robe gets untied, and she climbs backwards until she's sitting on the table. "Open your legs."

"Still hungry?" she jokes.

This isn't a joke, so I stare and wait.

She inches them apart slowly, until she's spread wide for me and leaning back on her elbows. I shift and then draw my mouth over her, savouring the sweet smell of musk, and watch her. She writhes the moment the width of my tongue starts playing with her, and moans as I put more pressure on it. Makes me lap longer and harder, running my tongue over her repeatedly to make a point about who owns it, until she's filling with juice and begging me to do something more than I am. "Abel, please," she groans.

I lift away, gently running the edges of my teeth along every part of her, before blowing cold air on her warmth. "You still sore, darlin'?" She moans again and hooks a leg over my shoulder, damn near forcing me to obey what she wants. "'Cause I'm hard enough to fuck you raw again."

"Bring it here," she says. "Just keep sucking on me. Please." I shift her leg and move around the side, angling my head across her stomach instead, and the second I do she's got her hand inside my pants and is grabbing hold hard.

"Fuck," growls out of me, as she starts me off.

My mouth stutters around her pussy for a while, guttural groans coming long and hard as she strokes my dick fast. It's exquisite, and the whole goddamn room starts spinning under her hold. I brace the table and keep sucking and licking, lifting her ass up to me so I can get deeper into her, but that talented hand keeps driving me to fucking distraction.

"Oh God, yes. There," she moans. "Jesus, right there."

Her legs start trembling, and I keep exactly where I was so I can get that cum on my tongue where I want it. Hard licks, heavy suction. I'm smothered in her and needing to cum so bad I'm barely holding myself back.

She comes on the next drive of my tongue, panting hard and heavy under the assault, and I lift up and grab for the back of her head. The other hand goes to her pussy, on automatic, and helps pull her across the table to get her mouth hanging over it and onto my dick. "You done it at this angle before?"

"No." She licks her lips, though, and I move forward.

"Swallow it down then. Relax. Let it all the way in." She does slowly. She sucks on me like her life depends on it, and I can't help thinking about how it does with every next pull on her throat. "That's it. All the way, darlin'." My eyes close, deep breaths staving off the inevitable, and my hand travels to her neck. It tightens, covering marks put there by another man, reclaiming what's mine, and enjoying the feel of her throat moving for me. She tenses immediately. "Don't you dare fight me. Relax and keep taking it. Trust I'm not going to hurt you and you'll be fine."

Her hands reach for my legs, pulling me closer. Fine skin stretches out in front of me, when I look back at her. Her legs are spread wide, and I keep pushing my fingers around her. Pressure starts building, making it hard to stay calm about this. "Fuck, that's good. Deeper." I'm desperate for harder, for more, for my grip to strangle, and my increased rutting shows it, but then I grunt with no want to hold back or force pain.

Cum floods out of me into her, and I watch the pulse in her neck as she swallows and writhes.

Fucking provocative doesn't even begin to cut it.

Groaning, I eventually pull out of her, listen to her choke on the move, and lean both hands on the table by her head. "Beautiful." She licks her lips and smiles up at me, running her own hands down to her pussy to play with it some more. "And that's a dirty fucking mouth you've got there."

"Why thank you, husband. You're not so bad yourself." She slowly spins herself and drops her legs down beside me, lifting herself up to my chest. "You could do with more training, though. There's some room for improvement."

My lips twitch. For a woman who's married to a trafficker, that was a stupid-ass thing to say with my background in forced orgasms. She must notice something about me change, because she drops her feet down to the floor and pushes me away. "Whatever you were just thinking, Abel, unthink it. I am not a challenge to be played with. I'm your wife."

"Well now, darlin', that's exactly why you're a challenge to be played with."

My phone rings on the table while I'm still thinking about

fucking her smart mouth out of her some more – Dante. Sore or not, she just set down a game I'm thinking about beginning.

Still, I swipe my arm over my mouth to clear it of cum and spit, grab my phone, and head out to the pool.

"You alright?" he asks.

"Fine."

"She alright?"

I look back at her in the kitchen and watch her making her way over for more coffee like everything's alright. It might be as far as fucking is concerned, but the rest is debatable. She holds my cup up, as if gesturing to make me one, so I nod in reply. "No."

"How far did that asshole get?"

"He didn't. Other than playing with her ability to breathe and slapping her around."

There's quiet on the end of the phone. I get it, and not only do I understand his frustration with that information, but I also feel his own self-loathing at the thought. We've both done the same. We've pushed and broken women, making sure they feel what it's like to defy us. I might not care that much about that, but him – the one with the heart and hope under his ferocity? He does.

"Well, it's been dealt with. Chance called me and let me know it was all done. You need me to do anything else?"

"Yes. Find out where Miguel Ortega is for the next few days."

"Why?"

"Because he caused it. I'm not a ray of fucking sunshine about that fact. Send me the details."

More silence. This time his end of the line is filled with as much goddamn revenge as I'm thinking about. Maybe he doesn't think about Lexi like I'm starting to, but she's an extension of me now as far as he's concerned, just like Wren is to me, and that means he's as pissed with the thought as I am. "And cover things for me for a few days. I need some time. Call me if there are any problems."

"Done."

He ends the call before I say anything else. Not that I need to. He'll be all over this business like the asshole he is, and no one will get a minute's peace now I've given him control of it.

I stare at the pool some more, potentially thinking about getting in it, or maybe going out with her to take her mind off everything, and then I choose to turn around and go back through the house. "Have you cried yet?"

She looks up at me with two coffee cups in her hands. "What?"

"In the shower last night. Did you cry? More than a stray tear or two."

Her chin lifts and she hardens everything about herself. "No." She shakes her head and puts the coffees down. "I don't do that about things like this."

"Yeah, you do now." I walk over and scoop her to me. "Everyone cries. Me included. We need to get that out of you. Up you get."

"What?"

"Jump."

She pulls back, putting space between us. "Where? What are you talking about? Unless you missed it, we just did sexy on the table and now you're talking crying? There's that damn whiplash again. And when the hell have you cried?"

"Stop talking and jump your ass up until you're wrapped around me."

She rolls her eyes. "Why?"

"Jesus, woman. Get the fuck up here."

My tone must counter her growing aggravation because she bounces and springs up, sliding her legs around my waist. "Fine. Now what?"

I swing her left and right for a while, letting the sound of the music keep her in that calm she's trying for, for the time being. She's nowhere near calm. She's hoping for it, and some orgasms might have helped, but if I know anything about women it's that no matter their hatred or fears or concerns, tears will always come. They glare using them. They shout using them. They bleed using them. We're getting them out of my wife whether she likes it or not.

"You feel safe on me, Lexi?"

She nods on my shoulder, crawling herself in tighter until she's got her lips by my neck. "I'm starting to."

"That's because you are, darlin'. Always will be now. But listen, you're gonna need to learn to bring tears at me every time you need to. You understand? Just me." Another nod and she rests her chin on my shoulder. "I don't care how they come. You just let them come."

Maybe I'll make them come if I need to.

CHAPTER TWENTY - FOUR

LEXI

I never imagined that someone like Abel, in fact, any guy, could be so open about emotion. That he's permitted me to be vulnerable is perhaps what brings the mist to my eyes.

I squeeze them shut, desperate to stop them from falling. They're a weakness, or at least that's what I've spent years thinking. Still, my arms tighten around him, and he shifts my weight, wrapping me in comfort and protection. It's a craving I didn't know how to identify before him, and now that I've tasted it, I don't want to let it go. Or Abel. If last night needed to happen to get us here, maybe there was something good that came out of everything.

"Abel?" Mariana's voice rings out in the house, and I feel his body tense. He murmurs something under his breath, and, reluctantly, I let go and slide down his body.

I sniff the emotion back and blink, pulling myself back together.

"Ever heard of calling first?" he mutters, levelling a look at Mariana as she descends the stairs to the kitchen.

"I'm sorry. Bringing your car back kinda implied I'd show up." She looks between us, and I watch Shaw walk in behind her. "Everything okay?" she asks Abel, but I can feel her gaze on me.

My hand automatically creeps over my neck to hide the marks I know are visible, and I pull away from Abel to head for the coffee machine. A wash of shame and embarrassment creeps over me, making me turn my back to all of them.

The conversation I'm waiting for between him and his siblings doesn't emerge, but I do feel a hand drop to my shoulder. Taking a breath and forcing my eyes wide and a smile over my lips, I turn and see Mariana standing by my side. She's not looking at me with pity or anger, but maybe understanding.

"I ..."

"You don't have to say anything." She leans in and puts her arms around my neck, pulling me closer soon after, "We've got you."

After a moment as personal and heartfelt as the one a few minutes ago with Abel, in some ways this means more. She lets me go, and I offer her a small smile and flash a quick look towards Abel and Shaw on the other side of the kitchen. Abel's studying me as if he's anticipating something.

Mariana's hand runs down my arm to my hand, and she gives it a squeeze. "Come on, Brother. Time to go."

She walks right by the men and heads up to the exit, confident that Shaw will follow. He does, and my body sags, causing me to lean against the counter when I hear the door close. Perhaps Abel's right, and I do need to cry. Maybe that will purge my body of the emotion that keeps welling up and threatening to drown me.

He approaches and twists me so I'm looking at him. "Don't fight it, Lexi. Let it out." I stare into his eyes and feel the cracking of the damn I've built inside, but there's still something holding me back – keeping me from showing him my weakness.

My phone buzzing interrupts, breaking the moment between us. And as I pick it up and look at the screen, a new sense of dread hits me like a wrecking ball.

"Who is it?" Abel asks.

"My …" He doesn't deserve the title of Father. He never did. To me, he's lost that right – he lost it the first time he gave me to one of his friends, only I was too young and naive to see it, and it's taken Abel to give me the strength I should have found myself to sever the connection.

The blackness inside of me – the poison he's tainted in me – can be harnessed as fuel for the rage that's simmering and aimed at him now. "It's Miguel. Why would he call?"

"Give it to me." He reaches for the phone, but this is my problem, my blood, and I want to know what he's calling for.

"What?" I snap, answering it. I click the button to put him on speaker, near crushing the thing.

"I'm not in the mood, Alexia. What the hell happened?" he clips, short and tight in tone. "You had one job."

Abel opens his mouth, but I put up my hand and shake my head. This is my fight, and while I can't express my gratitude for him saving me from that monster, I want to handle this on my own.

"One job? Fuck that. You set me up. Don't you have any concern for me?"

"You've handled plenty of men in your past, Alexia. Men much worse than Blackford."

"Such concern. Interesting given that you showed none for me last night. Glad to know I'm only worth what someone's prepared to pay for me."

"Cut the crap, Alexia. What happened, and where's my money?"

"Didn't he pay you? Oh, boohoo."

"Alexia!" he shouts down the line. I look up at Abel, who looks ready to murder someone. No, not someone, Miguel Ortega. "Where is he? What happened, and don't try to lie to me, or you'll have me to answer to."

"I don't know what you mean, Miguel." I draw out the syllables, emphasising the name. "After all, you had me taken to a room with the man," my voice rises, "and left me there. You left me with him, and he did whatever he wanted!" I swing my arms in anger as the emotion I've been holding onto morphs into a rage at the one person that's always let me down in my life.

"Stop playing games. I don't care if he defiled you, sodomised or passed you around to his colleagues while he watched. Because that's all you are, Alexia. A piece of meat, a commodity to sell, only you've never understood where you fit into this business. You've had your little power play. Abel Cortez should have straightened you out by now." The disgust is evident in his voice, and I watch as Abel storms to the sitting area. He shoves the coffee table with his foot and sends it sliding into the glass doors, cracking the pane and splintering it. "Where is Blackford? I want my fucking money and my deal!"

Abel snatches the phone from my hand. "You're a real piece of shit, aren't you? He's in the desert. Cut up and rotting. You dare touch something that's mine? Something that belongs to Cortez. Only I have the right to do that. You hear me, ONLY ME!" If the coffee table hadn't shattered the glass, Abel's voice would have.

His face is red with deep frown lines drawn into his forehead. I'm caught between wanting to offer him the comfort he gave me this morning and finishing the conversation with Miguel.

I take the phone out of Abel's hand and take a moment to compose myself. He'll never change. He'll never accept me as a daughter in our family like Mariana is to Abel and Melena. He'll never see me as he did Nicolas or even give me a chance. He even thought he could manipulate me after marrying into the family that would deliver him the power he's always craved.

"You've made a mistake, Miguel. You put me in a situation that you now can't undo. And you've made an enemy of me, and by extension, the Cortez family. I hope you know what's coming for you because, unlike you, they know how to treat family." My voice goes softer, quieter. "I want you to remember that you've done this to yourself. You made an enemy of the one person who could have saved you."

"Stop being so dramatic. Let me talk to Abel."

"No. You don't get to talk to my husband. He rescued me from that piece of shit you wanted me to please."

"Alexia, listen," his voice is pleading now, and I can hear the shake in it.

"No. It's over, Miguel. Abel is my family, and no thanks to you, I now know what loyalty feels like. You're going to regret crossing me."

Hanging up, I turn to my husband. His fury is only just contained, but for once, I know it's nothing to do with my actions. He's angry on my behalf, and it's that vision of him that burns my eyes and sets the tears tumbling free.

Hot, silent tears flood my cheeks, pulling at emotions that I've never given myself time or space to feel before. It's wild and raw, overtaking and engulfing me in seconds. Abel's arms catch me before I collapse to the ground. He pulls me to him, cradling me in a way that feels so natural I crave more. My arms reach up to pull myself closer to him, burying my head to his neck as I struggle to even my breath or pull oxygen into my lungs between the sobs.

I sniff and stutter and hiccup through the tears, and he doesn't say a word. He holds me close, making sure I don't fall. And in that moment, amongst all that pain, suffering and doubt that have shaped me into the person I am today, I finally feel safe and that I belong.

My knees crawl up as he sits, and I let him engulf me like nothing before. The notion of belonging to someone else used to repulse me. As a teenager, I associated it with the deeds of a woman who was abused and used. And then, as I grew up, I saw it as a sign of weakness because I only had myself to rely on and believe in. But belonging to Abel doesn't feel like any of those things. It feels like home.

I don't say the three little words that some might say encompass what I'm feeling right now. Instead, they seep back into my soul, pushing out the pain and anger that was always there, choking and poisoning my soul.

Eventually, the tears stop, and I'm left with dry, tired eyes. My body feels wrecked, and all I want to do is disappear, but that's not who I want to be. I want to keep the strength that these years have taught me, hone it, and become stronger for what I've been through. And now, with the purge of emotion, I can look at building the life I deserve as part of a family who'll protect and defend me.

"I'm okay. Thank you." My voice is clogged and sounds hoarse from the emotion, and, as much as I'd like to be fine about all of this, a tinge of embarrassment eats at me as I try pulling away from his hold.

"You're far from okay."

I nod. He's right, but I've got to get myself together. "I'm pretty drained. Plus, you might need to fix that window." I try moving again, but he clamps down on me hard.

"Couldn't give a fuck about the window. Do you want to talk about Miguel?"

I shake my head. "No."

We stay as we are, and I stare out into the house rather than look at him. I'm too exhausted to argue and almost too drained to move.

"I need you to stay here for a few days," he announces.

I muster my strength and look up at him with an attempt at a smile. "Why, Abel, I thought you'd never ask," I sass, needing some relief from all the heavy.

"I'm fucking serious, Lexi."

"I'm sorry." I raise my arms to his neck, attempting to appease him. "I know you are, and I have no intention of going anywhere."

Not yet, at least. Something or someone has to stop Miguel, though. He's not going to react kindly to what's happened.

"Good. No more bullshit between us. This is it now."

"I know. And if you don't think I believe that after everything we've been through, then I might as well walk away. I choose you, Abel. For everything you've done to me, for everything we've been through in these few weeks, you mean more to me than blood. It's time for us to both believe we can work at us."

He stares at me, then takes my face in his hands, cradling me before pushing his fingers through my hair and bringing his lips down to mine. Everything about him is sure and possessive and full of intent, and everything he speaks to me in that kiss locks in the pledge I just made – he's my family, he's my future.

The kiss deepens, and my heart quickens, and then he pulls back, resting his forehead against mine. "If anyone touches you, if anyone dares upset you, I'll kill them. You've seen me do it, and I'll do it again. Don't ever forget that. You're mine, Lexi." I nod in his hold, eyes fixed on his. "And if moving in is what you need, I'll have your stuff brought over tomorrow. You ready for that?" My eyes widen. Am I ready?

"Yes, but I thought–"

"It's done then. All in. Heed the warning, darlin', because we don't fuck up from this second on."

CHAPTER TWENTY - FIVE

ABEL

Suit on and I walk down the stairs, searching for her. She's nowhere to be seen. Suspicion might flick through my head for a half second, but it's gone before I give it any real thought. No one's getting in here without me knowing about it, and, after the last few days, I doubt she's going anywhere without me. What else does she have but me? Her father's a piece of shit. Her brother's dead, and, despite what brought her here, we're beginning to find something worth fighting for.

I drink the last of my espresso and look towards the open doors to the pool. She swims by, naked, rolling her body well enough that at least her abilities in the water aren't something I need to worry about. The thought sends me back a long time, to a place where we swam as kids and enjoyed the life we thought we'd have back then. White sands. A beach that stretched for miles. A new father I thought I could trust. He was good at it for a while. Turned out to be another piece of shit, though. Just like hers.

I walk out to the pool, snatching my car keys on the way. "Enjoying yourself?"

She smiles and looks over at me from behind her sunglasses. "You're not joining me?"

"No. I've got work to do."

"And what wonders do you have in store today?"

"New intake. Carmen's bringing them over to Berettas for me to look at."

She swims closer until she's at the edge of the pool, leaning her arms on the side. "Berettas?"

"Strip club."

"How exciting," she mocks. "Presumably, you don't need to fuck any of them to prove their use."

I crouch down. "You getting all insecure again, darlin'?"

"About other women? No. I am, however, bothered about how clean you are. I don't want their potentially diseased pussy anywhere near me."

A laugh bursts out of me, and I stand up again and look at her darkened hair, now it's wet. Suits her. Not that I give a damn if she needs it blonde, but it would be good to see her as nature intended. "You'll be alright here?" She nods, but I'm not convinced. She still has moments where I find her thinking about what could have happened. "You're as safe as you can be inside these walls. No one can get in but family."

"I'm fine. What's done is done. Time to move on. Besides, you've given me enough time, and what are you going to do? Stay here and not work?"

"I will if you need me to."

She smiles. "Well, that's enough reason for you to go then. I don't need you to."

"I'm wounded."

"I doubt that very much."

I chuckle. Doubt she'll ever admit to needing anyone. "Your things will be here by lunch. I'll be finished about eight, but I'm sending Shaw to pick you up. Dinner. He'll be here at seven thirty."

She pulls herself out of the pool, gracefully stretching her fine frame up until she's standing in front of me and pushing her hair back. "Or you could take a different car and I could just drive and meet you there?" Unsure how alright I am with that, considering the shit that's just gone down, I keep staring. Her wet hands land on my jacket, and she slides them up to the back of my neck. "Come on, Abel. You know it's in safe hands, and it's not like I'm going anywhere else anymore. I can't be locked up here. I need a little freedom."

"Hmm."

"I mean, you don't want a little woman who's incapable anyway. And if you think I'll be driven everywhere and coddled, you're wrong." My brow arches. She's damn right about that. Last thing on the planet I want is a woman who needs coddling, but I'm still fucking wary. "You're going to have to give in on this. You know it as well as I do. Whatever happened, happened. That's done now. We'll start arguing again if you don't let me and—"

"Fine." I take her hand from the back of my neck and pass her the keys. "Eight o'clock. Sharp. Do not be late. I'll text you the address." She skips back away from me and grabs her robe, smiling to herself about her win, as I turn to leave. "Don't trash my car and make me regret this." I turn back as soon as I've got the other car key and head back to her. She's still celebrating her win by twirling around as if she's dancing. I smile a little, amused by this version of her. "Don't leave until you're ready."

"Why?"

"You won't be able to get back in. I haven't set the security or access for you."

"Oh, right. Yes. Can't we do that now?"

"No. Eight. Sharp. Yes?"

She nods and watches me go, and I get in the car and leave her in my place all alone. It feels strange to think about as I make my way over to Berettas. I'd like to say it sat well, but I'm not sure it does. I never intended for a woman to be there with me. It was always supposed to be my space and mine alone. It's built for me, designed for me, and tailored to what I need it to be. Something about her in it just doesn't work.

I pull into the parking lot, get out, and look over the cars already here as I walk in. Carmen's and Knox's are already side by side, and I can hear Dante's coming along the road behind me somewhere. Goddamn Mustangs make too much noise for their own good.

Knox comes striding towards me as I make my way through the halls. I move sideways to block him. "We need to finish our conversation about Reed."

"Yeah, but I've got a meeting now." He looks up and behind me. "Jesus. Are you ever not covered in blood?" I turn my head to see Dante walking in.

He pulls his shirt off and wipes his face and hands over with it, tucking the shirt into the back of his pants. "You're the one who gave me the fucking list."

"It's ten in the morning."

Dante keeps moving past us, a dark chuckle rumbling through him. "Yeah, well, beatings come at all times of the day."

Knox starts moving again before I get a chance to stop him. "Look, I'm late. Call me and we'll get together. I've got more intel now and we need to plan it out. I'm not hiding shit; I'm just really late. Fuck knows why people do this time of day anyway." His hand goes up in the air, signalling he's finished discussing anything for now, so I scowl and carry on after Dante.

By the time I get to the main floor, eighteen women are attempting to pull all the moves to the kind of music we're used to in here. I go straight behind the bar and watch Dante sink a few drinks from a bottle of whisky, so crack open a couple of sodas and shove one in front of him. "You need to slow down on the booze, Brother."

He glares at me. "Fuck you. You see this shit on me? Just about every damn day it happens. Under your orders. If I need a goddamn drink to ease it off, I'll have one."

"I'll let Wren know you felt that way when we put you in the ground because of cirrhosis." Shock, or maybe fear, crosses his face. "Yeah. Or maybe I'll tell her the day she marries someone else and raises your kids with him."

"AGAIN!" Carmen pulls both our attention. She carries on shouting at one of the girls, reducing her to tears about some inadequacy. She whines and keeps crying, making herself pointless in my eyes. I don't even need to say anything before Carmen's dragging her off the stage to put her back in the cage she came from. Dumb-ass bitch had a chance here. Not anymore.

I keep watching the others and drink my soda, then cross the floor to get to the side of the podiums. My head tilts as I watch one of them. Red hair. Curvy and wearing just about nothing. She looks down at me and fucks that damn pole like she owns it, licking her tongue up it and trying to get me interested. I'm not. She probably fucks well enough by now, but I'm not interested in anything that reduces itself to this kind of life. They're nothing but dollar signs in my eyes. This one's gonna make me a lot of money.

"Carmen?" She leaves the other girl and comes over, meek in nature, considering our last conversation. "This one for Mariana."

"She's not one of the new intakes." I keep watching, as she swings high and splits her legs for me. Dante arrives by my side, swilling back his soda now he's understood what he might lose. "She's from Vegas. Looking for work. I thought I'd bring her down for you to see. Chance found her."

She comes to a stop and stands still for me, slowly turning herself around so I can get a good look at everything she's offering. "Hey, baby," she coos. Dante snorts and slaps me on the back, walking away and still chuckling to himself. She drops down onto her knees, moving her way to my face. "You wanna try me out first? I'll ride you real good."

"Back the hell up before I change my mind. Last thing I'm doing is fucking a whore." Her self-importance shrivels to the level it should be, and she slumps back on her sorry ass rather than try any more of that shit with me. Still, that's the kind of crap that works on other men, and she looks like she'll be good at doing what I need her to do. "Name?"

"Lauren Astley."

"Hmm. Let Mariana see her." I turn and head back to the bar. "She can make the call. If she says yes, get her branded up like the rest."

"Branded?" the woman shouts.

I stop and look back at her. "Yes." I angle myself so she can see Dante's frown in the darkness. "He does it. You want to work for me, then you sit like a whore should and you let him put our mark on you." She shrinks back towards the pole, probably not one bit fucking happy about that information. "Or you can just walk on out of here right now. What's it gonna be? I either own you or I don't. There's no in-between."

She keeps staring at Dante rather than me, then starts smiling like a bitch in heat. That's as stupid as trying to play me. No way is she going to change his mind when the time comes with what she's thinking about. "Okay," she says.

"Good."

We sit for the rest of the day and keep watching parades of women. Once the first lot are done, I scrutinise the next until I have a list of venues they'll all be transported to. Thirty of them aren't going anywhere near our places. They'll be shipped across the country and hired out to contacts. The rest of them will end up working here on rotation, where they'll dance and fuck to see if they can get the clients spending big.

They only get one shot at staying with us in San Antonio – either here or the Bourbon Lounge. One week in our lead venues to see if we can make a decent profit off them. They do, and they get the kind of life we can provide for them. It's as safe and secure as it gets. They don't, and I either push them to some of our lower ranking places, or I send them the fuck away and take my cut of the profit they make in some other shit hole. I don't need them bringing our reputation down. And there's always Chance's ventures for the truly useless.

A coffee gets placed down in front of me, and I look up to see Dante hovering.

"You all good?" he asks. I nod and drink the coffee, about done here and ready to get somewhere cleaner than this place provides. "And Lexi?"

"Yeah, she's fine."

"Do we need to discuss what you're going to do about her father?"

I pull in a long breath and stare at the last girl dancing. He'd be dead by now if I hadn't been thinking hard about it, but whatever I might feel about his behaviour towards her, or what that behaviour means to me and my business, I'm not sure killing the piece of shit is the right call. "He's still her father, Dante. No brother anymore. No mother. Nothing other than us."

He sits and nods, presumably knowing exactly how I'm feeling about the situation. "But she's your wife. And it's just plain fucking wrong. Using your child like that? Makes my damned blood boil."

The last girl leaves the floor in front of me, and I drain my cup. "He called her, asking why he hadn't had his money yet and if she hadn't satisfied her side of the bargain. There was no bargain. She didn't even know it was coming until she was in the middle of it. And before you ask, it was all on loudspeaker. I heard it first-hand." I reach into my jacket, pulling out my pack of cigarettes and lighting one. "Still doesn't mean I have the right to kill the only person she has left. No matter how much I want him dead."

Standing, I make my way over to Carmen and hand her the file with the girl's names and where they'll be going to. "Get these to Knox. He'll organise with Dante as usual."

She nods and walks off into the darkness, less mouthy than I think I've ever seen her be, and so I go collect my jacket. I've got dinner to get to, and hopefully, an on-time wife. Frankly, after an afternoon of watching mediocre pussy, and my head still trying to fathom what to do about an Ortega dick who needs putting down, I'm ready for some peace and a woman worthy of thought. "What are you doing tonight?" I ask, as Dante stands.

"Why?"

"Just asking a question."

"Heading to Austin."

"Why?"

"None of your goddamn business."

I laugh lightly and start moving for the parking lot. "See? You're better with no booze. I don't need to hear about your little Wren and her apparent dark side. Although, give my regards to Rick while you're there."

"The fuck?"

"There's only one reason you go to Austin. His place is it. I thought you'd have worked out by now that you can't hide shit from me. What's Wren up to at the moment?" Because Lexi needs some allies round here, and they could get on if they tried.

"Wedding bullshit. She's running three from the home office now. Gone solo and set up her own thing. Place looks like a goddamn florist. Might need to move just so I can get past them into the gym at some point."

Move.

We say our goodbyes and I watch his car drive out in front of mine, then turn in the opposite direction for the place we're eating at. Only takes fifteen minutes to get there, and before I know it I'm pulling in beside my own Challenger parked up in the back. She's leaning on the side of it, swinging the key ring around her finger and looking damn pleased with herself.

I look through the window at those legs wearing a short as fuck skirt, and smile. They're peeking out behind a long, blue, lightweight coat, showing off her deeply tanned skin. Nothing mediocre about any of that. That's fine and perfected, holding that line she manages so well. Not trashy. Not slutty either. Just sharp and precise, as if she knows the exact level of sexy I need to get turned on.

"You know," I muse, as I get out and slam the door. "You could get arrested looking like that."

She frowns. "Why?"

"Too damn beautiful."

Her face brightens. "Well thank you, but I doubt it. I'm a Cortez now. I don't think we get arrested for much at all. Apart from murder. When it's done passionately at least. Which you know all about."

I crouch down, gently easing the fine strap back into the buckle on her shoe. "True enough."

"We still haven't talked about that."

My fingers drag up the length of her leg, and I cage her on the side of the car and lean in to get a smell of her perfume. "No. Not going to tonight either." My mouth comes down to hers, mind thinking of anything but food. "You look good enough to eat, darlin'."

"Maybe so, but you smell like a cheap brothel, and I think I might be overdressed considering this place." She looks back at the barn come building. "What is it?"

I back off. "It's a secret for people who can afford it. We can."

A smile beams on her face, and she links her arm through mine and lets me lead the way through to the restaurant. Not that any of it looks like a restaurant. We need to go down a few floors for that. I open a heavy metal door at the back with a code, and usher her down the steps until we step out onto a decked area. The spread of San Antonio lies in wait for us, ten miles of it laid out like a light show starting to come to life.

"Well, that's impressive."

"Hmm." I keep us moving until we arrive at a reception area and we're led to a small table set up on the corner of the deck. White linen. Cut crystal glasses. "The chef moves the location every three months. This is the first time he's been in San Antonio. I went to his first place a few years back in Havana."

"I love Havana," she says, taking a seat.

"Let me guess, the laughter?"

She watches as a waitress approaches, offering us both Champagne. "Yes, I suppose so. But it's gritty too. I always feel like I can get lost there."

"That's a definite. You can get lost straight into the back of one of our trucks. Plenty of women do."

"Lowering the tone, are we?" she questions, lifting her glass of Champagne to drink.

"You're more than aware that it doesn't get much lower than me."

"Well, there's low, and then there's low with class. I think you're the latter." I stare, watching the way she seems relatively at ease with what I am under this suit and expensive finery. "Besides, I like your low. It's honest. No hiding anything. No pretending." She blushes. A real honest blush that seems like it's come out of nowhere.

"I'd like to know what that thought was."

She chuckles and looks at the table. "Where's the menu?"

"There isn't one."

"None?"

"No. You take what you're given." I lean forward, more interested in what that damn thought was than any food that might be coming. "What made you blush?"

"Blush? Me? I don't blush."

"You just did. Sexiest damn thing you've done since we met. Give it up."

She laughs and swings her legs back and forth, amused at my

insistence. "No. You'll have to wait. I think you probably need to wait every now and then anyway. Talk me through your day, husband. I want all the nasty little details."

"You want me talking about this now?"

"Yes. I want to know everything. Every morsel. Make it dirty and I might just show you what made me blush later."

So, I lean back again and drink some Champagne, then start talking her through exactly what I've been doing. She gets it all, as honestly and truthfully and dirtily as I can give. She gets to know about the redhead and her attempt at flirting with me, and about how many women we're about to make some profit from and what each one was like. No hiding it. No pretending about any of it either. The only thing I don't talk about is her father, and that's because I still don't know what I want to do about him and she doesn't need to think about him either. That's for another time. Now isn't it. Now is for flirting and getting to know each other some more. Later, it's gonna be about a whole lot of fucking. Probably involving forced orgasms and begging.

CHAPTER TWENTY - SIX

LEXI

I

    stretch, and a delicious ache heats my body as I do, a reminder of Abel's more generous side from last night.

The bed is empty, my husband missing, and, surprisingly, I'm a touch disappointed. After the emotional connection he drew, no, forced from me, I now find myself craving that connection.

I look around the dark room and tune in to hear the shower. I could go and interrupt, but my body has other ideas and stays motionless in the bed. My apartment back in San Diego is, or was, nothing like this place. It was full of light. Whereas Abel's is full of dark. Stylish, yes, but it's not a home. I wrap my mind around the word and consider it for a long moment. After all, a home isn't something I've been familiar with, but in my heart, I feel it should be something comforting and warm as well as elegant and sophisticated. A balancing act, for sure.

The shower stops, and a few moments later, he comes out of the bathroom, a towel slung low on his hips. A tantalising vision, and a tempting one, despite my sated body.

As he approaches me, I peel the covers back and knee-walk to the end of the bed.

"I could get used to this," I purr, my eyes eating up the view.

"I like that comment coming from your lips." He bends to seal his words with a kiss, sending a hum of satisfaction through me.

"Mmm. Good. As you seem to be in a good mood, I want to ask you something."

He steps away and heads to the dresser on the other side of the room, dropping the towel. "Go on."

"This house. I'm here now, and my things are here, but I'd like to put my own mark on it."

He doesn't seem interested in the conversation topic and continues to dress. "What did you have in mind?"

"Well, it's very masculine. It's stunning, but what would you say to a splash of Lexi?" I dramatically fall back onto the bed and spread out.

He turns to look, and I smile at him, letting his gaze take its fill of me draped over his dark sheets.

"Fine. Carmen arranged the interior. I'm not attached to anything particular, but the layout stays."

Carmen?

The name douses me in ice water, and the buoyant mood pops. "I'm sorry, Carmen? The bitch from work? You let her design your living space while I had to endure all that crap to even be invited in?" My voice betrays the anger this knowledge unlocks. And after my run-in with her, I have to question just how close the two of them were.

"Insecure and now jealous?" he teases. Not the best idea right now. "Darlin', you're gonna need to get harder real damn quick about—"

"Fuck off, Abel. Yes, I'm jealous. She's everywhere around us, and I hate the bitch. You don't see this as a problem?"

"Not if you don't make it one."

"I'm your fucking wife." I stand and storm over to him, not caring that I'm still naked.

He smirks. "You are."

"Then show me some respect, and don't make me live in the shadow of a woman you've slept with. I hate the fact that she's here, that she picked out your bedsheets. The same bedsheets you fucked me in last night." I shove him hard and whirl around, my frustration and jealousy clouding my mind.

"Lexi, calm the fuck down," he growls, grabbing for my arm.

I snatch it away. "Don't tell me what to do. You told me you wanted truth and emotion, well, here it fucking is. Listen to it, hear me and let me do something about it." My eyes blaze at him. And while this might be trivial to him, it's a huge issue if we're to build anything solid between us here.

Our marriage was arranged, a convenience for our families, but all of that's blown to shit. Abel's shown me what family can be, and now that's what I want more than anything, but I'm still on the outside until he lets me build part of our future together.

"I told you I'm not attached to anything." He turns and grabs a jacket, pushing his arms in. "If you want to pull the place apart, then be my fucking guest."

"Don't play with me, Abel. I'm not in the mood."

"You're my wife, Lexi. We don't play anymore. Get dressed. We're going out for brunch."

~

There's still tension in the air between us as he drives us through the streets. We're both on edge, and whilst the last few days have added to that, I think it's deeper than that alone. There's a fire between us – there has been from the start, and when it burns together, it can be incredible. But it also leads to arguments and fighting.

We just need to find the right balance between the two.

He parks at a small diner, closer in style to the places we visited back in San Diego, and rounds the car to open my door for me. His hand reaches in, picking up mine until I'm all but dragged into his hold, and he's slamming the door.

"You calm yet?" he snaps.

"Not particularly." His mouth is on mine the second I finish the word, body caging me on the side of the car. It's damn near an assault at this time of day and ignites the passion he's managed to unlock inside of me. My fingers thread into his hair, and I pull him deeper, wanting, no, needing the connection to bring us together again.

We both soften after a minute, and he pulls back, hands still on the surface of the car, so he can just stare at me up close. "She means nothing to me. She's a tool. No different than Ratchet. I'm not gonna have this argument again." I sneer at the thought but relent to his words to some degree. "Jealousy doesn't need talking about. I don't fuck anything but you. Understood?"

"It's not just about sex."

"No, but if you think she means anything to me but profit, you're wrong. Drop whatever bullshit you've got in your head. I'm your husband. We mean something to me."

Something gives inside me as he turns, and we head inside. His fingers grip my hand tightly, showing me that surety he's becoming so good at. First, the emotional connection he forced from me, and now words from him that show truth and feelings of some kind. I look at our hands rather than the venue, knowing I'm getting so close to something I've never had before.

The place is bustling with activity, and the smell of coffee and hot greasy food and spice is inviting as hell. "Not what I'd have thought for a lunch date," I muse, as he heads to one of the booths.

He drops my hand and sits me down. "No. But I'm not after someplace like Bellini's right now." He picks up the menu, as do I, scanning the mix of dishes. "And I want to see you eat real food. Might improve that mood of yours."

His phone rings as the waitress comes and fills the coffee mugs already set on the table. He notes the name on the screen and answers, and even I can hear who's on the other end of the call.

"Abel, your wife's maniac of a father is here looking for her."

My heart stutters at the mention of Miguel.

Abel's eyes flash up to mine. "Why is he there?"

"I thought he'd come to talk business!" Melena screams, and I have to assume she's shouting at Miguel and not Abel. "After all, this was our plan."

The shrillness of her voice must focus Abel's attention, because he's up and pulling me with him the second he hears it. "Are you safe? Has he touched you?"

"He's too gutless to hurt me."

"The gun pointed at your head should indicate otherwise, Melena." Miguel's voice is quiet, but the words are clear through the phone, as our feet rush the ground across the parking lot.

"Abel, he's crazy, and I don't trust him," I warn him quietly as he opens the car. "We've forced his hand, and I don't know what he'll do." The bite in his glare at me is so vicious I recoil from his anger.

"I want you and my fucking daughter here, Abel. You hear this, or I will have no hesitation in painting Melena's house with her blood." The line disconnects.

"Fuck fuck fuck!" He slams his fists into the steering wheel over and over before starting the engine and blasting out of the parking space.

My stomach rolls at the thought that he might lose his mother because of my idiot father, but then I wonder if he's really got the guts to go through with it. His game has always been power. He's hungry for it – blinded by it. And if he goes down this route, he's declaring war with the Cortez family. He already has, in a way.

Roads flash by outside, but I barely notice them. I'm too busy thinking about my father, about what he's attempting to do in this situation. "Abel, he won't hurt her."

"How do you fucking know that?" he spits.

"Because I know him."

"And you're willing to take that chance with my mother's life?"

"Are you willing for us to walk into a trap?" I counter.

"I don't take kindly to threats, Lexi." His fists wring the leather steering wheel. "You've seen what happens to people when they touch something of mine."

Abel might think this is all about him, but I know differently. This is about me getting one up on my sperm donor. It's because I'm in the power position, and he's been left with nothing to strengthen his business, and he can't stand that. It's the reason he's come looking for me. It's going to be his undoing because if he had any sense, he'd have returned to San Diego and been satisfied that he still has a business monopoly that brings in millions. But that's not him. So, like he used to do with Nicolas, he's schemed and plotted to his selfish benefit, but this time, he's lost.

It takes the longest time to reach the mansion. I was so pleased to be out of this house, but I feel disgusted that Miguel would come in here and turn it into a battleground. Melena should have known better than to let him inside, but I don't voice that opinion. After all, she can scheme with the best of them.

Abel drives through the manned gate and scowls at the guard. He races up the drive and abandons the car in his rush to march inside. On the surface, everything looks normal until we hear shouting.

Grabbing my hand, he pulls me with him, and we follow the sound until we open the door to the great room. Inside looks like war's been declared. The furniture in the room now forms an obstacle course between us and Miguel and Melena in the dining room through the double doors. He's holding her in his grasp with a gun in his other hand.

Abel takes a step forward, but my father shakes his head and narrows his eyes at our hands entwined. Discarded chairs and smashed liquor bottles cover the scene, the glass flecks shining against the dark hardwood floor. There are also two dinner plates and their remaining food scattered across the main dining table.

I pull the information together in my mind and see the cosy little lunch between them. What turned things around is yet to be seen, but I know Abel's processing the scene just like I am.

"What the fuck are you doing, Miguel?" he barks.

"I could ask you the same thing. You don't get to kill one of my associates with no consequences. You don't get to take your share of our deal and give nothing in return," he snarls, jostling Melena with every statement.

It's then that I see his face is marked with vivid red claw scratches, and I have to hand it to Melena for drawing blood.

"Let my mother go," Abel growls, low and menacing.

Miguel's response is to grab her hair and pull her closer to him, causing her to hiss and curse. The gun turns to her, and he digs the muzzle into her throat, shutting her up.

"No. Not until you fulfil your end of the bargain. You all betrayed me. After what you did to my son."

"There is no betrayal, Miguel. You needed us more than we needed you. You'll have your transport network. We've set that in motion. But you don't get to use my fucking wife in your games. That mistake was all on you."

"Abel, listen to him!" Melena snaps.

"How about a trade, then?" Miguel's eyes fix on me. "Your mother for my daughter."

Abel advances, anger vibrating from his body, but I hold his hand to keep him back. "She's not your fucking daughter."

"Oh, so she's done a number on you. Clever girl. Perhaps I've underestimated your charms in bed."

His words are crass and send a jolt of revulsion through me. All the years of abuse, disappointment, and frustration at being kept on the outside swarm in my stomach, filling my blood with a hatred so pure, it's terrifying. Add in that I know that the man standing next to me will tear down the sky for me, or any of his family if pushed into it, and that confidence is all I need to stand up to the bully that's in front of me.

"I'll switch. Melena can go. This is between you and me, right, Daddy?" I tilt my head to the side.

I let go of Abel's hand, and I hear his growl. "Lexi," he warns.

"It's okay." I fix my stare on my father. "This is about you and me, right? You didn't get what you wanted, so you need to take it out on someone." I climb over the chair in my path and round the table until I'm standing in front of Miguel, who still has the gun at Melena's throat. "Why are you so power-hungry, anyway? You have wealth, and the Ortega cartel is strong. And now you do this?" I hold my hands out at the mess.

I look at his reddening face and note the beads of sweat at his temples. He'd never come in here without backup if he'd thought it could end badly. My brain whirrs, trying to work out the missing information, but I need Melena out of danger.

"What did you say to him, Melena? Andreas isn't here. Miguel was invited in. What did you say to turn him against you?"

"Lexi," Abel cautions.

"No. Something went on between them today. After all, we're husband and wife thanks to their little arrangement to better each family. Perhaps Melena's been playing everyone all along?"

"Bitch, you're not good enough for my son," she seethes, throwing some curse or other at me despite the gun at her throat.

I turn my attention to the man who betrayed me, stepping even closer. "You're never going to get a single dime from this family,

Miguel. The Cortezes will end you."

The backhand explodes across my cheek, and I fall to the ground. My hands brace my fall, but more pain slices through me. Shards of glass and China cut into my flesh, drawing blood. I blink to focus myself and hear fumbling and movement, and I have to trust that Abel will have used that moment to get his mother free. And then I see it: a steak knife resting on the floor from their lunch date.

My bloodied hand reaches for it, and I squeeze the wooden handle tightly in my grasp, forgetting the sting of pain as I do and pulling myself back to my feet. I see my husband's now the one with the gun. It's trained on Miguel, with Melena behind him.

"On your knees, you piece of shit." His command is thick with anger, and I can tell he's only a moment away from turning into the man who drowned a guy in cold blood.

My father drops to the ground slowly, sneering at everything around him.

"Stop!" I shout as I move to stand between the gun and Miguel, blocking Abel's shot.

He doesn't lower the gun. "Lexi, for the love of fucking God, move the fuck away."

"No. I need you to trust me." I say the words for everyone in the room to hear. Melena's eyes narrow into slits – all that's missing is the actual hiss, and I'd swear she's a living witch.

Abel doesn't move, but he studies me.

He looks towards Miguel on his knees behind me.

"Do you trust me?" I ask.

My heart starts to thud, the pulse at my neck booming as a rush of adrenaline floods me, and I wait for my answer. He still doesn't give it. He keeps the gun raised and trained on me, as if maybe he doesn't trust me at all.

With my heart in my mouth, he finally gives me a subtle nod.

Melena screeches at Abel, but he doesn't respond to her, just holds her firmly out of the situation to let me lead it.

I turn around and see my pathetic lump of a father kneeling before us. His hands are raised in defence, and I have to wonder if he's resigned to the inevitability of the situation. My feet move, and I walk behind him to position myself. With every step, the blade grows heavier, yet my other hand snatches at his hair. I pull his head back, exposing his throat so I can put the blade just under his ear.

"You don't deserve to live for what you've done to me. So you can take this to the grave. I'll have everything you've ever dreamt of. I'll run the Ortega business with the Cortez family behind me while you rot away to dust." My voice drops to a whisper. "Revenge can be so sweet."

I look up at my husband as I press the knife harder against Miguel's skin.

"Alexia, please. I'm your father."

The words don't mean anything to me. He's pathetic for even saying them.

I yank his head back further and jab the tip of the knife into the side of his throat, where I expect to find his carotid, and with all my force, I drag the serrated edge down, sawing through his tissue and skin and opening him up to bleed out. His hands fly up to stem the bleeding, and his voice gurgles as he begins to choke. But it's too late.

I pull the knife out and drop it to the floor, as I straighten and watch the man who was responsible for so much of my pain crumble and slump forward. And then I listen to the silence. I don't look up. I stand and stare at the body in front of me as the blood seeps out and edges towards where Abel still stands, and I take a deep, cleansing breath. For the first time in my life, I really feel free.

I look my husband in the eye and feel a sense of pride wash over me with his gaze, and looking at him, I finally see a truth he's been trying to pull from me. This is the wife he wanted to see. My actions and my strength against the man who caused so much pain. Standing up for something and being unapologetic as to who I am. "We'll need to call Dante. Or Chance." I don't fight the smile that tugs at my lips.

CHAPTER TWENTY - SEVEN

ABEL

The air seems a damn sight more calm this morning. For two reasons. A piece of shit is dead. And my wife let her true colours emerge.

I look out over the pool, wondering how she feels about killing her father like she did. I don't suppose she has the same thoughts about it as I had taking Emilio out of our lives – the only real father I knew, but maybe she does. Maybe she has as much vengeance in her blood as I do. And maybe, going forward, I need to watch my damned back around her.

Chuckling to myself, I pick up my espresso and think of her in that moment. She shone. She glared enough that she could have shook the building around her with it. I'd like to believe it was protective instinct for her new family, but I'm not convinced it was in totality. I think it was years of disappointment and hatred let loose alongside it. Either way, I can use it, and so can she. We can build something more than I ever thought I'd find in a fine woman like her. In fact, I don't think I've ever felt as much pride in my life as I did watching her kill for both herself and me. Overnight, what was bordering on perfection, has become exquisite in nature. My perfect marriage, I suppose. A woman who understands my life and is part of this with me.

The phone rings, breaking my thoughts. Shaw's burner.

"Does she need to see him again before this happens? Last chance," he asks.

"No."

I end the call and keep looking at the water in front of me. I haven't asked her opinion on the matter, and I don't care if she does or not. She's not taking time to mourn the man she hoped he was, or worrying herself about what she's done. She'll remember the man he actually was and the look on his face when she finished his life for him. If that hurts her, so be it. She's got me to cling to now. We'll find a way to make it hurt less if she needs that. Watching a body get burnt in a make-believe meeting gone bad isn't going to help her, no matter the pleasure I might take seeing the finality.

I drink more coffee for a while and wait until I have to go wake her. We've got about an hour before the phone call will come, and so for the time being she can sleep and rest her thoughts. I suppose your first death deserves a bit of adjustment. Did for me, anyway. Although, my adjustment was alone behind bars and full of carnage. Hers won't be.

"Good morning," she says behind me somewhere.

"Do you have Andreas' number?" I call back.

She walks out and sits on the other side of the table, coffee in hand and her robe scuffed in tight to her frame. "Yes. Why?"

Because I might kill him for not protecting you. "Because you're the head of a profitable business now. You'll need someone to run it for you while you're here." She looks at the table and stirs her coffee, as if she's not ready to discuss that yet. "Lexi?" She looks up, and I see the tiredness in her features, which is at least useful for what's coming. "This needs dealing with."

"I don't even know if I'm the main beneficiary, he never acted like I would be."

"You will be whether you are or not. We have an attorney for that."

She nods and drinks some coffee. "I need time to—"

"There is no time. Your father's body will be found in a warehouse near San Diego in the next thirty minutes or so. The police will call you soon after, and you need to act the distraught daughter who doesn't know anything because you were here with me."

"What? Why San Diego?"

"Deniability. Dante and Shaw drove through the night. Knox is talking with our lawyer this morning to prepare him. You should call Andreas now if you trust him and get him organised."

She glares at me out of nowhere. "Why didn't you talk to me about this? He was my father. I need time to consider the next steps."

"Yes. But don't think it's going any slower for a while. You did this. I'm fixing it so we're in the clear."

Her chair scrapes the floor, and she stands, indignant and frustrated. "To protect your mother! And for my own self-worth. Why are you pushing me on this?"

"Sit your ass down. I'm not pushing, I'm being pragmatic."

"It was last night! I'm not ready to—"

"Shut your damn mouth. I am not losing the woman I love to the inside of a cell because I didn't act quick enough to protect her." Her mouth closes.

She damn near falls back into the seat, too. "Love?"

I stare at her mouth trying to find some more words.

I don't need any from her.

"Sit. Calm down." She does, fully. "I'm gonna say this once so you hear it loud and clear, and then, with any luck, we're gonna get on with the rest of our lives, yes?" She nods slowly. "You asked me once when I'd cried. It was inside Huntsville. Often. I know those walls. They're hard and they don't give one fucking inch. You think you can handle the guard's gang raping you? Because I've felt it first-hand from them, and you won't have a chance against that kind of menace controlling you, just like I didn't. So yes, I've dealt with everything here as fast as it needed to happen, and no, I didn't ask your permission or talk with you about anything. Mainly because you needed to deal with you last night. But right now, I need you to get with this program real fucking quick, darlin', and act like the Cortez you are because if you think, for one fucking second, I'd risk even the possibility of you going where I can't protect you, you don't know a goddamn thing about me yet."

We stare at each other for a while. No words and that's fine by me. I just need all that information to land so she understands why I've done what I've done and how my feelings for her affected my reaction. I held her last night. I let her deal with the immediate aftermath in my arms, and then I let her go when she drifted off to sleep and stayed up most of the night dealing with everything else. That's what this husband does for his wife. And if it comes to it and I can't make this work, I'll take the hit and go back inside for her as well. Sounds fucking dumb even to my own ears, but my decision's made. I can handle the inside of those cells. She can't. As far as I'm concerned, no one will ever know she killed her father and she will get everything he had.

"We haven't talked about love," she murmurs softly.

"You think you'd be in my home and sleeping in my bed if I wasn't thinking about it?" I watch her reaction to that, wondering where the hell she thought I was at. "That's what everything has been about since San Diego, Lexi. I wouldn't have bothered trying to find who you really are if I didn't care. I certainly wouldn't have given you a chance at being part of this family, but you defending my mother yesterday sealed it. You're in. Fully Cortez. Get with the program."

She can work the rest of that out herself in time, because, again, we have none and I'm tired enough to kill.

Standing, I check my watch and start walking back into the

house. "You need to get dressed and prepare yourself for a phone call." Soft padding feet follow me through the room. "The plane is ready whenever we need it, which should be about an hour after the police call."

"Abel?" I turn around to find her hovering, her mouth open as if she's got a thousand questions. This is not the time for any of them. "I'm …"

Reaching forward, I take her chin in my hand and kiss her forehead. "Don't talk. This is what I do. Just let me do it." I rub my eyes and hit the machine up for more coffee. "Go get dressed."

~

The phone call came as predicted, and then they asked her to get to San Diego to identify the body. She sat on the end of that call and kept her eyes fixed on me, reacting just as I needed her to in response. Shock, fear, overwhelming tears. I wasn't sure how real any of it was until we got on the plane and she spat a fuck load of curses around the space, mainly at me. I gave her that, because maybe I should have let her know she'd have to go see a burnt up body. But I didn't, and I didn't because I wanted her reaction to be as unprepared as it needed to be when we got there.

The detective at the precinct was pitiful. He either didn't care that Miguel Ortega was dead, or he had no interest in finding out who killed him. Both of which were useful to me, so I waited and filled out forms for Lexi while she went and identified the body. By the time she came out of that room, she was in floods of tears and acting the way we needed. She shouted at the detective, flinging insults at his ass to try improving the odds of finding the killer. He did nothing other than brush the crumbs off his dirty shirt and offer her counselling if she wanted it.

"A lot of people hated your father, Mrs Cortez," he said. "And a lot of people will be hiding what happened here. I don't see much other than dead ends and a long-running investigation. I'm sure you know as well as we do that his business dealt with high-profile cartels and crime gangs."

Couldn't help but smile a little privately about that. He wasn't going to do shit about finding a killer, mainly because Dante had already paid his captain off and threatened his kids earlier in the day. Not that Lexi knew any of that at the time, but I wasn't about to give her an inch of thinking she was in control. She needed to be real in those moments. Or as real as an actress who killed her father could be. It worked. And either way, any investigation about this was going to be dead in the water for the foreseeable. That's exactly how it needed to be.

"Do you think that worked?" she asks, as we drive along the road leading to her father's home.

The road sweeps around, climbing upwards. "Yes."

"So, it's done?"

"They'll have to process the body, and then you'll have to grieve at a funeral, and there might be an investigation into some of the business dealings, but yes."

"Investigation?"

"Don't worry. Grasby will be all over that side of things, along with the will and any other relevant papers. I'm sure the feds were up your father's ass most of the time. We'll deal with it."

"My father had his own attorney." A guy steps out in front of the car as we approach the gates. He looks in the window at Lexi and nods, swinging the gates wide soon after. "It might be easier if we can persuade him to be on my side of things in the future." She turns to look at me and I see a glint in her eye.

"And if he can't work with us, well, he'll die."

I take in the private compound, driving slowly around the vast circular driveway that leads up to the huge, white mansion house. Gardeners are working the lawns, feeding them water to keep the greenery that way in this climate. Wide steps lead the way up to the entrance, arches left and right of it to shade the veranda running around the whole place. I suppose it's all the way a man like Miguel Ortega would keep it. High end, classy, and whilst befitting my wife, totally at odds with the character he actually was.

I chuckle. "Nice place. I can see why my mother liked him."

Lexi gets out before me and leans back on the hood of the car, staring up at it with her arms crossed. I give her a few minutes to take it in. It's all hers now, as are the other places he probably had around the States and other countries. In fact, she might actually have more wealth than me, now I'm thinking about it. Not something I've considered before this moment.

I get out of the car. "How do you feel, Mrs Cortez?"

She sighs. "You've never called me that before, but stronger. I feel strong," she says, as I approach and lean next to her.

"I'm not surprised with all this at your fingers."

"I don't know if I hate this place or love it, though. So many bad memories, but a few good ones, too." I look at her rather than it, watching the way she sighs again. She turns to look at me, too, just holds her gaze with mine — soft and relaxed for a minute. "Either way, I don't need this place to feel strong."

"You know why I never defended you in front of your father that day yet?"

She looks back at the house. "Because you were trying to provoke me into action?"

"And?"

"Because I should have trusted you'd be there for me when I did attack."

"I'm glad we've clarified that. Don't ever forget it. Every damn time I'll be there."

And then we both hear footsteps approaching.

She pushes off the car and walks straight for a guy coming down the steps. "Andreas," she greets. He smiles and waits for her to get to him, before moving sideways and allowing her to lead the way in. So I follow with little else to say about anything at the moment. We haven't discussed how any of this will work, or how we could meld the businesses so it functions as it could. For now, it's just about her owning her new position in life. Within half an hour, it'll be about me owning this Andreas she seems to trust.

Letting them talk, I wander the house. I end up looking at the view from the main lounge's veranda rather than the floor to ceiling grandeur. Nothing but miles of sea looks back at me. I sit on one of the metal chairs, wondering how much money has been made around this table through the years. Much as I might despise drugs, it's a good business to be in. This place proves that.

A maid walks out halfway through my musings.

"Mr Cortez, could I get you a drink? An iced tea?" I nod and watch her walk away, then turn my gaze back to the sea. It doesn't take long before she's back in front of me and placing a full jug and crystal glass down in front of me, so I pick it up and keep my rising temper in check. It's nothing to do with where we're at in life, it's to do with a fucking asshole who chose to let that near-raping happen to my wife. Trust or not, Andreas needs a damn reminder about how to protect women of importance. I don't care if he would've died by helping her. I care that he didn't try. She would've had a chance then. She could have run.

Thankfully, they walk out to join me before I completely lose my cool. He offers his hand to me as Lexi introduces him. I don't take it. I stare at him from where I'm sitting instead, letting my face scowl at his seemingly arrogant self.

"Sit the fuck down," I snarl. He looks straight at her. "I'd keep your face directed at me, because I'm the one who chooses if you get to live or not." He unbuttons his jacket and sits, as does Lexi without any interruption. "Talk to me about why I should let you live." Seems that confuses him because he screws his face up and thinks about looking back at her again. "I wouldn't. That's not gonna help your cause in any way."

"I'm here to help," he says. "Alexia asked me to meet you both here. I thought this was about me running this side of the business for you and—"

"It is, but the fact is you let my wife get taken to a room when you knew what was going to happen to her."

He looks at the floor. "I tried to tell her."

"Little fucking late considering you had her number."

"Yes." I keep staring, waiting for something more to help me trust him with anything, let alone my wife's safety or my business. To his credit, he lifts his gaze back up to me and holds firm.

"Abel, he's apologised for that." I look sideways at Lexi, as she puts her hand on my arm. "I've known Andreas a long time, and he's always tried to warn me if he could. I trust him."

My stare goes back to him. "I don't."

"I understand that," he says. "I wouldn't if I were you either, but I do have her best interests in mind. I've had to watch her endure a lot under her father. And he never allowed me to influence how he should do things, despite my repeated attempts. Miguel favoured some of the others for leadership."

"And where are they?"

He shows me a snarl of his own. "Hiding out and wondering if someone's coming for them, too. I will be, as soon as I'm given the instruction to."

I look back at Lexi, watching as she nods at me. "I'm good with all of this. We've discussed it, and I was just about to run it by you before giving the order. I don't want any of them in my business any longer." My own smile broadens at her forthright tone, and I take a minute enjoying the fierce sentiment behind her words. She'll no doubt be a bitch to work under, and I couldn't be prouder of that if I tried. Anything Cortez needs that nature inside them. It's where we thrive.

"Don't fuck up again," I mutter at him, as I stay square with my wife and let her relaxed aura around him guide me. "You won't survive it. If she's with you, you die to protect her, yes?" She smiles at me. Just a quiet smile. Gentle lips.

"Understood."

"Time to make good on your words, Andreas. You've been instructed. Go get on with it," she commands.

He leaves in silence, giving me a chance to keep staring at my wife's beauty. So, I do. I keep staring and holding her gaze, perhaps thinking about bringing her down a step or two from her new position, until she starts looking a little shy about it. Her cheeks flush, bringing that pretty-ass blush with it.

She chuckles quietly. "Since when did my being domineering make you hot?"

"Thinking about fucking it out of you makes me hot."

"Of course." She chuckles some more and leans in, kissing me briefly before standing. "But I have work to do."

I pull her ass straight down onto my lap and get back to that kissing she just started. "Later."

CHAPTER TWENTY - EIGHT

LEXI

TWO WEEKS LATER

My world has changed. It will never be the same again. And for the first time in my life, I'm truly happy about that. If I can just get the contractors organised to strip every last detail that Carmen added to this house, then life will be perfect. That, and, of course, beating my husband this afternoon.

With all the recent drama, we hadn't set a date for the track day and had to push it back, but now it's here. I can't wait. I'll finally be able to show my husband just what he's messing with.

Mr Griffin, the Ortega attorney's name flashes on my phone screen. He chose the easy road and decided working with me as the head of the family was a much more profitable and lasting position than the alternative offered by Abel. And, so far, he's come through with everything we've asked.

"Yes, Mr Griffin."

"Mrs Cortez. I've had word from the Sheriff's office that they're officially dropping any open investigation regarding your father's death. As your father was still settling your brother's affairs and didn't have a will, his assets have been included in your father's estate. You will inherit everything as the only remaining heir and family member." I already knew I would. Abel's assured me of that, but hearing it formally makes it feel real now. "Congratulations, Mrs Cortez."

"Thank you, Mr Griffin. Let me know if you need anything else from me."

"I will."

"Problem?" Abel walks down to the kitchen and heads for the coffee machine.

"No. You're looking at the head of the Ortega business. Officially, now."

"Well, don't let all that go to your head. You're a Cortez, and you're gonna have to prove yourself this afternoon."

"Oh, don't worry. I will."

"Do you want to drive us to the track? Get warmed up?" I tease, as we leave the house a few hours later.

"Oh, darlin', it's you that needs warming up." He throws the keys to me as we enter the garage, and I take a moment to appreciate the Challenger before me.

Eagerly sliding in behind the wheel to get comfy, the smile on my face seems a permanent fixture. And as soon as we're clear of the automatic gate, I stomp my foot and let her slide through the traffic.

According to Abel, the family will meet us at the track, hired and paid for the afternoon's use – clearing the way for some good sibling rivalry. If the events of Knox's party are anything to go by, it should be a fun day out.

A fun day for the family. The Cortez family.

I'd wondered if it would be strange adapting to that name, but it's not. A thread of doubt about acceptance still infects my thoughts, though. Maybe I just need to beat them at their own game. Maybe I need to truly win something and prove I'm one of them to myself if no one else.

With that thought, I carve up a Porsche in front of me and make a turn, taking us out of town towards the track.

"Have you ever raced before?" Abel asks.

"Not properly. I ran a couple of quarter miles. My job was always entertainment. Behind the wheel, I wouldn't have been useful." He signals for me to turn, and I follow his instructions.

I've not had many moments when I've stopped to think about Miguel since the day I killed him, but I do now as the car eats up the road. It's a reflective moment, and I allow myself to take a breath.

"Snap out of it, Lexi. Game face time. You're racing for Cortez now, and you need to prove what you can do." He points up to the metal arch we drive under, entering the race grounds.

Following the road, I drive past the raised bleachers until I see a few other cars. As we approach, I spy the Camaro shining at me and Knox lounging against the door frame.

I pull up next to him and get out.

"You made it. Ready to race?"

"You bet. Ready to lose?"

"Fighting talk. Abel, you gonna let your wife speak to me like that?" He smirks, as he draws Abel into the banter.

"She can talk to you any way she likes, Brother."

I whip my head to look at Abel and see the grin on his face.

"Come on then, Lexi. You get to drive this baby. Show me what you got." He lobs the keys over the car, and I grab them in both hands. It was a superb car to drive back in San Diego, and having a track to play on, without the inconvenience of traffic or other cars, will be fun.

I slip into the driver's seat and start the engine, wagging my eyebrows at Knox through the window before I gingerly drive towards the entrance to the track. I keep my revs low to start with, but I know what this has under the hood. And as the wheels hit the tarmac, I shift, put my foot down, and enjoy the jolt of power pushing me back into my seat.

The speed climbs, and my smile is beaming. The track begins to bank at the far end, and I cruise around the incline before pushing the car even harder. My body wakes up as the adrenaline and excitement race around my system, giving me the guts to push again and see how far she can go.

The first lap is just a warm-up, and now that I have a feel for her, I focus on what the car can really do to show Knox and the rest of them what they'll have to do to beat me. The speed is insane, as the wheels grip the road, and I'm having far too much fun. I even giggle to myself as I turn out of the final bank on the last lap.

Heart rate slowing a little, I coast the car back along to the exit and park up next to the Challenger. Dante and Mariana are here now, too, and Shaw is parked up talking to Abel.

"Well, if I didn't like the Camaro before, I do now," Knox calls to me, as I open the car door.

"She's got all the moves." I hum to myself, sliding my fingers over the hood. "So, how does this work?" I look over at the Cortez siblings and their cars, waiting for clarification as I cross my arms. "An all-in race, or are we going head-to-head?"

"You know you'll lose in a head-to-head." Dante's confidence is loud and clear, and with his Mustang, it's not ill-placed.

"Well, let's put money on that," Abel says, stepping in.

The rest of the siblings all join in at this point, and there's a riot of drawn breaths, oohs and laughs.

"You fucking bet I will," Dante says.

"I'm not betting against Abel," Shaw mumbles as he lights a cigarette.

Knox looks between Mariana and me. "How about the girls race?"

Mariana shoves her brother, and he stumbles to the side.

"Sexist much. What's wrong, Knox? Scared I'll beat ya ass?"

"I'll race you, Knox," I cut in. "Mariana, you're welcome, too. Let's show him how girls can drive."

"Um, and what car are you driving Lexi? Because last I checked, you took my Camaro for a spin."

"She'll drive mine," Abel answers.

"That's a hell of a race, Abel." Shaw offers, and I wonder if he's a little intimidated amongst all of the horsepower on display. He shouldn't be considering his attitude at the party. And that Charger of his is close to what the Challenger's putting out and could certainly give it a decent race if driven well.

"I know. You joining?" Abel asks.

"I'll wait for the next one."

"You'll be racing me, Shaw. Might have better odds against your sister," Dante stirs.

"The more, the merrier, Dante." Mariana encourages him, but he just scoffs.

"Are we racing then? Half mile, laps, what's the deal?" I ask, looking between everyone.

Dante claps his hands together, and Knox and Mariana seem to be eyeing each other up. "Three laps. First past the line wins."

"Sounds fair."

"Don't break her, Lexi." Abel says, tossing me the warning as I climb into the car and make sure I'm comfortable.

I look up at him as he joins me by the side of the car. "Not helpful, husband. Don't you want me to win?"

"Oh, you better."

I put my seatbelt on and drop the window. "Who's starting the race?"

Dante jogs around the car and jumps in the passenger side. "I will." The smoke from his cigarette blooms inside the car. I cruise back out along the slip road and let Dante out before I line up the car at the start of the half-mile drag straight. Mariana pulls up alongside me, with Knox on the other side.

Dante stands in front of us all, and I get a little surge of anticipation as I wait. My foot hovers over the throttle, gently pushing down and making her purr. Total power sings back at me, deeply raw in its quiet rumble.

I look across at Knox, then to Mariana, and finally, focus my eyes on Dante. He raises his arm in the air, and the noise from all three cars picks up.

Any. Second. Now.

Dante drops his arm, and we all let rip, surging forward.

I take the early lead, but it's close.

The Challenger is faster on the straight. It's got more horsepower than the Camaro, but Knox can drive, and has me on the bank, even though I try to stay on the inside track.

As we come up towards the first lap, I'm close behind Knox, with Mariana behind me.

The second lap is almost a carbon copy of the first, but I'm gaining confidence on the bends and drawing back the distance, so I'm right on Knox's tail. I'm so close that I give him the tiniest nudge. What can I say? The devil made me do it.

His red brake lights flash up, and it gives me space to pull to the right, head out of the incline, shift, and take the inside line that he's left open for me. I look across as I pass him and feel the car begin to pull away onto the straight. Knox is too busy looking across at me, though, because he's forgotten about Mariana. She's hot on my tail and lets me pull her through and past her brother.

I watch her car behind me, making sure she doesn't try anything. It's beautiful – too beautiful to be playing out here, but that's her call. It's a work of art in reality, and either way, I'm pleased we both get to beat him.

The final straight is all I have to hold, and with the power of this car and Knox rattled, I push hard, refusing to give up. Dante is standing in the middle of the track, so I correct to miss crashing into him and cross first, with Mariana behind me, and Knox is last.

My smile is award-winning, as we all slow and hit the exit lane. And for the first time, it fills me with a sense of real joy I'd forgotten existed.

I ease back around to where the rest of the family is waiting.

"Abel, your wife is a fucking cheat."

"Cheat, did we establish rules?" He looks over to Dante, who's laughing to himself and shaking his head.

"Sore loser, hey, Knox? Maybe you just need to warm her up a little more," I call over to him, as I get out of the car.

"Beginners luck, Lexi. And you know what you did."

Mariana looks pretty pleased with herself as she heads straight for her brother to brag.

Abel's looking at his car. "Risky move."

I join him, looking at the front. There's a scuff mark, nothing more, and certainly worth bragging rights. "You told me to win."

"I did."

"All in, family race, no excuses this time," Dante calls out to all of us.

"Who's driving her?" I ask, still looking at the car.

Abel looks over at his brother. "Knox, you good with letting Lexi show you how it's done?"

The look he gives in return is pure venom, but he concedes. "Fine. But I'm with her in the car."

"I don't appreciate backseat drivers," I warn.

"I'll behave. Scouts honour."

"You wouldn't know shit about Scouts," Shaw mocks.

"Let's fucking race!" Dante's impatience is growing, but it gets us all moving, and my heart fills with some warmth I'm not used to. A sentiment grows for the people around me – a family I've never had the privilege of knowing before. It's like the party, only this time, I'm a part of it rather than the one on the outside.

I head towards Knox, anxious as to how he'll react to me

driving his new car again after pushing him out of the race.

"Win, and we're even, Lexi. Deal?"

I nod to him and climb in. "Deal."

"Try and tell me how to drive, and I'll have no hesitation in wrecking your car." I don't really mean it, I could never wreck this baby, but he doesn't need to know that.

I pull my hair back and tie it in a quick low-pony and start the engine. The urge to beat Abel itches beneath my skin, and my stomach churns as we drive out to the start line, one after another.

All the Cortezes line up, but instead of Dante starting this time, he points to the lights hanging above the track. They're red, and I keep my eyes trained on them. In a flash, they flick to green, and we all jump off the line. The thundering roar of engines fills the air, and the smell of burning rubber infiltrates the car, but it's an amazing buzz.

The green of Dante's Mustang creeps ahead, and he beats Abel to the first bank. I tuck in behind him, staving off Shaw and Mariana for the inside track. We hit the straight, and I pull around to see if I can outpower Abel, but I know what that car has, and Abel keeps me shut out.

"Come on, Lexi." I cut my glare to Knox and then snap my concentration back to the two cars in front of me. Abel's hustling Dante, and they're pretty well-matched. Mariana and Shaw are busy behind me, so I just need to find an opening or cause a disruption.

As we move around for the second lap, I'm still shut out, but I creep close to the Challenger.

"Don't be fucking stupid, Lexi."

"I know what I'm doing." But before I have a chance to nudge the car, Abel's popped out and around, pulling alongside Dante and squeezing his car down to the inner edge of the track, forcing the lead.

He slips past, and I follow, drawing up next to Dante. But he steers wide, defending the line, forcing me to back off.

"Fucker," I murmur as I change gear and try again. He won't be able to catch Abel, and as we eat up the second lap, I'm doubtful if I can beat him either. We bank, and I tuck in as close as I can to Dante. On the exit, I push the Camaro harder than ever and align the car against the Mustang. Any flinch or move from either of us, and we'll be touching, but I don't care. I tip the steering wheel, and Dante moves, adjusting, and I find the space to pull past him.

"Fucking hell, woman, he did not like that move!" Knox cheers from the passenger seat.

"Shut up!"

One bend and the home straight are all that's left, and Abel's in front, home and clear. We tilt on the bend, and I position the Camaro to take the outside line on the straight. It's just not enough track to take him, but just as we're about to cross, I see his car slow, or something, because we end up crossing the line together.

It's not a win, and a part of me is pissed he thought he needed to concede to me or give me the race. Maybe we'll have to settle that a little later tonight, but I don't let it sour a brilliant race.

Eventually, we all pull in. Doors slam closed, and the low-lying buzz of engines still running hangs in the air as cheers and congratulations start.

Dante's in my face immediately. "You are one sneaky bitch on the track, Lexi. Nice driving." I nod in thanks, feeling a little smug, as the twins snap and bicker. "I know where I'm coming if I ever need a driver."

I walk over to my husband, who's perched on the hood of his car. "You did that on purpose." I lean against the car.

"I don't know what you're talking about."

"Bullshit. But I appreciate the gesture." I reach for his hand, and he opens it, allowing me to thread our fingers together.

"We're heading to Ranger's Bar to finish this properly," Dante calls to us, his face looking pretty savage considering the outcome of the race.

I catch the nod from Abel towards Dante, and the rest of the siblings seem keen to keep the celebrations going.

"Are we going to join them?"

"In a minute." He stands and walks towards the driver's side. "I think you deserve this," he continues, as he slaps the roof of the car.

"The Challenger?"

"We did make a bet."

I think back to the conversation over dinner. So much has happened since then. It doesn't feel like I'm the same person, even. "We did. I'm not sure if I actually won it according to the rules of that bet, though."

"Doesn't matter. Nothing before matters now. But a Cortez wife needs a respectable car."

The slight smile that tugs at Abel's lips is infectious, and I walk to him and throw my arms around his neck in thanks. He lifts me a little off the ground, and I think it's the least-Abel thing he could possibly do, but it's perfect.

The perfect end to a pretty great day.

EPILOGUE

ABEL

I t's been a while, but this needs doing now.

Smells stale in here, like it needs air to breathe.

Not that he'll ever breathe again.

Dropping the keys on the hall table, I look around the place and sigh at the feel of him all over it. Everything's dark, just like my place is. It's filled with crisp edges, harsh furniture, and endless swathes of black curtains. I pick up a jacket abandoned on the couch and head through to the kitchen, gently putting it on a hook on the back of the door. It's as still in here as the rest of the place, with only the sound of a clock ticking to interfere with the sound of death.

It's been nearly six months now. I miss him. I miss his need to create havoc and chaos, to push me, to walk outside boundaries I set down and tell me I'm a pussy for thinking sensibly. He was the wild card of us all. The one who didn't conform to anything. I need some of that back. I need him cajoling me into the rhythm of destruction rather than sense. Fuck Knox's idea of being as we are. We can be more, and with Lexi behind me now, and the manpower that brings, I'm going to use it whether he likes it or not.

A knock sounds behind me on the front door, and I go back to swing it wide. Men walk in with boxes and tape, and I nod my head at them to start filling his shit into storage. I'll sell the place after that's done, and then maybe when I've killed the cunt that murdered him, I'll take some time going through his belongings. There won't be much any of us want because he lives in our hearts, irrespective of him being dead, but, I guess, there might be something some of us need. Dante especially.

Leaving the guys to it, I grab a framed photo of the six of us the day after I came out of Huntsville and head for my car because, other than this constant reminder of my own failure, life is good at the moment. It's stable, solid, and as dependable as it needs to be. Maybe we are chaos and carnage in some respects, just like Elias was, but we're united in that whether it's morally inept or not. And now we have a new addition to our cause – my wife. Never thought it would end up this way, but it is as it has become. And that fills me with a warmth I didn't think existed for men like me.

I smile at the thought as I get in the car and head into early morning traffic. I left her this morning before the dawn broke. We fucked in the dark, lazily, and she ended up swallowing my cum like a good wife should with my hand holding her down on me. I can still picture the look on her face as she crawled back up to me and kissed me after it, and still taste myself on her lips.

She laid there after with her hair fanned out and her tight body half out of the covers. Our rings clinked, as I unthreaded my fingers from hers, and then she watched me with a smile on her face as I dressed and backed out of the room. No questioning me on anything. No needy call for me to come back to her. She knows she doesn't need to do either. Anything I'm doing, I'm doing for us, and I'll always come back to her whether she likes that thought or not. She's in with no getting out now. That's what love is in this family. No escaping it, nor running from it.

I just drove for a while after that to get some perspective now everything has quietened around us. It's a big word considering what we now are because of our marriage. Our wealth has tripled, our reach the same. I suppose I did think for a while about calming us all down. Relaxing in that wealth and just being, like Knox said, but that's not who I am. He's right. I do want more. And not only do I want more, I want everything. I've spent a good portion of my life inside a fucking cell, looking at nothing but four damn walls and taking it up the ass by guards who thought they could control me. And yeah, they're all dead now, but there's always another someone who thinks they can tell me what to do, or another problem that thinks it'll beat me. It won't. Nothing will.

Taking the long route back to Mother's, I pass through the suburban neighbourhoods and eventually slow as I turn onto Kayla's avenue. Two of her kids are playing out front with a basketball, jumping hoops and living the life I've given them. They're not mine, but she had a home and money out of me all the same. Don't know why I did that for her. Penance maybe, for ruining her before she was ready for ruining. Either way, there is, and always will be, a low-lying moral compass that guides me still buried deep. It keeps us all together and strong. Maybe keeps us sane in the insanity we've become.

The eventual sight of the main house comes into view, and I drive through the gates and up the winding drive. I've got work to get on with today and a plan to put in place regarding Reed. A trip to New York might be in the cards. We can call it a honeymoon. Always have liked the place and the opportunities it brings me, and maybe with time, and thought and a little intel from Chance, I can make the trip worthwhile in other ways. A priest could also be useful before I use him as leverage, given that our marriage was never sanctioned under God. It wasn't real then, though. It is now.

Getting out, I walk around back to see if anyone's out by the pool yet. We all stayed here last night. A family meeting to get the next six months in order now Lexi's fully on board. The sound of raised voices coming from inside hits me instantly. Both Mother's and Lexi's. I stop and lean on the wall, listening to the argument rather than interfering with it. One thing they both need to get to grips with is hierarchy here, and that's something I need Lexi to find on her own terms.

"You will do as you're told!" Mother shrieks.

"Melena, there is no point using that tone. This is my business and–"

"Why you little bitch. It is not your business. It is my son's, and you'll heed my fucking warning."

"Don't you dare call me a bitch!"

"You're here because he accepted the terms. Don't think you're anything special. You're just part of a bargain made. A bargain I facilitated. We allowed you into our home, but you're nothing but profit to any of us."

"Maybe at first, but it's changed now and–" The piercing sound of a scream interrupts the noise – my wife's scream. Still, I wait and light a cigarette.

"You've drawn blood! If you ever touch me again, I'll end you," Lexi spits. "I think we all know I'm as capable as any of you."

"You wouldn't dare. Abel would kill you for even trying." My brow arches as I think that problem through. "You ever come at me, and your time will be done. You wouldn't be able to spread your legs and get out of that fucking scenario. He's my son. He does what I say." No, he doesn't. Not unless it suits me. "You're a bought package, Alexia. We got you for your business alone, and you will deliver on that."

"I will run my business as I see fit, Melena. My business!"

Scuffling starts, which makes me assume they're actually fighting now. More than likely started by Mother.

"BITCH!" Mother shrieks again.

"At least I'm not an actual fucking whore!"

I take a long draw on the cigarette as I turn for the door.

"MOTHER!" Mariana cuts across the noise. "Get the hell off her!" The sound quietens before I make it inside, so I wait again, trying to let them sort this on their own without me.

"How dare you touch me!" Mother snaps. "Get off, Mariana. This has nothing to do with you. You're as fucking stupid as she is."

"When you're intent on belittling something Abel loves, you're damn right it has something to do with me. Leave her and calm down."

"Perhaps if you weren't such a fucking witch, you'd have some manners," Lexi snarls. "Push me anymore and this is going to get real fucking nasty, Melena!"

"Stop, Lexi," Mariana tries. "Leave it now."

"I will not be spoken to like I'm nothing. Especially from an old whore who should know better than to try baiting me!" My mouth tips up. There's my wife's nature shining.

"WHAT THE HELL IS GOING ON!" Dante's voice shouts.

Everyone goes quiet for a second or two.

"Maybe we can all calm down and—" Wren's voice tries.

"And you're fucking useless, too. Get out of my house!"

"You better close that damn mouth before it gets you in trouble," Dante mutters.

Another slap rings out loud and clear in the room.

Mariana shrieks this time. "MOTHER!" she shouts. "What the fuck is wrong with you? I'm done with you hitting me!" Dante's back is coming out of the door before the question is even finished, his hands towing Mother with him until he turns and shoves her onto the same deck I'm standing on.

"Get a fucking grip of yourself!" he snaps.

"She's the fucking problem! They all are," she spits back. "I will not have another woman in my house thinking she runs my businesses!"

I stare as she starts ranting off in Spanish at him. She's halfway through her tirade about pathetic women and the problems that brings, cursing Dante and everything he is at the same time, when she finally notices me. Her mouth stops as I blow a fuck load of smoke out. She immediately stiffens and tries gathering her temper back in to act hurt and fragile. It's pretty pointless, given that I've just heard everything she's said.

"Abel," she starts, taking a small step towards me.

I glare. She stops.

Dante turns to look at me, fury heavy in his features about that slap she just sent Mariana's way and her trying to eviscerate Wren. My foot crushes the last of the cigarette down, and I push off the wall to look into the room. Lexi's pacing, glaring at anything she can, and Mariana's just standing there as if biding her time.

"Lexi, let me look at your face," Wren offers. She turns, showing the three scratch marks embedded in her skin. What was mild irritation turns damn offensive inside me.

I swing back to look at Mother, hardening my glare and thoughts. "Lexi's business is just that. Hers. You'd do well to apologise and try making amends." She looks instantly affronted, all rage and ire sending her straight back where she was before she thought she could use me to help her. "You'd also do well to remember who my father was. I'm only an inch away from his kind of evil. Don't make me treat you like he did." She strides at me without words, raising a hand to try slapping some manners back into me. I catch it before she manages, twisting her wrist to force her downwards. She whimpers then. Her knees hit the deck and she whimpers and moans her distress. I'm damn close to causing more of it, considering the scratch marks on my wife's face.

"Abel, please," she says, quietly. I sneer and keep staring. "I'm your mother." Hmm. "Dante, help me!" she shouts. There's no movement behind me.

"Apologise," I say. "Now." That fucking goads her into hatred again. She tries turning out of my hold and getting to her feet, so I do cause her more pain. It's enough that she ends up fully on the ground with me crouching at her side to keep her face down there.

"Brother?" Dante questions.

His hand touches my shoulder as if ready to draw me away.

"Get the fuck off me." I can't see anything other than reasons for this witch of a mother to understand her new place under me. "Lexi, get here."

Her heels move, and then something sends me sideways.

Crashing against the railings, I roll and get myself straight back up to deal with whatever the hell that was. Knox is in my face instantly, two hands on my lapels and his head aimed at mine. I rebound off it, as it hits me in the forehead, and then shake the feeling off to go at him for fucking daring. He's all front and aggravation in front of me, a hard sneer of his own levelled back at me.

"What the hell is wrong with you?" he snarls. Dante moves in between us, both his arms outstretched to try breaking this up. "In fact, what the fuck is wrong with this family?" I move sideways, glaring around Dante so I can keep focused on Knox. He blows out a breath and tries pulling back his sense. Mine's long gone. "Abel, did you even see what you just did?" He drops his hand to help Mother up from the floor she's still on, then turns back at me again. "This is the sort of shit that gets us in trouble. We're supposed to be united, and I come down to find this? Get out of your fucked-up head."

Silence. Dante stares me down, no emotion on his face. I glance behind him at Lexi, still full of rage about those goddamned scratch marks, and watch Shaw walk over to the scene. She just stares back, knowing all too well that this isn't about her in totality. This is about people doing exactly what I want them to do, when I want them to do it, without fucking questioning me.

I'm around Dante without any other thought, grabbing Knox and sending him straight down the steps towards the lawn. His ribs shunt into the rails on the way, body tumbling to the ground and arms flailing for support.

"ABEL!" Lexi shouts.

Hard hands land on my shoulders from somewhere, the arm attached going around my neck. I twist, lever my body weight against him, and slam my fist straight into Dante's jaw. He grunts, but barely moves, so I do it again and again and again until he finally gets the fucking hint and backs the fuck off me.

Lexi's in front of me before I get a step further towards a still reeling Knox, her hands splayed and her body trying to block me. "Stop!" she spits. I don't. "ABEL. STOP! Melena's sorry!" She looks behind me, practically begging Mother to comply. "Aren't you?" No fucking answer. I look back at Knox. "Abel, please. Listen to me," Lexi continues. "This is what she wants. Everyone fighting. She's got control then." My head swings back to look at her up there on the deck with Shaw, some sense coming back into my thoughts. "You're fighting the wrong person here. Please. Knox isn't the problem. Think."

Think.

I turn fully away from him and Lexi and head back past Dante, watching him step out of my goddamn way, as I pass. Mother's chin tips up at me the second I get to her. "Pathetic," she snaps. "You're being led with your dick. I taught you better than that, Abel." Shaw moves away from her, damn sure he's not going to cause me any problems in this mood. "She's a bought product. A slut for you to use. A barter that we now own. Don't you dare let her manipulate this and–" I grab the top of her hair and start pulling, towing her through the house, because I am not being led by my dick at all. I'm being led by the same feelings that guide me all the damn time. Love and respect.

She bitches the entire way to the car, deciding that cursing me like she does Dante is useful to her cause this time. It isn't. I don't feel a damn word of it. Cortez or not, I'm my father's son. He was a cruel son of a bitch, too, and he didn't give one fuck about sentiment – good or bad. He revelled in his barbaric nature. He coerced and filled the world around him with menace and hatred.

She's damn lucky there's even a scrap of decency in me, considering the dark life she built for these genes to exist in and rule.

I look back at the house, as I slam the car door behind her, and listen to more of Mother's bitching. Dante and Shaw are half holding Knox up, who's still intent on glaring at me despite the pain I've delivered to him. Wren's quietly waiting, watching and analysing everything. And then there's my wife. Mariana shadows her as she folds her arms in front of her and smiles. It's the only smile there is on show for me, but it's as true as it can be, given our combined savagery. She might as well be ordering a murder with that look because there's no doubting her intentions now she's part of something bigger than her alone. She needs this family strong as much as I do. She needs it wrapped around her and protecting the one thing we should all aim for in our fucked-up existence.

Harmony.

I'm about to make damn sure that happens.

READ MORE FROM THE AUTHORS

House of Skin Series

Darker Shades
When Sinners Fall
When Sinners Hate

TWO EXTERNAL NAMES ARE MENTIONED IN THIS SERIES - BRODERICK AND CANE.

Meet Landon Broderick and the other Broderick siblings in:

The Broderick Saga.

Four scorching stories of Scandals, Secrets, and Lies.

The Muse
The Lawyer
The Writer
The Fallen

You can also meet The Cane Family in:

The Cane Novels.

Five interconnected Dark Mafia Romance novels.

Innocent Eyes
Devious Eyes
Vengeful Eyes
Forbidden Eyes
Tortured Eyes

Printed in Great Britain
by Amazon